Either way, she would lose

She heard the swing creak behind her as the marshal rose and approached. Jo closed her eyes, feeling his nearness. He was going to touch her.

He laid a hand on her shoulder. She felt his breath on her neck, knew he was smelling the flower water she'd splashed on before supper. Her skin tingled, and she wanted to touch his hand.

The marshal gently squeezed her shoulder, and she took a shaky breath. It had been too long since she'd felt the warmth of a man's touch, felt the desire to open herself up to someone who wanted to hear her sorrows and understand them, understand *her*.

Her heart was beating wildly within her breast, imploring her, pushing her.... She bowed her head, fighting it.

Then the marshal withdrew his hand. Jo felt a chill of regret move though her like an icy wave....

* * *

The Marshal and Mrs. O'Malley
Harlequin Historical #564—June 2001

THE
MARSHAL AND
MRS. O'MALLEY

JULIANNE MacLEAN

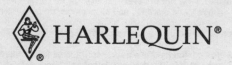

HARLEQUIN®

TORONTO • NEW YORK • LONDON
AMSTERDAM • PARIS • SYDNEY • HAMBURG
STOCKHOLM • ATHENS • TOKYO • MILAN • MADRID
PRAGUE • WARSAW • BUDAPEST • AUCKLAND

ISBN 0-373-29164-7

THE MARSHAL AND MRS. O'MALLEY

Copyright © 2001 by Julianne MacLean

This edition published by arrangement with Harlequin Books S.A.

® and TM are trademarks of the publisher. Trademarks indicated with ® are registered in the United States Patent and Trademark Office, the Canadian Trade Marks Office and in other countries.

Visit us at www.eHarlequin.com

Printed in U.S.A.

Available from Harlequin Historicals and
JULIANNE MacLEAN

Prairie Bride #526
The Marshal and Mrs. O'Malley #564

Please address questions and book requests to:
Harlequin Reader Service
U.S.: 3010 Walden Ave., P.O. Box 1325, Buffalo, NY 14269
Canadian: P.O. Box 609, Fort Erie, Ont. L2A 5X3

For you, Stephen.

Acknowledgments:
To the Kansas State Historical Society and the
Kansas Heritage Center. To editors Melissa Endlich
and Tracy Farrell, and my agent, Paige Wheeler.
To Cathy Donaldson, Tammy Sisk, Julia Smith,
Paulette Phillips and my mom and dad, for much
appreciated publicity. To my critique partners,
Tory Leblanc, Ruth Maclean and Georgie Phillips.
And to my dear cousin, Michelle,
for your love and friendship.

Chapter One

Dodge City, Kansas, 1882

Josephine O'Malley's stomach clenched tightly with panic as she peered through the night along the dusty street, looking for potential witnesses. She couldn't let anyone recognize her in these clothes that had once belonged to her husband, God rest his soul. Especially after she pulled the trigger.

Fighting to keep calm, she opened her long slicker and palmed the walnut handle of her Colt .45—the handle her husband had worn smooth over the years. Her boots tapped lightly over the aging planks along the boardwalk while her spurs chinked a slow rhythm. Music from a tinny saloon piano across the street seemed muffled beneath the erratic pulse that drummed in her ears, but she continued on, soberly watching the mannish lines of her shadow as she walked under a hanging lantern.

When she finally stopped outside Zeb Stone's Dry Goods Store, she took a deep breath and tried to relax. Over the past six months, raw fear had compelled her to learn how to handle her late husband's guns, preparing for this day, should it come. Hadn't she pictured this moment over and over in her mind, wanted it, known it was necessary? Wasn't it supposed to be filled with righteous determination?

Instead, she looked up at the huge painted sign bearing Zeb's name and felt only a sickening knot of intimidation and a horrible surge of dread. She'd never killed a man, never thought she could. It went against everything she ever believed in.

But she had to do it now. *Didn't she?* She couldn't stand by and watch her son, Leo, choke to death in a noose like her husband. Leo had been poking around the finer points of his father's murder lately, and Zeb, with his black heart, was beginning to take notice.

No, the time had come for Jo to face Zeb once and for all. The law had done nothing to help her. If she was going to protect Leo now, she had to help herself.

Jo raised the red bandanna over her nose. As she reached for the brass doorknob, her hand trembled. She pulled it back and paused to fight the pulsing knot in her stomach, then pushed the door open. Bells clanged as she made her way quietly across the threshold.

Zeb Stone stood behind the counter wearing a black waistcoat and starched white shirt. His black bowler hat rested on the counter; his head was down as he scrawled in a notebook.

"We're closed," he said, his voice flat with disinterest. "Come back tomorrow."

Jo shakily drew one of her weapons and held it with both hands in front of her. Anxiety spurted through her, but this was not the time for that. It would take a cool head to carry this through.

She crossed the room in three swift strides, stopping

at the glass counter and breathing fast with panic. She shoved the barrel of her gun against her enemy's shiny forehead.

Zeb's fearless gaze rose to meet hers. The familiarity of those black eyes sent a hideous chill through her. "You're out of luck," he said, not recognizing her face behind the bandanna. "The money's already gone to the bank."

"I didn't come here for money," Jo replied in a calm, low-pitched voice, but inside, her heart was beating a breakneck rhythm.

"What do you want, then? Supplies? I'd best warn you, mister, nobody steals from me and gets away with it."

Jo stood motionless. So much of this did not seem real. It was as nightmarish as tossing that handful of earth on Edwyn's casket!

She swallowed hard as a wave of desperation washed through her. She had to see this through no matter how terrible it seemed. Finish it once and for all.

She touched her thumb to the hammer of her gun and felt her stomach churn with debilitating dread. "Are you ready to die, Zeb Stone? Because I'm ready to do you in."

Marshal Fletcher Collins led his horse to the Dodge House Hotel and flipped the soft leather reins around the hitching rail. He reached into his shirt pocket for half a carrot and stroked Prince's warm muzzle. "Here you go, boy. I might be a while. I gotta make the right impression my first night on the job, if you know what I mean."

Fletcher stepped onto the boardwalk, nodding to the

cowboys sitting on the hotel steps. "Howdy, boys. Mighty fine evening."

One man tipped his hat. "Welcome to Dodge, Marshal Collins. Headin' down to the Long Branch for a drink?"

"Not tonight. I'm on duty."

One of them called after him. "That never stopped Marshal Lewis from filling his holster!" The other two exploded with rowdy laughter.

Fletcher stopped and turned around. The laughter quickly died. Straightening his hat, he continued on his way.

A buckboard wagon rumbled by, lifting a cloud of dust. When the clatter of hooves faded into the night, Fletcher listened with a keen ear to the hoots and hollers from the dance halls across the street, the boisterous banjo music, the laughter and foot stomping.

He passed in front of Meuller's Boot Shop and glanced through the dark window. Looked quiet. In fact, he probably shouldn't be wasting his time over here in the business district. He should be enforcing the gun ordinance over in the Comique, where there was bound to be some fool packing iron.

Fletcher paused on the boardwalk for a moment, then decided to finish this block. He walked by Zeb's store and glanced through the window, but tensed when he saw Zeb—backed up against the wall with his hands in the air, facing an armed robber.

Fletcher hugged the brick wall just outside the door and drew his Peacemaker. He checked the cylinder for bullets, then clicked it shut and peered inside again. The thief looked like he was just itchin' to shoot.

Fletcher took a deep breath. No do-si-do for him tonight. Dodge City was a trial by fire for the new marshal, and he sure didn't aim to get burned.

With growing panic, Jo stared into Zeb's dark eyes and rubbed the clammy pad of her index finger over the trigger. She clenched her teeth together. She *had* to do this.

He paled visibly, perhaps realizing she meant business. "You won't get away with this. I have friends who—"

"I know what kind of friends you have. They're gutter swine." Jo pressed the barrel of the gun harder against his forehead. He squeezed his eyes shut, not so fearless now. It was a moment of terror he greatly deserved after all the pain he'd caused others.

A film of perspiration appeared around his dark mustache, but his voice stayed calm. "I'll give you anything you want. Just don't shoot."

Good Lord! She couldn't do this! But what choice did she have?

Zeb cautiously opened his eyes.

Just then, the door flew open and slammed against the inside wall and the doorbells clanged and clattered to the floor.

Without thinking, Jo drew her second weapon. She aimed it at the flash of movement in her peripheral vision, hearing the man's commanding voice before she could focus on him. "Drop the gun! Now!"

With a heavy weapon in each hand, Jo glanced back and forth from one opponent to the other. The stranger moved closer. She saw his tan Stetson and his long brown coat open in front, but it was the barrel of his gun that held her attention—a small black hole pointing directly at her.

"I said drop it!" he yelled.

"You drop it, or I'll kill him," Jo replied, deepening her voice as best she could without it breaking.

"Do that, kid, and you'll be waiting in line for a coffin."

Perspiration dampened Jo's face. Her bandanna began to slide down her nose. If it fell, she'd be done for. "This ain't your fight, stranger."

"I own every fight in this town." He opened his coat to reveal the steel badge pinned to his brown leather vest.

Jo's stomach did a sickening flip. Who in tarnation was this man? She'd been counting on Marshal Lewis taking his early evening nap in the jailhouse. She'd assumed this stranger was one of Zeb's men.

Feeling her fate grow more precarious by the minute, she gave the marshal a more mindful once-over, concentrating on his face this time to see what she was up against, what manner of man could aim a gun at an opponent who held *two* of them—one in each hand— and still be as heartily confident as the day was long.

To her dismay, he was calm—too calm—and his bold self-assurance made her teeter alarmingly on her already unstable courage.

He must have been watching her carefully because he seemed to know she was faltering. He took another slow step closer and spoke in a subtle Texas drawl that crumbled her grit to dust. "I'm the new marshal, kid, and my patience is dyin' fast. Either drop both guns now, or prepare to meet your maker."

She glanced back at Zeb and saw a bead of sweat trickling down his cheek.

The lawman took a few steps sideways toward the counter, his movements smooth and fluid. "I can see you don't want to kill anyone. Now do the right thing and lower your weapons.''

Jo's mouth went completely dry at his gentle command. Her palms were wet and slipping on the handles of the guns. She didn't want to die and she couldn't go to jail, not with Zeb alive to kill her son. But this man was right. Somehow he knew she wasn't a killer and his calm presence was stirring something inside her—something she didn't want stirred.

Was it shame? Or was it compassion for a cold-blooded killer who did not deserve it?

Strangely, she found herself backing away, lowering her arms to her sides. She could not fight this man, this unexpected intruder.

The lawman moved forward, his gun still fixed on her, his green eyes flickering with reassurance. Something in his expression spoke to her. *You're not a killer,* he seemed to say, without uttering a word. The oddness of it all made her feel weak and dizzy.

She had done the right thing, she told herself. She had to stay alive for Leo. He was only eleven years old. He needed her.

All of a sudden, Zeb bent forward. Jo froze. She watched transfixed as he drew a pistol from under the counter, the steel barrel rising up to confront her.

A surge of clarity sliced through her mind. She had come here tonight to kill Zeb Stone. If she was going to plunge into hell in the attempt, she would take him with her.

Jo cocked both her guns. She raised her arm in a flash and aimed at her enemy, then shut her eyes and pulled the trigger. The gun blasted, kicked back in her hand, and she heard a body drop to the floor with a dull thud. Feeling almost sick, she opened her eyes.

Oh, dear God. Jo stared numbly at the man lying in front of the counter. She felt as if her heart had stopped beating.

She'd shot the lawman!

A thunderous boom sounded and a bullet from Zeb's gun ripped painfully through her shoulder. The impact knocked her off balance and she stumbled back.

Nausea weaved through her stomach. She clenched her pistols as she staggered about in disbelief, fighting the reality of what was happening. Dazed, she felt warm blood stream down to the top of the corset she wore beneath the disguise. Jo heard a click and recognized the sound—the hammer of Zeb's gun. Her eyes darted up to that dark barrel again, and she knew he wanted her dead. No mistakes this time.

Determined to save herself, Jo leaped through the air just as Zeb fired. The gun boomed like a thunderclap, and behind her, a bag of flour exploded in a cloud of white dust. Jo hit the floor and rolled, pain stabbing her in the shoulder with each frantic breath.

Rising to her feet, she saw a window, her only escape. She heard Zeb cocking his gun again. There was no time to think. Fighting panic, Jo yanked her hat down over her face, took off in a run and threw herself into the glass.

Panes smashed and shattered all around her. She flew through the air and landed hard on the dry dirt in the alley, scrambled to her feet and ran around the back of the buildings, brushing the glass off herself as she went.

Panting uncontrollably, Jo fought the pain where the bullet lodged. Her stomach burned with fear. She heard Zeb yelling after her, heard his pistol fire two more times, but she was out of range.

She hugged her arm to her side to steady her aching

shoulder and ran through the darkness like a hunted animal. Her boots pounded over the hard ground. Her frenzied breaths matched the rhythm. She had to reach the privy before anyone saw her.

She skidded to a halt, swung the door open and spun inside. A turn and a *click*...the door was latched. The thick stench of stale excrement assaulted her senses. A grunt escaped her. Thank God, the lantern she'd left here was still burning.

Jo dropped to her knees and felt around for the loose board, raised it and pulled out her bag. She ripped off her coat and pain sliced like daggers down her arm.

Within seconds, she was fastening the tiny buttons on her bodice with shaking fingers. "Faster, faster," she whispered, trying in a panic to hurry, trying to ignore the blood that had soaked her chemise and was now staining her bodice, the blood that would drain the life from her if she did not somehow get out of here.

Voices echoed in the street, ricocheting off buildings like bullets. Jo tied her muslin bonnet ribbons under her chin, but pushed the bonnet back from her face to rest on her back. She swiftly stuffed the disguise into her bag, set it back into the compartment beneath the floor and lowered the boards.

She took a quick glance around the privy, then blew out the lantern. Blackness enveloped the fetid, makeshift haven, which would have been as silent as the grave, if not for Jo's small, frantic breaths.

Outside, desperate screams cut through the dark night. Footsteps. Hoofbeats. The town was alive in a mad search for the outlaw. They would not find him, she told herself, and tried to gather some courage from that fact.

Suddenly aware of the sick feeling in her stomach,

Jo's head began to spin. She tried to lean on the splintery wall, but toppled back onto the bench. An icy chill seeped into her veins and she began to shiver. She tried to calm herself, to take deep breaths to stop the shaking, but it was no use. She'd never felt so out of control.

She needed to get to a doctor. She stood, then staggered in the darkness, her trembling hands fumbling over bristly wood in search of the door latch.

Please, someone help me. I'm not going to make it.

Suddenly the door whipped open and she stared into another gun barrel.

"Mrs. O'Malley! You're bleeding!"

Jo couldn't look up until the gun lowered and dropped easily into a holster. A pair of hands were reaching out to her. Where was she? What was happening?

Arms encircled her and she fell into them. "Help me," she mumbled.

"I've got you. It's Deputy Anderson."

Relief poured through her as he hoisted her into his arms and carried her into the night.

Chapter Two

Flat on his back on the examination table, Fletcher tried to focus on a small black spider crawling across the white ceiling instead of the stabbing pain in his right thigh. Nothing against Doc Green, but the man seemed to be using a knitting needle to stitch him up instead of a surgeon's needle.

"You're a lucky man," Dr. Green said, pulling the needle through the bloody mess on Fletcher's thigh. "Bullet barely even grazed the muscle. This should heal in no time. It's your head wound that worries me. I want to keep you here overnight."

Fletcher grit his teeth. Some city marshal he was—shot in the leg and collapsing like a schoolgirl, right into Zeb's glass display case. Dead to the world before he even hit the floor. "Thanks for the concern, Doc, but that's not necessary."

"You were out cold when they brought you in, Marshal. Even with guns going off like the Fourth of July, you didn't flinch."

What else had he missed? Fletcher wondered as he covered his eyes with one hand and sighed, trying not to wince when the doctor pierced the wound again with that aggravating needle. For all Fletcher knew, the kid in Zeb's store tonight might have killed ten men on his way out of town.

The doctor tied the thread and began to dress the wound. Fletcher's head throbbed where he'd knocked himself out, but it was his leg that ached and burned the most, even though he tried to withstand it.

It could have been a lot worse, he supposed. He'd seen other men shot before, and most times they didn't live to see the dawn, so in that way, the doc was right. Fletcher should count himself lucky.

Just then, the door opened. Startled, Fletcher leaned up on one elbow to see Deputy Anderson hurrying inside with a woman in his arms, looking like an anxious groom carrying his bride over the threshold on his wedding night. But this woman was no bride. She lay lifeless like a rag doll in the deputy's arms.

"Another casualty, Doc," Anderson said. "It's Mrs. O'Malley. I found her in the privy behind Zimmerman's. She must have gotten in the way of a stray bullet."

Dr. Green quickly cleared off another examination table. "Set her down here."

Anderson laid her on the table and her face tilted away from Fletcher. He saw the disorderly twist of honey-colored hair at the back of her head, then his gaze fell to the accompanying blood stain on her shoulder.

This was what happened when men didn't respect the law. Innocent, law-abiding folks got hurt, and if they weren't lucky, they got killed, too. He hoped this poor woman wouldn't be one of the unlucky ones.

Her long skirts fell over the side and touched the floor like a fancy tablecloth. Fletcher noticed with some interest that she wore men's work boots.

The doctor searched for a pulse at her neck. "Was she conscious when you found her?"

"Yes, but she fainted straight away."

Doc began to unbutton her bloody bodice.

Wanting to do something to help, Fletcher tried to sit up but felt suddenly nauseous and dizzy. He dropped back down and watched the ceiling spin over his head.

The deputy approached. "Marshal! Thank the Lord! I heard you were shot in the head."

"No, just the leg," he answered.

"What's this, then?" Anderson asked, pointing at the bloodstained dressing around Fletcher's head.

"Don't ask."

"He knocked himself out on the corner of Zeb's jewelry case," Doc answered.

"Well, I'll be," Anderson said. "Your first showdown in Dodge and you didn't even get to see how it ended."

Fletcher ignored Anderson's teasing tone. "Did anyone catch the guy?"

"Not yet."

"Who's the woman?"

Anderson walked around the table, watching Doc examine the wound. "Josephine O'Malley. Her husband was killed about six months ago by some horse thieves. Right in his own barn."

Fletcher shifted uncomfortably. "Did anyone ever catch them?"

Anderson shook his head. "No witnesses."

Fletcher glanced at Mrs. O'Malley, her arm hanging limply over the side of the table. "Where was *she?*"

"In the house, I reckon. Now, she keeps to herself. A bit of a recluse. Doesn't even let her kid come to town. She lives out on her ranch with a bunch of cowhands and that causes a lot of talk in town, if you know what I mean.''

The doctor glanced at Anderson with disapproval, then began unfastening the woman's corset. ''Deputy, you'll have to wait outside.''

Anderson left the office and closed the door behind him. The doctor gathered his instruments.

''Need any help, Doc?'' Fletcher asked.

''No. But I suggest you look the other way if you're feeling queasy.''

Fletcher lay flat on his back and stared at the ceiling, searching for the little spider who had distracted him last time, but as luck would have it, he was gone. So Fletcher turned his attention to the bookshelf, but reading the spines of all those medical books made his head pound harder than a steel mallet, so he resigned himself to staring at the empty ceiling again.

If he could've relaxed, he would have been fine, but all he could think of was the woman beside him, her delicate skin being sliced open, all because of a small-time thief who didn't seem old enough to use a razor.

Fletcher touched the blood-soaked dressing on his forehead and tried to fight his anger. He'd taken this job to try to stop the killing, to uphold the law, to be strong where his father had been weak. A fine job he'd done tonight. Gunfire in the streets and innocent people shot down.

The woman moaned and Fletcher couldn't help but turn to look. The doctor stood over her with a bloody scalpel in his hand. He set it down and began digging around with another instrument. Fletcher felt ill, but at the same time, he couldn't tear his eyes away.

The doctor soon began to work with a needle he held in a clamp.

The woman groggily turned her head, and at last, Fletcher saw her profile—her tiny upturned nose and her moist, full lips the color of a pale red rose. Her long, delicate lashes were swept down upon her cheeks, and she moaned again in a delirious stupor that seemed almost sexual to Fletcher, who immediately chastised himself for thinking such a thing. The doctor quickly reached for a bottle, tipped it over a white cloth and pressed it to her face. Within seconds, her head fell limp toward Fletcher. The moaning stopped and the doctor went back to work.

Seeing her face for the first time, Fletcher took note of how pale she looked, albeit tanned. Obviously she possessed an unfashionable preference for sunshine. And her tiny, rough hands told him she had not abandoned her husband's chores after he died. Fletcher couldn't help but feel sympathetic toward her for all she must have endured.

Dr. Green cleared his throat. Fletcher looked up at him and saw the perspiration dotting his forehead. "You okay, Doc?"

He nodded. "I've never seen such a close call. If the bullet had gone in any lower—and I'm talking the width of a thread—she would have bled to death."

The wound in Fletcher's leg throbbed as he leaned up on one elbow. "Will she be all right?"

"I hope so. There's always the risk of infection, but like I said, she was lucky."

Fletcher's blood burned at the thought of her suffering. It was so damned unnecessary.

He would catch the man responsible for this, he swore to himself. He would see him brought to justice in front of everyone in a court of law, and he would show this town that—where their new marshal was concerned—*the law was the law.*

He wondered if Mrs. O'Malley would remember what had happened to her. Fletcher closed his eyes and decided to be there when she woke to ask her that very question. If this woman survived, she would see justice.

He would give her his word on it.

Consciousness bloomed slowly, as if from an empty, black abyss. Jo heard the murmur of voices, but could only lie immobile, trying to awaken her mind from its dazed stupor, all the while becoming more and more aware of a throbbing ache in her shoulder. She had to concentrate to force her heavy eyelids open.

Where was she? she wondered, trying to sit up. In someone's bed, no doubt, but whose? Nothing seemed familiar. Her sleepy gaze darted from the blue gingham curtains on the window to the unpainted pine washstand, then across the small room to a kerosene lamp flickering atop a tall chest of drawers.

She heard the voices again. They spoke quietly, probably in the next room if her ears were working properly. What had happened? Was Zeb still alive? And what about the lawman? Had she killed him?

Good Lord, she hoped not.

She began to sit up, but even the slightest movement gave way to her broken body's protest. She let out a low groan, squeezed her eyes shut and touched her injured shoulder.

"Land's sakes," she whispered, feeling the large dressing over her wound. Someone had tended to her and put her in a borrowed nightdress. Was she in the doctor's clinic?

Her ears suddenly tuned to footsteps and a man's

voice just outside her door. Perhaps someone was coming to arrest her. Perhaps the world now knew that a vengeful heart had lived inside the breast of a desperate widow. What if a lynch mob was forming outside. What would she do?

Telling herself these fears were irrational at this point, Jo watched nervously as the brass knob turned. The white-painted door squeaked open and Dr. Green walked in. Jo let out a tightly held breath and prepared herself for whatever fate held in store.

"Mrs. O'Malley, you're awake," he said, closing the door with a light click behind him.

Jo wet her dry lips and tried to bring the approaching doctor into focus. She had to gather her thoughts, carefully plan her responses. Was it too much to hope that her identity had not been discovered? "Yes, I...what happened?"

Dr. Green approached the bed, his black sleeve stained with blood. Was it her blood? she wondered, worrying not just about her own wounds, but about whoever else might have been hurt because of what she had done.

"You were in the wrong place at the wrong time," the doctor said.

Jo paused, contemplating before she spoke. "Who brought me here?"

"You don't remember?"

"Not exactly."

Dr. Green cupped his fingers around her wrist and took her pulse, which was probably thumping faster than he could count. "You were shot. Deputy Anderson found you in the necessary behind Zimmerman's." He glared down at her, and Jo thought she saw suspicion in his brown eyes. "Do you remember?"

"I...I'm not sure."

The doctor looked closely into both her eyes, pulling each of her lower lids down with his thumb. "You were lucky. The bullet went straight through without too much damage. I closed the wound and it should heal just fine. I want to keep you here, though, for at least a day or two to watch for infection."

Jo barely heard a word the doctor was saying. All she could think of was how lucky she was to be alive, and what Leo would have done if he'd had to bury another parent.

"I've already sent word out to your ranch. Your son will want to see you, I reckon."

Jo smiled weakly at him. "Thank you."

How was she going to explain this to Leo? she wondered. She was supposed to have been running errands when all of this happened.

As the doctor turned to leave, Jo thought again of the lawman she had gunned down in Zeb's store. A mental picture of him, sprawled out on his back and bleeding onto the plank floor, made her heart wrench. "Wait, please, Doctor. Was anyone hurt tonight?"

"Besides you? Why, yes. The new marshal took a bullet."

"He's not dead, is he?"

At that moment, a knock sounded. Dr. Green crossed the room and opened the door.

Jo suddenly found herself staring in stunned silence at the man she thought she'd killed. Her heart did a quick *pitter-pat,* then her mind was struck numb by the strangeness of it all—how she could be so plagued by him one moment, then so happy to see him the next.

"Why don't you ask Marshal Collins yourself?" Dr. Green suggested.

Leaning heavily on a cane, the marshal limped like a Civil War veteran into the room. A white, blood-stained bandage was wrapped around his head. He wore black wool trousers and a white shirt with the sleeves rolled up, a dark brown vest, no hat, and his light chest-nut-colored hair spilled in rippling waves onto his broad shoulders.

"Ask me what?" he drawled good-naturedly.

Jo couldn't find words to reply. She was too busy trying to keep herself from spilling out her relief in a gigantic wave of apologies and confessions and useless reparations, all of which would land her in the county jail.

The marshal glanced questioningly at the doctor.

"She wants to know if you're dead," Dr. Green answered.

The marshal's lips parted with a grin that revealed straight white teeth and deep dimples around his mouth, and his eyes sparkled flirtatiously. "There are days, ma'am, when I think I might be. Thankfully, this ain't one of 'em."

The two gentlemen shared a chuckle, but all Jo could respond to was the charming, congenial glint in the law-man's eyes—so different from the threatening glare he'd produced in Zeb's store when he first burst through the doors.

When the moment of humor passed, however, the marshal looked at Jo and his smile faded. She swallowed nervously, not wanting to think of all the things he could say to her at this moment, all the accusations she deserved to hear.

He limped a little closer, his cane tapping twice on the floor. "Are you well enough to speak with me, Mrs. O'Malley? Or would you prefer I come back later?"

She would have to face this man at some point, she knew. She might as well get it over with now and try to learn as much as she could about the situation. Jo tried to speak with a steady voice. "I believe I could manage it. Please, sit down."

He took a seat in the corner rocker, wincing subtly when he bent his knee. The doctor stood just inside the door.

"I'm very sorry about what happened to you," the marshal said, leaning his elbow on the armrest. "I can't help feeling responsible."

Knowing it was the most absurd thing for him to say—considering it was *she* who had shot *him* in the leg—Jo waited in silence for him to continue.

"As luck would have it, today was my first day on the job. It was my intent when I walked in on that holdup to disarm the man who shot you."

The marshal still believed the outlaw was a man....

"You must have been in the wrong place at the wrong time," he continued. "Where were you, exactly?"

"I was in the privy."

Marshal Collins stared at her intently. "But there were no bullet holes in the privy walls, I'm told."

"I mean, when they *found* me," she added.

"I'm aware of that much. I was here when Deputy Anderson brought you in."

So much had happened while she was unconscious. She was groping for an explanation in the dark with both hands tied behind her back. "What happened to you?" she asked, stalling. "Were you badly hurt?"

"Thank you for your concern, ma'am, but I'm fine."

Dr. Green interrupted. "Rumors are going around that he was shot in the head and laid out cold as a wagon tire. But as you can see, he hasn't hung up his holster yet.''

Marshal Collins shot the doctor a rankled glance, then looked back at Jo. ''I was wounded, is all.''

Jo gestured to the bandage on his head. ''What happened there?''

''It's nothing serious—''

''He fainted,'' Dr. Green said.

The marshal shook his head. ''I didn't faint, ma'am. I took a bullet in the leg and cracked my skull on the counter when I went down.''

''The bullet just grazed him, actually,'' the doctor added.

''If you don't mind, Doc, I'm trying to interrogate a witness.''

Witness. Jo felt some of the weight lift from her shoulders.

The marshal looked back at Jo, his expression sobering. ''I'll have to ask you again. Where were you when you were shot?''

Jo did her best to answer sensibly. ''I was late in running my errands today and I was on my way to the privy before heading home.''

''A lady like yourself shouldn't be walking the streets alone after dark. In the future you might want to be more careful.''

''A woman like me doesn't have the means to be careful, Marshal. I'm raising a son and running my late husband's ranch. If I need supplies, I get them. I don't pay much mind to whether it's the sun or the moon lighting my way.''

Something unreadable flickered in the marshal's eyes as he digested her reply. He hesitated a moment, staring, before steering the subject back to where he wanted it. "Did you see the man who shot you?"

"I didn't see him. I only heard gunfire, stopped to look in the direction I thought it was coming from, then felt the bullet strike. I have no idea where it came from, or who shot me. Then I ran to the privy and locked the door. I was quite frightened."

"Of course you were." He narrowed his eyes and his inquisitive gaze routed some of Jo's resolve. "Would you excuse us for a moment, Doc? I have some questions of a private nature, and I'm sure Mrs. O'Malley would want her answers kept private as well."

She felt a rush of anxiety. What would this private conversation be about?

Jo nodded her consent at the doctor.

"I'll be right outside the door if you need me," he said. "But you go easy on her, Marshal. She's in a delicate state."

As soon as the doctor walked out, the pain in Jo's shoulder grew worse, if that was possible, but she tried to ignore it. She had to keep the situation in focus. Her future depended on the marshal's questions and what she might learn from them. She had to protect Leo from his father's killer, and if that meant skirting the law until she had a chance to meet Zeb again, then so be it. The most important thing now was to lead this marshal away from her masquerade.

He leaned forward in his chair and the muscles in his sun-bronzed forearms tensed, then relaxed, distracting her from everything. Accordingly, Jo tried instead to concentrate on his voice, but that wasn't much better. His slow drawl had the same calming effect it had had in Zeb's store when he'd told her to lower her weapons. And she *had* lowered them.

Oh, if she wasn't careful, she would confess everything.

"You were on your way to the privy?" he asked again.

"That's right."

"Mrs. O'Malley—" he tilted his head "—I don't think you're telling me the truth."

Jo's heart began to race harder and faster until she could hear it pounding in her ears. "Of course I am."

"In order for me to do my job, I need you to trust me and tell me where you *really* were when you were shot."

How could he know all this? It wasn't possible. "I don't know what you're referring to, Marshal."

He watched her with discerning green eyes that told her she could hide nothing from him. "I know you weren't injured in the dress you were wearing when Deputy Anderson brought you here. After Dr. Green transferred you from his operating table to this room, I was curious about the extent of your wound. Please forgive me, but I examined the bodice of your dress. There was no bullet hole."

Jo stared blankly at the marshal, knowing she couldn't stand up to him much longer. Surely, she was done for.

"So let me ask you again, Mrs. O'Malley. Where were you when the bullet struck your shoulder?"

Chapter Three

Marshal Collins sat with his forefinger resting on his temple, studying Jo and seeming to find her as guilty as the last fox who'd emptied her chicken coop.

All Jo could do was stare into those green-and-gold flecked eyes and scramble for an explanation. Why wouldn't she have been wearing her dress when she was shot? she asked herself. What possible reason could there be?

"Mrs. O'Malley, I only want to know the truth so I can arrest the man who shot you."

"The truth."

"Well, yes, ma'am."

She tried to imagine herself not wearing her bodice outdoors in the full dark of night, why any person would ever do such a thing, anyone respectable, that is. At the same time, she knew what folks had been saying about her living on her ranch with all those cowhands in her bunkhouse, and those same folks probably wouldn't be the least bit surprised to hear she'd been out behind the saloons in her unmentionables.

Maybe those rumors might get her out of this—at least temporarily.

Jo pursed her lips. What did it matter if she told a little lie? After all the gossip, she couldn't possibly do any more damage to her reputation.

She tried to speak with conviction. "I...I was with someone."

"I'm not sure I understand."

"Marshal, this conversation is highly improper."

At that instant, he seemed to grasp her meaning and his elbow slipped right off the armrest. He quickly pulled it back and cleared his throat.

"This is awkward, I know," she said, lowering her eyes. "That's why I don't wish to speak about it any further."

The chair creaked as he shifted uncomfortably. "But perhaps whoever you were *with* might have seen something more."

"No, he'd already left."

"Left...left where? The privy? You were in the privy together?"

"No, we were in back of Zimmerman's. As I told you before, I was on my way to the privy before heading home when I was shot."

The marshal seemed reluctant to believe it. "Can I have his name? He might have seen something."

"Absolutely not."

"Mrs. O'Malley, this is a deadly situation. You have my word as a peace officer that I will do my best not to repeat what you tell me."

"I'm sorry, Marshal Collins, I can't say."

They lingered in a thick silence while Dr. Green paced the hall outside, his shoes clicking lightly across the plank floor.

After a few minutes, the marshal took in a deep

breath and sighed. Jo braced herself for whatever he was about to say next.

"I'm sorry to tell you this when you're in such a state, but your refusal to answer my question is an obstruction of justice. Are you aware of that?"

Jo could only nod, still unable to look up at him after the lie she'd just told. She'd told so many lies tonight and they were all taking their toll on her conscience— a conscience that by now was rapt with guilt and regret and a dozen other things that could make her toes curl if she let them.

"I'd like to go easy on you," he went on, "given the circumstances, but when it comes to the law, I'm about as inflexible as a branding iron. I need to ask this person some questions, so if you don't give me his name, I'm going to have to take you to the jailhouse."

By the firmness of his voice alone, Jo knew he meant every word. She had to put an end to this discussion, and fast.

"I'm waiting, Mrs. O'Malley."

"It's not what you think," she said, stalling. "It's not that I don't *want* to tell you, it's that I can't."

"I beg your pardon?"

"I can't because…I don't know his name." She was digging herself in deeper and deeper. She just wanted it all to end.

He rubbed his stubbled chin with his large, masculine hand, the same hand that had pointed a gun at her earlier that evening, and her skin prickled at the frightening image.

"I see. He didn't *hurt* you, did he?"

"No, no, it was nothing like that." Good Lord, what was she saying?

"So let me get this straight," the marshal said, rubbing his forehead in disbelief. "You were out behind Zimmerman's with a stranger, not wearing your bodice. The stranger left you there, you were shot, then you took the time to put your bodice back on and refasten all the buttons?"

"That's right."

"Why did you go to the privy? Why not just go straight to the doctor's office?"

Jo tried to stay alert, but it was proving more and more difficult with all these questions. "I was afraid of being shot again. I was in search of a safe place to hide." She met his gaze head-on. He wasn't going to outsmart her. "Marshal Collins," she said, in her best no-nonsense voice, "I don't know the man's name, I probably wouldn't even recognize him. It was dark. Now if you don't mind, I'd like to get some rest."

She swallowed hard, unable to believe what she'd just said but knowing she'd had to come up with something to explain herself. Biting her lip, she heard the marshal rock back and forth in the creaky chair. Why wasn't he leaving?

"I don't mean any disrespect, ma'am, but I intend to find the man who shot you, and if that means I have to ask questions that might dent your sensibilities, well..." He shrugged.

Frustrated and exhausted, Jo closed her eyes. She wished with all her heart that this night had never happened, that she could go back to a day when her husband was alive and there was never anything more distressing in her life than a damaged corral fence or a few too many chores to complete before breakfast. Those things, those little problems, seemed so insignificant to her now, so easy to mend and put away. Her life had been simple once; there had been nothing to fear.

Or at least that was what, in all her precious innocence, she had believed.

"I just want to go home and be with my son."

"I understand that, Mrs. O'Malley. I'm…I'm just
hoping you can help me out. That gunman broke the
law, and with first impressions being what they are,
folks are going to think their new marshal is a little soft,
and that just ain't the case. To be frank about it, I got
a score to settle here." He stopped rocking and locked
his large hands together. "Besides, Zeb Stone wants the
man brought to justice and I owe it to my sister to see
that it happens."

Jo's breath caught in her lungs. "Your sister?"

"She's married to Zeb."

"Zeb Stone is your…your brother-in-law?"

He nodded. "That's right. And besides being family,
he's the one who convinced the town council to hire
me. I owe him."

Jo could only stare in stunned silence as her enemy's
kin rose from his chair to stand tall before her, his words
leaving her whole body chilled to the bone with dread.

Fletcher gazed into Mrs. O'Malley's wide-open blue
eyes and struggled to keep his hopes from sinking.
She'd given him nothing that would lead him to the
gunman. And now she was obviously going to be ill.

"Doc, could you come in here?"

The doctor hurried in to her bedside. "What's the
problem?"

Mrs. O'Malley put her hand over her mouth and the
doctor saw what was about to happen. He reached for
a pan and held it under her chin while she was sick into
it. Fletcher stared at his boots, shaking his head with a
note of irritation.

Not so much at Mrs. O'Malley, of course—she couldn't very well stop herself from being sick after what she'd been through. He'd just hoped for something more to go on.

"It's a reaction to the surgery," Doc said, then turned to Fletcher. "You'll have to leave. She's answered enough of your questions."

Hearing the doctor's chilly tone, Fletcher felt a hint of guilt, then backed out of the room. He closed the door behind him and leaned his weary forehead against it. Perhaps he had been too hard on Mrs. O'Malley, but when it came to tracking leads, he found it difficult to see past his own nose.

Fletcher turned away from the door and took two painful strides down the hall. Suddenly the image of Mrs. O'Malley having a willing "encounter" with a stranger hit him like a brick in the face: Mrs. O'Malley, doing *that* in the dark of night, out behind Zimmerman's hardware store?

Fletcher stiffened uncomfortably. Was it really a stranger? he wondered, finding it almost impossible to believe. Had Mrs. O'Malley sought the man out or was it the other way around? She must have been as hot as a two-dollar pistol to risk such a scandal, especially with what people were saying about her. But why outside by the privy? Why not somewhere more private?

Fletcher started off again, leaning on his cane, reminding himself that he was an impartial lawman, and what Mrs. O'Malley did with her personal life, no matter how outlandish and risqué, was none of his concern.

He reached the doctor's front office and sat on the straight pine bench by the window, pulling the lace curtain aside to peer out into the predawn darkness. Except for a mangy rat terrier sniffing around the water troughs,

Front Street was about as quiet as a turkey pen after Thanksgiving.

The sound of hoofbeats and a jingling harness alerted him to an approaching wagon. He leaned closer to the window as a rickety buckboard came to a slow stop in front of the doctor's office. A young boy hopped down and landed with a thud on the dry street. An older woman set the brake and tied the reins, and with some difficulty, wiggled her wide bottom down from the high seat.

Before Fletcher had a chance to stand, the door opened. "Where's my ma?" the boy asked in a panic, pausing in the open doorway. "She was shot."

Fletcher stared into the same wide-eyed, fearful innocence that had thrown him off balance in the back room a few minutes ago.

"I just met your ma. She's fine. What's your name?"

"Leo." His shoulders relaxed slightly.

The older woman appeared behind him. "Go inside and close the door, Leo. The mosquitoes are getting in."

As they moved into the dimly lit room, Fletcher managed to rise to his feet, silently cursing his sore leg. When the woman noticed him, she pulled her black shawl tighter around her shoulders and raised her chin. "You're not the doctor."

"No, ma'am. I'm the new marshal. And you are…?"

"Shouldn't you be out looking for the man who shot Mrs. O'Malley? From what I hear, and no thanks to you, he's roaming the town as free as a prairie dog."

Fletcher's annoyance doubled as he hopped to keep his balance. "It's being taken care of. And your name is…?"

Indignantly, she lifted her double chin even higher.

Her cheeks were fleshy and red like a couple of ripe tomatoes. "I'm Matilda Honeyworth. I work for Mrs. O'Malley. Where is she?"

Fletcher gestured toward the back room. "The doctor's with her."

"Can I see her?" Leo asked, his dark eyebrows drawn together with worry.

When Fletcher remembered the tragic details about the late Mr. O'Malley, his heart went out to the boy. He must have been terrified when he heard about his mother. "You'll have to ask the doctor, son. He should be out in a minute or two."

Leo leaned into the front hall and tried to peer past the stairs. "So you're the new marshal?" He turned to Fletcher and held out his hand. "I'm a rancher."

"Is that right?" Fletcher replied, trying to suppress a smile that might insult the young man's proud spirit. "I'm Fletcher Collins." He shook the boy's hand.

"Did you see it happen?"

"If you mean did I see your ma get shot, no, I'm afraid I didn't."

"But you saw the rest of it? Were you there? Is that why you got that bandage around your head?"

"Leo! That's none of our business!" Mrs. Honeyworth scolded.

Leo ignored the reprimand. "Did you shoot anyone?"

"Leo!"

"Gunfighting's a serious matter, son. I do my best to avoid it. When I can."

Dr. Green walked into the room and stopped in the doorway. "Mrs. Honeyworth, it was good of you to come."

"How's my ma?" Leo asked.

The doc smiled down at him. "She's going to be fine. Would you like to see her?"

"Yes!"

"Come this way, both of you."

Fletcher watched them walk down the hall. He limped to the bench and sat down again, looking out the window at the slowly brightening sky, then he rubbed his tired eyes and listened to the quiet laughter coming from the back room. They seemed like a nice enough family. Been through a lot lately.

Hell, he didn't want to tarnish Mrs. O'Malley's reputation any more than it was already, especially after meeting her son, but the lover she was protecting might have seen something that would help solve this case. Was Fletcher to set aside his personal oath to uphold the law because he felt sorry for her and her son? Wasn't that the same kind of thing that had caused his own father's tragic death?

Fletcher pinched the bridge of his nose, thinking. It was impossible to leave that rock unturned, he knew. The way things stood at the moment, he had nothing to go on, not a single shred of a clue, and that didn't help his present mood. It was the kind of situation that would grate across his conscience until he caught that gunman and brought him to justice.

One way…or another.

Chapter Four

Hearing footsteps in the hall outside her room, Jo felt her pulse quicken. Had she left another clue somewhere? A trail of blood perhaps?

The doorknob turned, the door slowly squeaked open, and there stood her darling, dark-haired boy. He wore a plaid shirt with suspenders, and duck trousers that had recently become too short and now showed off his loose socks pooling almost comically around his ankles.

"Leo," she said with a rush of relief that could not compare to anything she'd ever known. The pain in her shoulder seemed to disappear momentarily as she regarded her son.

He ran in, his loosely laced work boots stomping noisily across the floor, and gave her the hug she so desperately yearned for. "Ma, are you okay?"

She loved him so much, her heart *ached* with it. She squeezed his slender body and, feeling his boyish weight upon her chest, she wished that life could go back to what it had once been.

As she considered it further, however, she knew she could never go back, even if Leo's father could somehow return from the dead and take over his duties on the ranch. After what she'd gone through, nothing would ever be the same again: she was not the same person she was, not the trusting woman who took safety and well-being for granted. She began to wonder ridiculously how the change in her personality would affect her marriage to Edwyn. Would he even notice? Then she swept the thought away and squeezed Leo tighter. It was a foolish, foolish notion to imagine Edwyn ever coming back from the dead.

Leo withdrew from her embrace and, reluctantly, she let him go and noticed Matilda standing just inside the door. The older woman smiled warmly, her concern showing. She hadn't known what Jo had set out to do, only thought she was running errands, and she must have been devastated to learn what had happened.

"We're very glad to see you," Matilda said.

"I'm happy to see you, too," Jo replied, wishing she could confide in Matilda about all of this, but afraid the knowledge might put her at risk. Matilda was a friend Jo could not do without.

"When can you come home?" Leo asked.

"The doctor says I'll have to stay here for another day so he can keep an eye on me."

"But you're going to be all right, aren't you?"

"Yes, I'm going to be fine, but I don't think I'll be gathering any eggs for a few weeks. I'm going to need you to take over some of my chores."

Leo considered that a moment, then sat up straighter. "I can do everything. Don't you worry about a thing, Ma. I'll take charge."

"Thank you, Leo. Matilda and I will be sure to depend on you."

He smiled proudly, then his dark brows rose with

excitement. "It must have been some gunfight. The marshal got shot, too, and he's all bandaged up."

"You saw him?" Jo asked worriedly, then she tried to sound casual and unperturbed. "What in heaven's name did you talk about?"

"I asked him if he saw you get shot, but he said he didn't."

Matilda gazed at a framed sketch on the wall. "I didn't like the look of that lawman. There was something about him..."

"Oh?" Jo questioned.

"I'm not certain what it was. Perhaps the way he asked my name. As if I was some sort of criminal."

Jo shifted, trying to ease the pain in her back from lying still for so long. "Don't fret, Matilda. I believe he's suspicious of everyone. He told me quite plainly that he was inflexible and that Dodge would soon learn he was in charge."

Matilda adjusted the small, round spectacles on the bridge of her nose. "Just what our town needs—another power-hungry man running things. What's his background?"

"All I know is that he's Zeb Stone's brother-in-law. That's how he got the job." Jo wished she knew more.

"Strange. I hadn't heard anything about that. Whatever happened to Marshal Lewis?"

"I don't know. When he rode out to check on us last week, he didn't say anything about leaving Dodge."

Leo broke in. "What's everybody so surprised about? I knew Marshal Collins was coming to town. I saw Zeb Stone on the McCaffrey land the other day when I was fixing the fence. He came over to talk to me."

Jo winced at the sound of Zeb's name on her son's lips. "You didn't tell me about that."

"Sorry, Ma, but you didn't ask. You haven't asked about much lately."

It was true, and she regretted having become so obsessed with Zeb, and the fear he provoked in her, that she had neglected the person she loved more than anyone or anything in the world. She tried to hide the fact that she was so shaken and got straight to the heart of the matter. "What did Mr. Stone say to you?"

"Nothing much, except that he was on his way to the depot to meet the new marshal."

"That's all? You didn't bother him with any questions about your pa, did you?"

For the past six months, Jo had tried to keep a low profile and steer clear of Zeb's watchfulness, but Leo's newfound interest in solving his father's murder had become such a dangerous problem it had driven her to desperation. *Good Lord, what was she going to do about all this?*

"No, ma'am." Leo lowered his gaze.

Jo's head was pounding. She knew Leo must have said something and was afraid to tell her.

Matilda gave Jo a nod. "We best be getting on home. Your mother needs her rest."

Leo moved forward to hug her.

"Be a good boy for Mrs. Honeyworth until I get home," Jo said, patting Leo's back and trying to keep her voice from quivering around the lump forming in her throat. Oh, she missed him so terribly much, and he was becoming a man so fast, changing every day, it seemed. She didn't want to let him go.

"I will." He gave her a carefree smile that only a child could muster, then walked to the door.

Matilda leaned down and kissed Jo on the forehead. When the door swung closed behind them, Jo looked at the window. Through a crack in the closed curtains, she could see the first glimmer of dawn, but sadly, the new day did not carry with it new hope.

With the morning sun uncomfortably hot on his back, his cane in hand, Fletcher limped down a Front Street boardwalk to get some breakfast. He could feel the curious stares from the townsfolk, ladies standing around with parasols, shopkeepers and barbers gathered in groups at their windows, chatting quietly. People wanted to get a look at the new marshal who had *fainted* in the middle of his first gunfight in town.

Fletcher clenched his jaw. What a circus. Now he had a reputation to fix. Hobbling around Dodge like a wounded dog didn't exactly strike terror into the hearts of the local criminal element. He tugged the brim of his Stetson down over his forehead to cover the bandage and wondered if he could manage without the cane.

When he reached the Dodge House Hotel, he walked into the wallpapered dining room, removed his hat and chose a table by the window to watch for Deputy Anderson and his posse.

"You must be the new marshal," the dark-haired waitress said, approaching. She carried a silver coffeepot and a newspaper, which she promptly set down on the white tablecloth. "Pleased to make your acquaintance. I'm Gert Bezel. My husband owns the place. Coffee?"

"Yes, thank you."

She turned over the flowery china cup already placed in front of him and poured the coffee. "It's a downright shame what happened to you last night. I saw them carry you off to the doctor. You looked like a big sack of flour. Most people thought you were dead."

Fletcher felt his cheeks grow hot. "I'm still breathing."

"Mr. Stone's done so much for Dodge. It's a pity he was robbed like that."

"He's a good man, for sure."

Mrs. Bezel smiled warmly, but Fletcher knew he had some fancy footwork to do if he was ever going to regain confidence in this town. He leaned his cane against the dark wood wainscoting under the window.

"What can I get for you this morning?" Mrs. Bezel asked.

He ordered a plate of fried eggs, bacon and corn bread, and when Mrs. Bezel took her leave, he flipped open the newspaper, but the front page headline turned his appetite sour.

Frontier Fun
Dodge City's Newest Marshal
Swoons at Gunpoint

Fletcher dropped his forehead into his hand and read on.

Last evening, Zeb Stone's Dry Goods Store was held up by the man citizens are now calling "Six-Shooter Hank, the scariest man alive." Marshal Fletcher Collins took one look at Hank and gracefully retired to the floor, not forgetting to introduce his head to the glass cabinet on the way down. For a few confused moments, it seemed as if the coroner and undertaker might have something to do, but a closer examination of the town's new guardian revealed he was merely resting his eyes. Collins continued his nap while gunshots flew freely in the street, injuring Mrs. Josephine O'Malley, wife of murdered rancher, Edwyn O'Malley. Six-Shooter Hank made off with unknown amounts of cash and a posse on his tail. Marshal Collins has awakened from his nap and sources say he is recovering affably.

Fletcher leaned back in his chair and gave up trying to control his temper. He clenched his fists and hoped he'd be able to find a lead soon—anything to help him catch that outlaw.

Just then, four men on horseback rode into town, Deputy Anderson bringing up the rear.

Hopes rising, Fletcher slid his chair back and took his hat with him to the front door. "Anderson, any luck?"

The deputy walked his horse to the hitching rail. "Afraid not, Marshal. Didn't find a trace of anything."

"Did you talk to any of the cowboys out on the range?"

"Sure did. Nobody missing, nobody bragging about a gunfight, but I reckon nobody wants to be a rat, either."

Fletcher removed his hat and pulled the bandage off his head. With the posse's failure, it was up to him now, so he decided right then and there that he would spare nothing to catch Six-Shooter Hank. Fletcher's tarnished reputation depended on it. And as far as Hank being the scariest man alive…well, Fletcher would just have to see about that.

Chapter Five

Growing more irritated by the minute, Jo slapped yesterday's newspaper down on the bed. Marshal Collins had probably read the front-page headline and spent every waking hour since the alleged robbery trying to capture Six-Shooter Hank.

Six-Shooter Hank! Didn't people have anything better to do than invent nicknames for criminals who had no business with fame?

She tapped her hand repeatedly on her leg. Her criminal disguise had been nestled beneath a public privy floor for two days, just waiting to be discovered by a disgruntled city marshal. She huffed in exasperation. Where was the doctor? He said he'd be in this afternoon to change her dressing and check her wound before releasing her. It must be past three by now, and she had to retrieve her bag and sneak it back home before anyone found it and turned it in.

Finally she heard footsteps in the hall and the door opened. "Good afternoon," Mrs. Eisenbein said, walking in with a lunch tray. "How are you feeling?"

"I'm feeling fine. I'm ready to go home, if the doctor would complete his examination—"

"Yes, yes, I understand. The doctor will be in after he's seen his patients."

"His patients? Are there many out there?"

"A few." She set the tray down on Jo's lap and began to spoon-feed her the hot broth.

"How long will it take him? Because I really have to be on my way—"

"Open up," Mrs. Eisenbein said, not waiting for Jo to finish. Before she knew it, she was swallowing the hot, salty-tasting liquid.

Just then, Jo looked up to see Marshal Collins standing in the doorway, his walking stick gone, his bandage removed.

Her insides whirled with alarm as she stared at him. He wore a clean white shirt and black vest, his black leather gun belt buckled loosely on an angle over his narrow hips. Jo eyed the shiny silver bullets, each with their own tiny pocket on the belt, and imagined those dangerous hands meticulously inserting each bullet while he imagined all the gruesome ways he would like to settle the score with Six-Shooter Hank.

Mentally shaking herself to force the disconcerting image away, she sank back onto her flat pillow, hoping he wasn't here with her disguise already in hand.

"Is the patient giving you trouble, Mrs. Eisenbein?" he asked.

Jo wasn't sure if he was joking or not. He wasn't smiling.

Mrs. Eisenbein, on the other hand, grinned and set the silver spoon into the bowl. "No, Marshal. She's just anxious to get home, is all, and the doctor hasn't tended to her yet."

Holding his tan-colored hat in his hands, the marshal leaned at his ease against the doorjamb.

The steel badge pinned to his vest flashed brilliantly, reflecting sunlight from the open window. "Well, maybe I can speed the good doctor up a little. I'll just threaten to polish his head with my six-shooter."

Mrs. Eisenbein chuckled, but Jo was less inclined to see the humor. She was too busy trying to think clearly while battling her rapid pulse.

"And how are we feeling today?" the marshal asked, directing his gaze straight through her.

"Fine, thank you, Marshal. Any luck catching that outlaw?"

"Six-Shooter Hank? Not yet. But I'll get him."

Not if I keep my wits about me. "Did the posse come back?"

"Yep, but they didn't find anything. I'm not through with this yet, though. A man couldn't disappear into thin air."

"No, of course not. Could I have some more soup?" Jo asked Mrs. Eisenbein, trying to change the subject.

The woman gathered up the bowl and began feeding Jo again.

"So what's the hurry?" Marshal Collins asked, crossing one brown leather boot over the other. "If I'm going to convince the doc to see you before his other patients, I'd better have a good reason."

"Tea, please?" Jo asked.

"You don't like to answer questions, do you?"

She glanced up long enough to get the impression he found her responses frustrating, which was only natural, she decided. She *was* avoiding his questions. "I'm hungry and I'm in a hurry to get home to my son, who is probably taking years off Mrs. Honeyworth's life."

"They expecting you for supper?"

"Yes, and Mrs. Honeyworth serves it precisely at six."

"Well, we'd best get you on your way, then." He leaned back to peer down the hall. "Doc should be done soon."

Jo tried to sip her tea delicately, but was annoyed to find she couldn't stop her fingers from trembling. In the silence of the room, the fine china cup rattled against the saucer.

Self-consciously, she glanced up at the marshal and saw that he was watching her. What would he do if he knew he was staring at the person who had caused that ugly lump on his forehead and the scar that was probably already engraved on his thigh?

She glanced at that thigh, able to see quite clearly the broad expanse of muscle, the hard contours beneath his light brown trousers. He was a large man and a strong one. No wonder Zeb wanted him as the city marshal.

She cleared her throat, telling herself to keep her eyes to herself, stop jiggling this teacup like a dunderhead, and get out of here and back to the privy.

"Just so you know," Marshal Collins said, interrupting the uncomfortable silence, "we'll be spending some time together this afternoon. I rented myself a buggy and I'm going to take you back to your ranch myself."

Jo tried not to choke on her tea. "But Mrs. Honeyworth is supposed to come for me."

"I told her *I'd* get you home."

"But why would you want to do that?"

"Maybe I enjoy your conversation."

Mrs. Eisenbein's playful gaze flicked up at Jo.

"What is it that you want to discuss with me?" Jo asked pointedly. "Whatever it is, you can ask me now."

"There's nothing to discuss. I just want to see you get home safely. Mrs. Honeyworth isn't coming and your ranch is four miles outside of town, I hear. That's at least an hour's walk and it's powerful hot out there. Not a good risk in your condition."

"Thank you, but it's not necessary. I wouldn't want to trouble you."

"On the contrary, it would trouble me if you refused." His eyes darkened with a cast-iron message that Jo understood clearly. He could see through her charade and wanted to knock her off balance, get her to say something incriminating.

She set her cup and saucer on the side table and looked at Mrs. Eisenbein for help, but the woman lowered her eyes and began to gather up the tray.

"Something tells me you won't take no for an answer," Jo said to the marshal.

"Something tells me you're right."

She stared at him, considering her options. If she refused, he'd become even more suspicious than he was already, and probably follow her to the privy. But if she said yes, she'd have to leave her bag there for another day.

Without waiting for her response, the marshal backed into the hall. "I'll go get that buggy and fetch the doctor." He placed his hat on his head and disappeared from sight, the rhythmic sound of his boots lingering on the surface of Jo's frayed consciousness.

"That was kind of the marshal, don't you think?" Mrs. Eisenbein said, the dishes clinking on her tray as she stood.

But Jo knew with plunging hopes that the marshal's offer had nothing to do with kindness.

* * *

After the doctor came to the room and checked Jo's wound for infection, Mrs. Eisenbein entered with Jo's laundered gown and helped her slip into it. A few minutes later, Jo was at last being escorted down the hall to the front office.

While she arranged payment, the door squeaked open and the distinctive rhythm of the marshal's heavy boots rattled her nerves as he came up behind her. "All set to go, Mrs. O'Malley?"

She faced him. "Yes, but it really isn't necessary for you to take me. I'm perfectly capable of walking. I do it all the time."

"Not with a bullet hole in your shoulder."

"The marshal's right," Dr. Green said. "No sense taking chances. It's best to have someone with you, in case anything happens."

Marshal Collins settled his hat onto his head. "There, you see?"

Why did he have to be right all the time?

They walked onto the sunny porch and the marshal took her elbow as she descended the stairs. Feeling the stability of that hand on her arm only made her more uneasy, but she fought the urge to pull away. She had no choice but to allow him to assist her. Any hostile behavior might alert him to her apprehensive feelings, and she had to keep a calm head if she wanted him to leave her alone long enough to retrieve her bag from the privy. She only hoped it would remain there untouched until she could return for it.

"Careful now," the marshal said, helping her into a black canopied buggy with a shiny red seat. The leather creaked as she slid across.

"It's been a while since I've driven one of these."

He climbed in beside her and gently flicked the long leather reins. ''I'm usually sitting back in a saddle.''

The buggy lurched forward and the harness jingled as the black horse flicked his ears at the cloud of flies hovering around his head.

They rolled smoothly down Front Street in silence, the round buggy wheels grinding two straight tracks down the dusty street. The marshal paid the fare to cross the toll bridge over the river, then they drove onto it and faced the wide-open prairie, speckled with longhorn cattle as far as the eye could see. The buggy wheels rattled over the wooden bridge, the horse's hooves clopping while Jo mentally went over the alibi she'd given to the marshal the other day. She only hoped she would remember it correctly if he asked about it again.

Once the buggy rolled off the edge of the bridge, the ride grew rougher and Jo hugged her arm to her chest to keep her sore bones from knocking into each other.

''You okay?'' the marshal asked, then they leaped over another bump.

''Ouch! I'm fine.''

He bounced toward her and his knee touched hers. She felt a keen awareness of it and slid away.

''I could slow down,'' he offered.

Going slower meant spending more time with him in this confined space and she wasn't sure that was such a good idea. ''I told you, I could have walked. And slowing down won't make the ruts in the road go away. Why don't you stop and let me out?''

''I don't think that would be wise, ma'am.''

''You can follow along behind me if you like.''

''It's a long way.''

''I know how far it is. I'll be fine. I feel wonderful

right now.'' They bounced one more time and she winced noticeably. "Except for the bumps."

He drove another few yards, then pulled the lumbering horse to a halt with a gently spoken "whoa." They were surrounded by hundreds of longhorn cattle, idly grazing. The horse nickered and shook beneath the harness.

"You don't want to talk to me, do you?" Marshal Collins said, all too perceptively.

"Where would you get such a notion? I simply prefer to walk, that's all."

He stared at her a moment, his eyes calculating. "All right. You can walk if it's easier for you. I'll drive behind in case you get tired, but don't overdo it."

"I won't get tired." She tried to step down, but had some difficulty holding on to the thin steel rail. Before she knew it, the marshal appeared with his hands around her waist. Her insides did a flip as he lowered her to the ground, her calico skirts billowing upon the wind. He remained there looking down at her for a moment.

"Thank you," she said politely, staring at the short, stubbly grass with the pretext of examining the toe of her boot, all the while relieved that she could hide her eyes beneath the brim of her heavy white muslin sunbonnet.

"You're welcome. Just watch where you're walking and don't hesitate to get back in the buggy if you feel ill. You've been through a lot."

Stepping back out of his arms, she struggled to gloss over the awkward feeling that was niggling at her, telling herself that she had merely *imagined* he was looking at her lips just now.

"There's a cow about to sniff your boots," Jo said, more than grateful for the distraction.

Marshal Collins turned. "Go on now. Go back to your herd."

The animal shifted direction and plodded away without argument, and by the time the marshal turned to face her again, Jo had started walking. "Let's get going before we become fodder."

She didn't let herself look back. She only listened to the sound of the buggy's springs bouncing and squeaking, then the horse's hooves thumping over the grassy road. Marshal Collins was following along behind her and that was just fine as far as she was concerned. At least they didn't have to talk to each other, and she didn't have to make a fool of herself answering any more of his prying questions.

Chapter Six

Not far to go now, Jo thought wearily as she forced one foot in front of the other along the narrow prairie road, the wind blowing her bonnet ribbons every which way. She couldn't wait to get home, rid herself of these heavy clothes and collapse into her soft bed to sleep.

She just had to make it the rest of the way. She'd walked at least two-and-a-half miles and the marshal hadn't asked her any more questions, thank heavens. He simply drove behind her—but she could *feel* him staring—and he hadn't made a peep except when he clicked his tongue at the slow horse.

With a dizzying sense of apprehension, Jo eyed the next hill. If she could make it up and over the other side, she would be fine. The rest of the way was as flat as a cornmeal griddle cake.

She climbed the grassy rise and began to breathe harder. Oh, this wasn't promising at all. Her nose was beginning to feel hot and sunburned, and when she reached the top of the rise, her vision grew blurry. Dizziness overtook her as the blue sky and rolling, tawny hills all began to fold into one another and take on a silvery hue. She stopped and touched her gloved fingers to her forehead. *Oh no, not now...*

She hesitated and heard the muffled hoofbeats behind her come to a slow stop. The horse jingled its harness. Her stomach exploded with nausea and she knew that if she didn't climb into the shaded leather seat in the next few seconds, she would swoon.

She turned around, but a fresh wave of nausea crashed over her and she staggered to the side.

Her gaze locked with the marshal's and she took some comfort that he knew what was about to happen and was going to do something about it. He leaped down and ran toward her, but all she could do was stare blankly, dimly aware of her knees crumpling beneath her and the sight of his leather cowboy boots as she fainted dead away at his feet.

Jo's mind floated in a sea of calm blackness. She couldn't speak, couldn't open her eyes. She could only lie immobile in the stiff grass that was needling the back of her neck, while she listened to that easy drawl.

"Mrs. O'Malley, wake up. Wake up, ma'am. You fainted."

Her eyes fluttered open to see the inside of the marshal's tan-colored hat, fanning in front of her face— back and forth, back and forth, the cool breeze beating against her cheeks and eyes and lips. Jo tried to speak, but all she could do was let out an embarrassing guttural groan.

The hat moved aside and she found herself blinking up at the marshal's green eyes. Behind his head, a black hawk soared against the blue.

The marshal donned his hat and pressed it down tightly. "You feeling okay?"

She didn't want to answer. She only wanted to lie here a little longer and look up at him. But all at once she remembered who this man was and why he was here.

Angry with herself for letting down her guard, she jolted upright in a ridiculous attempt to rise, but the sudden movement made her shoulder throb painfully.

"Hold on, now," the marshal warned, touching her good shoulder and laying her back down in the grass. "Not so fast. You need to rest."

Feeling a headache coming on, she tried to keep it at bay by rubbing her temple. "How long was I out?"

"Only a minute or two. You were strolling along just fine, then all of a sudden, whoosh." He knelt on one knee, his arm resting across his thigh. "You dropped like all your bones turned to the kind of oatmeal my mother used to make."

"What kind of oatmeal was that?" she asked warily.

"It was runny, ma'am. But don't get me wrong. It was tasty…in its way."

Amused—though trying not to be—Jo sat up and he helped her to her feet. "You sure you're feeling well enough to stand? You lost a lot of blood the other night. It's no surprise you took a fancy to the ground."

She held on to his hand for support. Her head spun in a dizzying circle and she had to concentrate on not falling into his ready arms.

"I'm fine, but I think I'd prefer to ride with you the rest of the way."

"I reckon that's a wise choice." He led her to the buggy and helped her up, then climbed in beside her and they started off again.

Jo remembered how he had tried to convince her to stay in the buggy in the first place and wished she hadn't proven him right. At least he wasn't saying *I told you so*.

"It's not much farther," she mentioned, swaying from side to side.

"I reckon we're a little more than halfway." He took his eyes off the road to study her for a moment and she felt vulnerable, as if her secrets were printed on her cheeks in bold red ink. "You're worried I'm going to ask you more questions about the shooting."

Jo tried to appear unruffled. "I said all there was to say about that."

"Uh-huh—then what's with the toe tapping? You've been doing that since you sat down."

Realizing he was right about one more thing, Jo stilled her boot. "I always tap my foot. It's a habit."

She pulled her toe in to hide it under a petticoat ruffle. "If I'm worried about anything, it's about whether or not you're going to deliver me home in time for supper."

He glanced toward the western sun. "I reckon we'll pull into your yard just as Mrs. Honeyworth is spooning up the gravy." He licked his lips. "Mmm, gravy on just about anything would go down nice right now."

Recognizing the hint for an invitation, Jo didn't bite. "Maybe you should get yourself a wife to cook for you."

The corner of his mouth turned up in a cynical grin and he chuckled. "No, I don't think so."

"Ah, I see," she said knowingly.

"What do you mean, *ah, I see?*"

Jo knew his type well enough. She'd seen enough roaming cowhands to get a feel for the kinds of things they wanted. "Married life isn't good enough for you. Too dull, I suppose."

"Dull. No, I never imagined married life would be dull, especially on a ranch like yours, with kids around. The ranch I grew up on was anything but dull."

Jo was surprised to hear he'd grown up on a ranch. "If it was so interesting for you, why aren't you there now?"

His jaw twitched. "It's kind of personal, ma'am."

"Oh, I'm sorry, I didn't meant to—"

"No harm done."

They drove on in silence for a while and Jo felt like a complete fool for having been so ill-mannered.

After a few minutes, he spoke up and his words nearly knocked her over. "My father was murdered five years ago. That's why I'm not at the ranch anymore."

Shaken, Jo took a few seconds to respond. "I'm very sorry."

"I appreciate that, but it's all in the past now."

"What happened, if you don't mind my asking?"

He spoke offhandedly, revealing no sadness or regret, something Jo found strange. "My father was a judge, and a man named Garrett Robinson was on trial for murder in his court."

"Garrett Robinson. I heard about him. He robbed trains and stagecoaches."

Fletcher's jaw twitched again and she wondered if maybe he *did* mind talking about it. "The night before my father was to hand down a guilty verdict, Garrett's gang sent him a message saying that if he convicted Garrett, they would hunt down his family and do to us what Garrett did to all the people who got in his way. We didn't know anything about it, of course. We were as shocked as everybody else when the verdict was 'not guilty.'"

Jo shifted in her seat, needing to hear the rest. "If he did what they said, why didn't they just leave it be?"

Marshal Collins shook his head. "Men like that don't know much about honor. They killed my father on his way home that day, three hours after he let them go free. I heard the shots from the ranch house and saw the gang ride off. They were hootin' and laughin' like a bunch of kids playing hide-and-seek. I had to run a mile up hill, climb over three fences, and I knew I wasn't getting there fast enough." His Adam's apple bobbed and he paused. "My ma died of typhoid that winter, leaving me and Elizabeth to run the ranch, but neither of us wanted to live there anymore. Too many memories.

"We sold off the herd and Elizabeth went to college in Chicago. I'd always imagined I'd be a rancher, but I ended up a U.S. marshal." With a shade of indifference, he added, "Funny how things turn out sometimes."

Jo knew exactly how he felt. How many times had she wanted to pack up and leave, to start a new life somewhere else and forget about the old one? She most certainly would have if she wasn't certain Leo would return someday to claim the land that was his birthright and avenge his father's death.

"What about Garrett and his gang?" she asked, wondering if the marshal and his sister had received the justice Jo herself was still seeking.

He flicked the reins. "I dragged each one of them back to jail and watched their trials, and those who hanged saw my face in the crowd. The others are still rotting in prison."

"You dragged *all* of them to jail? Without shooting anyone?"

"Oh, I used my weapon plenty. Knocked 'em over

the head with the handle most times. So when I said 'dragged,' I meant it in the literal sense.''

Jo stared at him, dumbfounded. ''That was you? You're The Bruiser?''

''I reckon that's where the name originated. You heard about that all the way up here in Kansas?''

''Yes, and that you've never shot a man in your entire career.'' She couldn't take her eyes off him now, this celebrity beside her. She'd had no idea....

''I have too much respect for life to go around killing people willy-nilly. Though if I could turn back the clock, I might have shot the gunman who tried to rob Zeb the other night. Wounded him at least.''

At the mention of Zeb and the shooting, Jo quickly forgot her newfound fascination with the marshal's celebrity status. ''Why is...*he* so different from the others?''

''He's not different. He's the same. They all are. Men who don't respect the law need to learn they'll get caught eventually. You see, I'm not like my father. I don't believe in bending rules. If he had been a stronger man and had done his duty instead of being afraid, those men wouldn't have killed him, wouldn't have gone free for another year, killing other innocent folks.''

Jo thought about what she had done, or almost done, the other night. How she had felt there was no other choice left to her. Not surprisingly, she could sympathize with the marshal's father.

''Your father thought he was protecting his family,'' she tried to explain. ''Someday, when you have children, you'll understand it better. You'll be ready and willing to walk through fire for them. You'll do anything to keep them safe. Even break the law when you feel the law can't help you, and frankly, the law isn't always able to help innocent folks around here. You can't begrudge your father for what he did.''

Marshal Collins gave her a steely glare. ''There's never an excuse for breaking the law.''

''That's very idealistic.''

''Maybe so. But you can't argue that that's the way things *ought* to be, and we owe it to this world of ours to keep striving for what's best. My father could have protected us another way. Sent us somewhere safe until the rest of the gang was caught. He shouldn't have done what he did. He was a judge.''

The marshal's voice had grown almost hostile. ''And to answer your question about last night's gunman, I wish I'd shot him because he made me look incompetent, and when it comes to the law, I rely on my reputation to help me run a tight ship. With it, outlaws are more likely to give up without a fight and no one gets hurt. Without it, all hell breaks loose and hell ain't no place for decent folks. Tarnation, that man shot you, an innocent bystander, shot me in the leg and tried to rob my sister's husband. She's been through enough after what happened to our parents. If she'd lost her husband, too…''

His voice trailed off and Jo saw how truly angry he was over this.

''The town thinks their new marshal is a buffoon and all because I wanted to avoid gunfire. It's going to take a lot of time and energy to earn back any respect, and who knows what might happen in the meantime? I should have known better than to think that gunman would lower his weapon, but I thought I saw something in his eyes. Something…''

Jo leaned forward, curious. ''Something what?''

''Something frightened. Something…'' He hesitated

again, as if searching for just the right word. "Something sad."

A lump formed in Jo's throat. The marshal had seen through her that night, and if Zeb hadn't raised his pistol, she *would* have lowered her weapon. She would have confessed everything to Marshal Collins.

Not knowing, of course, that he was Zeb's kin.

Desperate to change the subject, she cleared her throat and forced a smile. "Heavens above, I'm sitting beside the famous Bruiser. You're not what I imagined."

"No? And what was that?"

Jo felt suddenly uncomfortable. "I was expecting someone…bigger."

She saw humor dance across his face, then he laughed. "Well, it doesn't take size to whack someone over the head with a pistol. It only takes a sober mind."

"I suppose." They drove past a patch of white elderberry and pink clover, and in the distance, Jo recognized bright yellow sunflowers. She breathed in the deep aromatic scent of the blossoms and, with some surprise, felt the tension lifting between her and Fletcher. He was gazing toward the sunflowers, too, the set lines of his face relaxing somewhat, so that he no longer looked like the rigid, vigilant lawman that he was.

Realizing she wasn't the only one letting down her guard, Jo decided to take advantage and ask some questions of her own.

"How did your sister get hooked up with Zeb Stone?"

"He met her in Chicago just before she finished school. They hit it off but he didn't stay around long, with his business back here. They only knew each other a few weeks before he sent for her, asking her to be his wife. You don't know her?''

Jo shook her head. She'd made it a point not to get to know Zeb's wife. "How long have *you* known Zeb?"

"Since the wedding this past spring." He didn't look at her when he spoke. "I thought I was the one supposed to be asking all the questions."

Jo clasped her hands together in her lap. "Just making conversation. It's a long drive."

"But not much longer." He nudged his hat back with his thumb and squinted at the blue sky. "Looks like you'll be home in time for supper."

Jo settled into the seat and tried not to think about everything the marshal had said. With all the tragedy he'd seen, it was no wonder he'd retreated from the ranching life he'd known to become a lawman. It was plain to see that he thought he could make up for his father's mistakes, that he was dead set on protecting his sister's happiness. The way he saw it, she was the only survivor left in the family, the only one with any hope for the future. He wanted to protect his own, and that meant protecting Zeb Stone.

And Lord help Jo if the marshal ever discovered he'd rented a fancy buggy to escort his enemy home.

Chapter Seven

By the time the marshal drove the buggy up the last rise, the strong wind had died away and the meadowlarks were singing their hearts out. Though the ride had been bumpy and painful at times, Jo was glad she had decided to drive instead of walk. She only wished she had come to that conclusion sooner and avoided the unfortunate fainting episode.

The horse nickered softly when they crested the last hill. Jo spotted the ranch, where a couple of the cowhands were leaning against the bunkhouse, sipping water. One more was shaving, and she heard their easy laughter in the distance, along with the clucking chatter from the henhouse. Wood smoke rose from the kitchen chimney and melted into the sky.

She sat forward when the front door of the house swung open and Leo ran onto the covered porch. He clutched the corner post and waved, then called for Matilda, who promptly came out, wiping her hands on her long white apron and waving. Jo waved back and couldn't stop herself from letting out a little squeal, and she sensed the marshal noticed it with some surprise.

She stood up in the buggy, but felt the marshal's hand

cup her wrist. "Sit down, Mrs. O'Malley. I don't want to kneel over your unconscious form twice in one day."

They hit a bump and she dropped down into the seat. "Trust me, I'm not much in the mood for that, either." She waved her good arm at Leo and Matilda.

The marshal drove the buggy into the yard and pulled the horse to a gentle halt next to the white plank corral fence.

"Ma!" Leo called out, leaping off the porch and hurrying to take hold of the horse's harness. "You're all better!"

"Not quite, Leo, but I'm on the mend and happy to be home."

The marshal hopped down and walked around the buggy, appearing at Jo's side to help her down. She glanced quickly over the top of his hat at the ranch hands looking on and wished one of them had been quicker to assist her instead of *this* man.

She reached for the marshal's hand, but he took her by the waist and lifted her like a feather to the ground. "Wouldn't want you to fall," he said.

She quickly withdrew her hands from his shoulders.

Leo approached Marshal Collins. "Did you catch Six-Shooter Hank yet?"

"Not yet, but I will. And Leo, don't believe everything you read." He winked at him, and Leo smiled brightly.

Matilda approached.

"The marshal insisted on driving me home," Jo said, trying to explain herself to her housekeeper.

"It was a good thing I did." He rested his hands on his hips, gazing down at her as if they shared a special secret.

She cringed at what people must be thinking.

"Are you all right, Josephine?" Matilda asked, worried.

The marshal removed his hat. "No need to worry ma'am. She just felt a little tired, is all."

No one said anything for a minute or two, and the long silence was more than a little awkward. Surely everyone must be wondering what he was doing here.

Determined not to let her uneasiness show, Jo spoke up. "Well, thank you for the ride home, Marshal Collins." *You can go now,* she wanted to add, but of course held back the rude remark.

"It was no trouble at all." He moved to put on his hat, but Leo stopped him.

"Why don't you stay for supper, Marshal? We're having beef stew with dumplings."

If the last silence had been awkward, this one was downright painful. Matilda stared in shock at Leo, whose face colored sheepishly. Marshal Collins stood waiting for someone to say something, while Jo wanted to bury her head in the nearest haystack. If he stayed for supper, he'd have more opportunity to ask questions about the night of the shooting and she just wasn't sure she could handle any more of that.

"Of course, you're welcome to stay, Marshal," Matilda said coolly.

He looked down at Jo, telling her with his eyes that he knew she wanted him to leave.

Which was precisely why he intended to stay.

That didn't sit well with Jo. Not one bit.

"How can I refuse?" he said, patting his firm, flat stomach. "A man's gotta eat."

Fletcher pulled off his shirt and washed up outside the bunkhouse, where the ranch hands kept their shaving equipment on a white painted shelf under the window. Leaning forward, he splashed cool, soothing water from a wooden bucket onto his face and over his chest and arms, lathering himself with lye soap, trying to clear his mind.

He thought about the drive and how he'd gotten none of the information he'd wanted from Mrs. O'Malley. He'd been struck foolish with some kind of tongue-flapping disease, spilling out his soul to her about his father. He hadn't spoken about personal things to anyone in years, but her interest had seemed genuine, he'd thought. She'd been through something similar not long ago, and maybe that was why she wanted to talk and why she seemed to think she understood.

Which she didn't, of course.

Fletcher splashed more cool water on his face and rubbed his fingers over his tired eyes, trying to get his mind back on track. He straightened and looked across the yard at Leo, who was walking toward him carrying a clean white shirt. Fletcher toweled off and summoned a smile.

"Ma said to bring you this to wear at supper," Leo said. "It belonged to my pa."

Fletcher toweled his hands and face dry, eyeing the shirt with some hesitation. "Much obliged."

Leo handed it to him and Fletcher shrugged into it. It was a bit small through the shoulders, but he managed to fasten all the buttons, and at least it was clean. He pulled his vest on over it and buttoned that, too.

He felt a little strange wearing a dead man's clothing, though. How would Mrs. O'Malley react when she saw him wearing it? Would it make her think of her husband?

Just as Leo was about to turn away, Fletcher stopped

him with a question. "Tell me, does your ma spend much time in town?"

The boy leaned his back against the log wall of the bunkhouse. "Not since Pa died. She only goes for supplies when she has to, and even then, she'll put it off or get Mrs. Honeyworth to go for her."

"Does she stay out here alone when that happens?"

"Nobody's ever alone out here this time of year. I mean, there's always ranch hands around."

Fletcher knew that, of course, having been raised on a ranch, but he needed to steer his questions gradually. "What about in the winter? Is it just you and your ma and Mrs. Honeyworth? Any visitors?"

Leo kicked the dirt with the toe of his boot. "Not since Pa died."

"I heard about your pa," Fletcher said gently. "You must miss him a lot."

"Yeah. Things were different when he was around. He used to let me do more stuff."

"Like what?"

"Like helping with the spring roundup. It's different now, that's all."

"Your ma didn't let you do that?"

"Nah. She barely lets me out of her sight sometimes. She won't even let me talk to people we don't know."

Fletcher tossed the towel over his shoulder. He could hear the frustration in Leo's voice—a boy desperate to be a man and stand in his father's empty shoes, and a mother who was afraid of losing him like she'd lost her husband. "I think you just need to give your ma some time, Leo. Things will get better."

"But she never used to be like this."

"Maybe that's because your pa made the decisions about you. Now your ma has to do a lot of things by herself. A lot of things she never had to do before, and I would guess that losing your pa broke her heart and she's real scared of losing you, too."

Leo's voice was quiet. "Maybe. I just…" He stopped talking altogether.

Fletcher rested his hand on Leo's shoulder. "If you ever need to talk to someone about your pa, I'd be happy to listen. I lost my pa, too, and I know what it feels like."

"Really?"

"Yes. It might not seem like it now, but it *will* get easier."

Just as Leo stared up at him hopefully, Mrs. Honeyworth opened the front door of the house and rang the tarnished brass dinner bell on the porch. The clanging echoed off the barnyard walls as four ranch hands left the corral, swung the wide gate closed behind them and headed toward the house.

Leo pushed away from the wall and brightened a bit. "Supper's on."

"Everybody eats in the house?" Fletcher asked, watching the dusty cowboys climb the front steps. Back at his old place, the hired help ate in the cookhouse.

"Yeah. Unless they're out at the range camps. Then they settle for the chuck wagon. Pa always wanted it that way and I guess it makes Ma feel like some things haven't changed. Even though they have."

Leo walked off and Fletcher stood for a moment, watching him and feeling a deep sense of sadness for this boy who had lost his father at such a tender age. At least Fletcher had been a man of twenty-five when it had happened to him.

But as he considered it more, he doubted that his age

made much of a difference. Grief was grief. At least Leo still had his mother. And this land.

Fletcher let his gaze wander over the green rolling fields beyond the fenced corral and felt a pang of regret. He looked at the windmill behind the barn, listened to the purr of its wooden blades as they sliced the wind. A large herd of cattle grazed quietly in the front pasture. There was much to remind him of the home he had once had, the ranch his family had owned back in Texas when life was simple and cheerful and filled with luxuries he, for one, took for granted. He wasn't talking about the luxuries money could buy, either—though they had plenty of those. What came to mind now was the laughter and the sense of belonging, the warmth of the big house on stormy winter nights when the fireplace was roaring and the wind was whistling down the stone chimney and they all sat in the front parlor talking and laughing and reading aloud to one another.

But that was another life, he thought wistfully, another time. Those days were gone and nothing could bring them back. He was a lawman now and he was devoted to something else. He went where he was needed, and if that meant the idea of "home" had to be modified a bit, then so be it. There was no point reminiscing about it.

Leo turned back and yelled across the yard, "You coming, Marshal?"

Startled from his thoughts, Fletcher replied, "On my way!" Then he looked toward the small creek that babbled near the road, the wooden barrels stacked outside the barn, and the smokehouse next to the chicken coop. This place was probably already engraved on Leo's soul, Fletcher thought with some melancholy, just like *his* Texas home had once been engraved on his, and

Leo probably didn't know it. Fletcher decided he would make a point very soon to tell the boy how lucky he was to have this place. His birthright.

He tossed the towel over the side of a half-full water barrel and started walking toward the house, laboring to force all thoughts of lost dreams from his mind, and keep only two others.

Beef stew and answers.

"So what brings you to Dodge City, Marshal?" one of the ranch hands asked, as he passed a plate of thickly sliced rye bread down the large table. The red-checkered tablecloth was barely visible beneath all the serving bowls full of steaming potatoes, corn and green beans. Forks clinked against plates as eight hungry men chowed down as if it was their last meal.

Knocking elbows with the man, Fletcher accepted the china plate and picked up two slices for himself. "My sister, really—Elizabeth Stone. She came here this past spring and I thought it was high time I live near my kin. At least for a little while."

Mrs. O'Malley sat next to him at the head of the table. Her gaze remained lowered as she ate her stew. "Bread?" he offered.

Without looking up, she took the plate. The pads of their fingers touched beneath it. Fletcher tensed at the swift surge of awareness and wondered if she had felt something, too, and if that was why she refused to make eye contact with him.

Bowls passed from one end of the table to the other and Fletcher was glad when the conversation picked up again. "Where are you from, Marshal?" one of the men asked.

"Texas. My family owned a ranch there, but after my folks passed on, Elizabeth and I sold the place."

"That don't make a lick of sense to me," the man said. "A place like that is worth a—"

Mrs. O'Malley interrupted. "Mr. Birk, I'm sure the marshal has his reasons and it's really none of our business. Pass the lemonade, please, Marshal, and would you be kind enough to pour it for me?"

Somehow she had sensed how he felt—that he didn't want to talk to these people about why he'd sold his ranch—and Fletcher was grateful to her for sparing him that task. He wanted to lean over and quietly whisper "thank you," but instead, all he did was pour her lemonade.

During the remainder of the meal, he thought about everything she'd said to him that day and about what her life must be like on a daily basis. Judging by the faces at the table, he knew she held everyone's respect as the head of the household. She was intelligent and strong, to be sure. He could tell by the condition of the ranch. She'd kept things going efficiently around here, and done it without a husband. Most women probably would have packed it in and gone back to their families. Did she have a family to go to? he wondered. He wanted to know so much more about her.

With some uneasiness, he realized that he wasn't curious because it was his job and she was a witness. Something more personal was stirring inside Fletcher now. He wanted to make up for what had happened to Mrs. O'Malley the other night and make sure it didn't happen again. She already had enough pain in her life. Anyone could see that.

One of the cowhands handed the plate of bread down the table and Fletcher passed it to his hostess.

"Thank you, Marshal," she said, and he felt something friendly pass between them.

"Thank *you*, ma'am, for inviting me to supper. The stew is delicious."

"Sure beats beans and bacon!" someone said, and the whole table cheered.

After that, Fletcher's mood lightened and he settled in to eating. It was a busy meal, bowls and pitchers being passed along for second helpings. By the time everyone finished their stew and there was nothing left of the bread and vegetables, Fletcher was stuffed. Mrs. Honeyworth gathered up the plates and disappeared into the kitchen.

At the opposite end of the table, sitting at the head, Leo leaned back and laced his fingers together over his full belly, just like some middle-aged banker after a big meal. Fletcher couldn't help but grin to himself, and when he glanced at Mrs. O'Malley, he caught her doing the same thing, trying to hide it as well, and they smiled at each other.

The kitchen door swung open and Mrs. Honeyworth swept into the dining room with a tray of desserts and served Mrs. O'Malley first. Then she set a glass pedestal dessert cup in front of Fletcher, filled with what smelled like raspberry cream custard, and finally she poured coffee for everyone from a shiny silver pot.

"What's it like to be a lawman, Marshal?" Leo asked, delving into his dessert.

Fletcher was grateful for the conversation to distract him from thinking about his hostess. "It can be dangerous, son, if you're not careful. But I try to be careful most of the time." He considered the question some more over a sip of hot, black coffee. "I reckon the best part is when I help somebody.'' He felt Mrs. O'Malley's gaze studying him but didn't look up.

''If I were a marshal, I'd catch all the outlaws,'' Leo said, playing with what was left of his dessert. ''Especially the horse thieves who—''

''Leo!'' Mrs. O'Malley burst out.

Fletcher saw the look of shock on her face, then saw a similar emotion dance across Leo's.

''May I be excused?'' the boy asked.

Mrs. O'Malley stared at her son, her womanly facial features tightening, then her authoritative tone vanished. Clearly, her love for her son was her number-one weakness. ''Are you finished with your dessert?''

''Yes, ma'am.''

''Then yes, you may be excused.''

He shoved back his chair and walked quickly from the room, which had gone deathly silent.

Fletcher glanced at Mrs. O'Malley. She leaned an elbow on the table and covered her mouth with two trembling fingers. After a moment's deliberation, she made a move to rise, but winced and touched her shoulder. Fletcher saw the frustration as her eyelids fell closed.

''I'll go,'' he said, lightly touching her hand.

''That's not necessary.''

''Someone has to go.''

''But not *you*,'' she whispered, looking up at him with narrowed eyes, both pleading and commanding at the same time.

Fletcher hesitated, confused by her desperate expression. ''Trust me,'' he said simply, then he walked out, feeling every eye watch him as he left the quiet dining room.

Chapter Eight

With Matilda's help, Jo managed to rise from the table and say good-night to the other gentlemen. She had to follow the marshal and prevent him from talking to Leo, from getting too close to him. Leo was vulnerable now. He needed a father figure, and a lawman sworn to protect Zeb Stone was the last person her boy should turn to. Just the thought of it made her stomach turn.

Walking quickly, she reached the front hall, peered out the window and listened for voices on the dark porch. She heard nothing but crickets chirping and cows lowing in the distance. She pulled the door open. The moon hung like a lantern in the clear black sky, lighting the barnyard.

She knew where Leo had gone.

A wave of apprehension swept over her. Ever since Edwyn's death, Leo had chosen the barn as his private hideaway, the place he went to think. Jo's heart ached with the painful realization that he chose it because he knew it was the one place his mother would not go.

As she crossed the yard, she tried to calm her erratic pulse. After everything she'd lost, was she losing her son, too?

She reached the barn door, which had been left open a crack, and stopped outside to listen. Hearing the faint murmur of voices and seeing light from a lantern coming from the tack room, she tried to find the courage to go inside, but icy terror licked at her flesh.

It had been six months since she'd been in the barn, and if not for Leo and the other men, the animals never would have survived. Each time Jo went near the huge gambrel-roofed building, she could still smell death, hear the rope creaking as it swung back and forth like a pendulum. She could see Edwyn's well-worn boots suspended only a foot above the hay-strewn floor, his body limp, his bare hands bleeding from trying to defend himself against Zeb's two hooded henchmen, who had beaten Edwyn before dragging him inside.

She wished she had heard Zeb say *why* he had murdered Edwyn. Then there might have been a way to convict him.

Squeezing her eyes shut to force the memories away, she tried to listen to the voices inside the barn but could hear nothing clearly from where she stood. She worried about what the marshal might say to Leo. Or worse, what Leo might say to him. But should she go in? *Could* she go in?

She sucked in a deep breath of cool air to fill her tightening chest. She'd had the courage to confront her enemy with a loaded weapon a few nights before. Why couldn't she face the spot where her husband had died? Why must it continue to haunt her with such terror?

Feeling defeated, she rested her head against the timber wall of the barn and closed her eyes. She needed a moment to think and began to make excuses, as she always did: Perhaps she didn't *need* to go in. More than a few things the marshal had said to her during the day had surprised her and cast doubt upon his involvement with Zeb. Perhaps he wasn't such an adversary after all. She wished she knew. Maybe what he was saying to Leo privately would reveal something. Give her hope that some lawmen could be trusted. That Zeb didn't own everything in Dodge City.

Hearing laughter from the tack room, Jo knew she would not be going into the barn tonight. And though it would drain her already depleted patience, she would have to wait to find out what the marshal with the questionable integrity had said to her son.

Precisely fifteen minutes later by her pocket watch, Jo sat on the porch swing tapping her foot. What was taking them so long? What could they be talking about?

At last, the light from the barn went out and the door swung open. Jo stood up, pressing her palm to her chest, relieved to see her son appear from the dark and silent interior where Edwyn had gasped his last breath.

Leo stepped into the moonlight, then the marshal walked out and closed the barn door behind them. As they approached the house, he rested a hand on Leo's shoulder and Leo laughed at something. It made Jo feel disturbingly territorial. Until tonight, Leo would not speak to her—or anyone, for that matter—when he disappeared into the barn. What was it about the marshal that he admired so much? Was it because Fletcher had lost his father, too? Had he spoken of that to Leo?

They reached the porch and only then did the marshal look up and notice Jo sitting there with her watch in her hand. She forced a smile, stood up and walked to the top of the steps. "Is everything all right?"

"Yes, Ma. Can I go to bed now?" Leo replied.

Jo swallowed the urge to ask him anything more. "Yes, you may."

"Night, Marshal Collins. Night, Ma."

"Good night, Leo."

Jo watched her son go into the house and heard his footsteps tap eagerly up the stairs. She took a deep breath and turned to face the marshal, not knowing what to expect.

When their eyes met, her emotions dipped alarmingly. He stood at the bottom of the porch stairs with one boot resting on the second step, his hand on his raised knee. He gave her a subtle, reassuring smile and the attempt only served to confuse her.

"What happened?" she asked, unable to control her curiosity.

"Nothing much. We just talked."

Just talked. Leo hadn't *just talked* to anyone in six months. "What about?" She tried to sound nonchalant.

The marshal didn't answer right away. He walked calmly up the stairs, moved around Jo, sat himself down on the porch swing and leaned back. "Care to join me for a minute or two?"

The invitation—the thought of sitting so close to him—made her insides swoop with nervousness. She tried to smother the reaction and stiffly made her way to the swing and sat down, keeping her backside perched forward on the wooden seat to avoid touching his arm, which rested across the back of the swing.

"How's your shoulder?" he asked.

"It still pains me a great deal. I'm anxious to retire."

The corner of his mouth turned up, as if he was amused by her never-ending attempts to get rid of him. "I see. Can you stay awake long enough to hear what your son had to say?"

"Of course. I'm always interested in what Leo has to say."

"I'm sure that's true. Only problem is, he doesn't think so."

Jo felt as if she'd been blasted by another pistol, this time straight through the heart. She knew she and Leo had been having problems since Edwyn died, but she didn't want to hear it from Marshal Collins.

"He'll come around in time," she said, working hard to be guarded and abrupt with this man who seemed to be pushing to get closer, to understand her and Leo. Could that be true? Could he be as sincere as he sounded?

The marshal leaned forward, rested his elbows on his knees and laced his fingers together. "He told me what happened to your husband."

Jo let her eyes follow the erratic flight of a bat overhead. *But he didn't tell you the truth. I'm the only one who knows what really happened.*

The marshal continued. "You can't let that stop you from letting your son grow up. He thinks you don't trust him with things, that you don't have any confidence that he can take over the ranch."

"He's just a boy. Taking over the ranch is a long way off."

"Not in his mind. He's ready to be a man. He needs some freedom."

Jo knew this already. She'd known it for a long time. She just couldn't bring herself to give that kind of independence to Leo. How could she, when she knew he only wanted to be out from under her protective wing so he could investigate his father's murder?

Part of what angered her now was that she was being told this by a man who had no business with her family.

In fact, he was the last person on earth she wanted involved.

"Did he talk to you about Edwyn?" she asked, hoping desperately that Leo hadn't tried to elicit the marshal's help in finding his father's killers.

"He said things were different when he was alive."

"Of course they were different—" She heard her angry tone and cut herself off before she spilled out all her woes to the marshal right here and now.

But oh, how she needed to spill her woes to someone. It had been so long since she'd had anyone to trust with the workings of her heart—her doubts and fears in the middle of the darkest nights....

"I know how you feel," he said gently, and his kindness, which she had been working hard to deflect, nearly broke her.

She had to move away from him. She stood up, and the swing twisted to and fro. The porch planks creaked beneath her feet.

"Just try talking to Leo," the marshal said. "Let him know why you're prudent, and maybe you could relax the rules a little. Let him do the things he used to do."

A chilly evening breeze blew her skirt as she stood resting her hands on the white-painted porch rail, gazing across the dark hills. "I can't," she whispered, feeling as though the ground was slipping out from under her.

"You have to. Or you'll lose him."

Jo swallowed the sob that rose in her throat. Either way, she would lose.

She heard the swing creak behind her as the marshal rose and approached. Jo closed her eyes, feeling his nearness. He was going to touch her. She sensed it, but she couldn't bring herself to ask him to leave, even though she knew she should.

He laid a hand on her good shoulder. She felt his breath on the back of her neck, knew he was smelling the orange flower water she'd splashed on before supper.

Her skin tingled and she wanted to touch his hand. To thank him, oddly enough, for wanting to help Leo, even though she'd not wanted him to. It had been a while since Leo had looked to anyone for advice. None of the ranch hands seemed wise enough. Mature enough.

The marshal gently squeezed her shoulder and she took a shaky breath. It had been too long since she'd felt the warmth of a man's touch, felt the desire to open herself up to someone who wanted to hear her sorrows and understand them, understand *her*. She could respond to him now, turn around and…

Oh, how she wanted to. Her heart was beating wildly within her breast, imploring her, pushing her…

She bowed her head, fighting it. She felt so terribly confused. Even if the marshal was ignorant of Zeb's crimes—and she couldn't be sure of that—he would still feel some duty to protect him. Zeb was his sister's husband, after all.

A few seconds later, the marshal withdrew his hand from her shoulder and stepped back. Jo felt a chill of regret move through her like an icy wave.

"I must be on my way," the marshal said, his voice revealing his disappointment. "I'll just get my hat."

The door squeaked open and Jo looked up at the starry sky, so impossibly distant. She heard the marshal thanking Matilda, then the door squeaked again and he stepped onto the porch. The evening crickets chirped a steady rhythm.

He stood behind her for a moment, and she realized

he had not asked her any more questions about the shooting. Had she managed to convince him she'd said everything? Or had Leo simply distracted him from it?

Jo turned around and faced him. Her polite smile was agony to muster, but she forced herself, while inside her heart was aching more than she could bear.

But aching for what? And why?

He donned his hat. "Thank you for supper, ma'am. I'm much obliged. Good night, now."

With that, he breezed by her and walked to the rented buggy. It bounced as he got in, and the horse nickered. The marshal flicked the reins and turned the buggy around in the yard, gifting Jo with one last look as he passed by the house.

For a long moment, she felt as if she were floating. He touched the brim of his hat, staring a little longer than would be considered proper, but Jo stared back all the same, wishing she could trust him to take care of all this for her, to make it all go away.

Just before he looked away, she raised her hand with a goodbye. A glimmer of intimacy shone in his eyes.

Confused, she stood on the porch watching the back of the buggy until it disappeared over the moonlit hill. The relief she was expecting from his departure eluded her. All she wanted, strangely enough and in the most unsettling way, was for him to return.

Fletcher drove away from the O'Malley ranch, fighting the urge to turn back and take that reclusive widow into his arms and satisfy the desires he'd been trying to fight all night long. He was certain he'd seen something in her eyes that said she didn't want him to go. That delicate wave had been more than a simple goodbye.

He drove over the hill and just had to pull the horse

to a halt. Something in him didn't want to leave Mrs. O'Malley alone after what she'd been through with the shooting the other night. After that pleading look in her eye just now, he began to wonder if there wasn't something more going on here. Maybe she'd actually seen the gunman, and that's why he'd shot her. Maybe that's why she was so secretive. She was afraid the gunman might come back to finish her off if he knew she could identify him.

But it still didn't explain why there had been no bullet hole in her dress, Fletcher thought with some irritation. After spending time with her, he was finding it harder and harder to accept the explanation she'd given him, despite the rumors about her.

Come to think of it, he was finding it harder to accept the rumors, too.

Unable to make sense of this, Fletcher sat alone on the dark prairie, squeezing the soft leather reins in his hands. He wanted—needed—to protect her from whatever danger he sensed she might be in.

But how was he to stay on his toes and maintain his professional objectiveness when all he wanted to do now was touch her and smell her and tell her he'd keep her safe? He hadn't wanted a woman in his life for a long time, and he certainly didn't want one now. It would never work and he'd known that when he chose this career path. He shouldn't be having these doubts.

He took a deep breath and tried to think rationally. If he went back there, it would be a personal thing, not a professional one, that much he knew, and it made him clench his fists in frustration.

But despite it all, he flicked the reins and began to turn the buggy back toward the ranch, with no idea what he would say when he got there.

The fragrant prairie breeze cooled Jo's flushed cheeks as she stood on the porch, watching the dark horizon. All she could think of was the intimate conversation she'd just had with the marshal when she knew he was a man she could not trust—the brother-in-law of her husband's murderer and the man her son had confided in instead of her.

Why then, was she staring after him?

She waited a few moments, then sighed heavily and went into the warm, lantern-lit house where all was quiet. Leo was in bed, Matilda in the kitchen and the ranch hands had retired to the bunkhouse.

Jo stood in the front hall staring at Edwyn's large tilting portrait. The black-and-white photograph had captured him well—his brown eyes serious, brows in a straight line, mouth covered by a long bushy mustache that made him appear to be frowning even though he wasn't.

She reached her hand out to straighten the gilt frame, trying to remember the long-ago days when they were first married. Had he ever made her body respond with fluttering heartbeats as the marshal had tonight when he touched her shoulder and she could feel his breath on the back of her neck?

No, she did not remember anything like that. Edwyn was a kind man. A decent man. That was why she had married him, and they'd had a good life together all these years. But there had been no passion for either of them in their union. Her husband's touch had never inflamed her senses like the marshal's had tonight.

She stepped back and stared a little longer, feeling guilty for so many things.

Of course, Edwyn must have had his share of guilt, too…

She walked into the parlor and sat on the sofa, letting her fingers roam idly over the deeply buttoned crimson upholstery. She thought about the marshal, and imagined her fingers roaming over the strong lines of his jaw, through the wavy hair at his nape. Though she tried to chase the thought from her mind, she wondered what it would feel like to kiss him....

Fletcher sat quietly in the buggy in Mrs. O'Malley's yard, wishing he'd not returned to see what he'd seen through her front door—a young widow staring so intently, so longingly at her dead husband's portrait, she'd not noticed the man in her yard.

Perhaps it was best, he tried to tell himself, flicking the reins to head back to town. Perhaps that's why fate had urged him to return here just now—so he could see the way things *really* were and put an end to this ridiculous distraction before it got too out of hand. Before it turned into something he sure as hell would have to be crazy to want.

Chapter Nine

Leo blew out the lantern by his bed and snuggled down under the patchwork quilt. He stared at the ceiling for a few minutes, then out the window where the moon shone brightly onto the hills in the distance. He looked at a star, the brightest one, and watched it flicker.

Listening to the sounds of cattle far away, he closed his eyes and thought of the things Marshal Collins had said to him. *Your ma loves you very much. She just misses your pa.*

He tried to remember the last time he'd seen his ma laugh, but couldn't. He tried to remember the last time he'd seen her cry, but couldn't. Where had his tender mother gone? Why was she always so angry with him?

Leo wished Marshal Collins were here so he could talk to him some more. Then he thought of his pa, and he clutched the quilt in his fists.

"Pa? If you can hear me, I want you to know that I'm gonna take care of Ma. She's been sad since you left us, but I think part of it's because she's afraid of losing me, too. At least, that's what Marshal Collins said. Marshal Collins is a real nice man. He promised to show me the jailhouse someday."

Leo thought carefully about what to say next. He wanted to get it right.

"I'm gonna take care of things, Pa. I'm gonna see that the men who robbed us get taken to jail, and then Ma will feel better and not worry so much about losing me, too. Maybe she'll start smiling again."

Leo turned onto his side and looked at the star. It flickered brightly in the sky, and he watched it shine until he couldn't keep his eyes open any longer.

Today was a day for new beginnings, Jo thought, looking up at the bright sun and feeling more optimistic than she had in a long time. Heading into town, she sat beside Leo on the squeaky, bouncy wagon seat, heeding some of the marshal's advice by letting her son drive.

She'd also told him he could run the errands for her in town—all by himself—which gave him a reason to eat breakfast in a hurry instead of fiddling with it endlessly just to prove a point. This way, Jo could accomplish two tasks at the same time: patching up some of the lost love between her and her son, and sneaking her bag out from under the privy floor.

Of course, there was a third very important task.

"Tell me, Leo, what did you and the marshal talk about in the barn last night?"

Elbows to knees, Leo held the reins loosely. "Some talk between men is private."

Jo pulled her shawl tighter around her shoulders, realizing her optimism was a bit premature. "I didn't mean to pry."

He hesitated a moment, as if considering whether or not to continue the conversation. Jo waited, determined to prove she could give him the space he desired. After a few more minutes, Leo leaned back and said,

"Fletcher told me you were just worried about me, and that you miss Pa. He said you were lonely for companionship, having to run the ranch all on your own."

"Lonely for companionship?" she blurted out, then wondered why it should matter what the marshal thought about her. "Of course, I'm lonely for your pa," Jo said, trying to sound casual, "but I have everything I need in you."

His eyes beamed briefly. "Did you know the marshal has sent more than sixty men to prison? Some of them were horse thieves. He's a real good tracker. He chased some of them for weeks."

"Leo, we have to put what happened to your pa behind us, otherwise it will eat away at us forever. The men who robbed us are long gone and the trail is cold. We did what we could."

He shook his head and spoke softly. "No, we didn't."

Her heart throbbed at his words. She knew Leo felt powerless and understood his frustration, but she just couldn't let him act upon it. Not while it was still so dangerous. "Yes, we did, Leo. You know I spoke to the sheriff about it. I told him everything and he looked into it. There was nothing that could be done to catch those men."

"But maybe Marshal Collins can help us."

"No, Leo."

"Did you ask him?"

"Of course not."

"Well, I did." Leo shifted in his seat, as if he knew how angry Jo would be and was preparing himself.

She stiffened, trying to control her voice. "What did you tell him?"

"I told him what those horse thieves did and that the

sheriff couldn't find them. Fletcher said *he* wouldn't have stopped hunting them until they were brought to justice.''

Jo swallowed hard. ''Is that all?''

Leo cleared his throat nervously. ''I asked him to see what he could do.''

''You what!''

''Why won't you let me do something? I want things to be right again.''

It was bitterly ironic that Leo had no idea how much she wanted that, too, and how far she was willing to go to get it. If only she could explain it to him. But if he knew what she knew, he would not survive the day.

''You're all I have left, Leo, and I don't want you getting mixed up in it.''

''But Fletcher said he'd do all the work. He's going to look into it for us. You don't have to worry.''

''There will be no looking into it, do you understand?''

Leo flicked the reins and said nothing more.

Stunned to speechlessness, Jo stared straight ahead. As desperately as she'd wanted to mend the broken feelings between her and Leo, what he was asking of her was the very thing she could not give him. Trusting Marshal Collins to investigate Edwyn's murder was too great a risk. What if he was with Zeb right now, telling him that a young rancher boy was dead set on finding the man who had killed his pa?

Jo needed to stop Zeb on her own, without anyone's help, particularly the marshal's. Her son was growing more and more determined every day and the new marshal with his shiny revolver was giving Leo false hopes he'd do better without. On top of that, she'd actually thought about *kissing* the man.

Ah, her choice was clear. The best thing for everyone now was to stay as far away from Dodge City's new lawman as was humanly possible.

After finally retrieving her gunman's disguise from the privy, Jo returned to the wagon and hid her bag under a worsted blanket in the back. She stood for a while under the hot sun, thankful for her wide bonnet brim shading her eyes, and waited for Leo. When she heard people cheering at the other end of Front Street, she turned to look and saw a crowd gathering near the water tower.

Jo picked up her skirts and walked curiously along the boardwalk past the saloons and mercantiles, her boot heels clicking a steady rhythm over the uneven planks until she reached the far end of town where the smell of burnt pastry wafted out of the bakery.

Jo stood on the boardwalk shading her eyes, squinting up at the raised platform, and when she saw the speaker, her heart began to race.

There, in a black suit and top hat, his dark mustache waxed into curls, his deep eyes gleaming with the charisma that had gotten him everything his black heart had ever wanted, stood Zeb Stone.

And what was this? He was announcing his candidacy for mayor!

He looked down and spotted Jo in the crowd. For the briefest of seconds their gazes met, and she saw the sparkle of recognition, the hint of a smile. Her stomach clenched tight with fear.

The crowd erupted in applause and Jo looked around without the slightest idea of what he had said to gain such approval. She hadn't been able to hear anything above the thundering rhythm of her blood pulsing through her veins.

Then she remembered Leo and tried to spot him. He was probably watching from up front. A sea of colorful feathered hats and Stetsons blocked her view, so she stepped onto the street and circled around the audience, going by the tall water tower, still searching. Then, one word from Zeb caught her attention. *Family.*

She stood off to the side, watching. Zeb's voice gentled. "I want to introduce my beautiful wife, Elizabeth, whose support has been and will continue to be my greatest bounty."

"Isn't she lovely?" the woman next to Jo said, her gloved hands muting the sound of her clapping.

A warning voice whispered in Jo's head telling her not to look, but she couldn't help herself. She lifted her gaze for one peek. A suffocating sensation squeezed around her chest.

Elizabeth Stone was lovely, without question, but that was not what nearly knocked Jo over onto her backside. The young woman with the dark features possessed an uncanny resemblance to her brother.

Elizabeth smiled down at the citizens of Dodge, making shy eye contact with them. It was not surprising Zeb had chosen her for his wife. She was any politically ambitious man's dream.

Zeb bowed before her and kissed her white-gloved hand, a well-thought-out spectacle that made the crowd cheer and whistle. Elizabeth blushed sweetly.

"And I must also introduce," Zeb went on, "a gentleman who I am confident will bring pride and dignity and restraint to our growing city. My brother-in-law, Marshal Fletcher Collins."

The audience held back their applause, murmuring

with gossip about the shooting and the way their marshal had decorously collapsed before the gunman. A flicker of infuriation passed across Zeb's face. Jo rose up on her toes to see Fletcher.

He climbed the platform steps, appearing relaxed and confident despite the crowd's quiet chatter. Jo felt the tension for him, as if it was she who was up there facing the difficult crowd. He didn't speak, only touched the brim of his hat. He and Elizabeth said something to each other with reassuring smiles.

"And I want to take this opportunity to clear up some misconceptions about our new marshal," Zeb said. A hush fell over the crowd. "Whatever was reported in the newspaper about Tuesday night's shooting was grossly inaccurate. I witnessed the event, and let me assure you, the marshal did not flinch or cower. He walked into my store with his weapon drawn, ready to fire, and that gunman had agreed to surrender. He was, in fact, shaking in his boots!"

A hum of approving laughter filtered through the crowd. "Marshal Collins was wounded in the line of duty because that outlaw was so terrified, he shot his pistol off by mistake!"

People began whispering to each other. Some laughed, and Fletcher shifted his weight, clearly uncomfortable being the focus of so much attention.

Zeb added, "But what this city needs to know, is that I did not bring this man here because he is my brother-in-law. I brought him here because we need someone to clean up our town's disagreeable reputation. I have brought to you, good people of Dodge—The Bruiser!"

The roar of merriment nearly shook down the water tower. Jo was bumped on either side by men unable to control their excitement. Hats were being tossed into the air.

She looked up at the platform where Zeb was shaking Fletcher's hand. Smiling, they patted each other on the back like true blood brothers, hearing the cheer below them and feeling their power grow.

Searching for Leo, Jo circled the crowd and spotted him up front, clapping his hands over his head, leaping up and down. "Leo!" she called, sidling along the platform. She reached him and grabbed his hand with her weak arm. Gritting her teeth against the pain, she pulled him through the crowd out into the open.

"Ma! What are you doing? Didn't you hear? Marshal Collins is The Bruiser!"

"Let's go, Leo." She started off toward their wagon down the street, but Leo didn't follow.

"Don't you want to hear the rest of the speech?"

She turned back, her temper rising and overflowing. She'd never been so furious with Leo. He'd never given her reason to be. "Leo, you have disobeyed me enough. Come with me now."

"But Ma!"

Just then, Zeb raised his hands to quiet the crowd. "As president of the city council, I can report that the election for mayor will be held one week from today. The election for county sheriff will be held as usual in November, and I believe…" He paused, then his voice took on a humorous tone. "I believe, judging by the enthusiasm I hear today, that we may have a suitable candidate in our very presence!" He gestured toward Fletcher and Jo shook her head in disbelief.

"I want to thank you all for your support, and I'll see you on election day!" The crowd applauded and cheered.

"All right, Leo, it's over. Come with me now."

"But Ma! If Mr. Stone's going to be mayor and Marshal Collins is going to be county sheriff, maybe they can help us find the men who killed Pa!"

Before Jo could stop him, Leo turned and ran into the crowd toward Zeb.

Chapter Ten

Breathing hard, Jo followed Leo into the crowd. She pushed her way to the center of the shifting mass, but others were eager to brush elbows with the future mayor. Ambitious businessmen butted ahead of her, bumped her in the shoulder, knocked her off balance and into other equally aggressive money-grubbers. Shouts and laughter came at her from all angles as people swarmed together like bees.

"Leo!" she called out, but the noisy mob smothered her voice.

Forcing her way forward, she found herself stuck somewhere in the middle of the hubbub, not sure which way to go. She grunted and pushed at someone, then felt a hand squeeze her arm and pull her back.

"Are you looking for Leo?" the familiar voice asked as they emerged from the mob. Jo whipped around to face Marshal Collins, just as a breeze lifted his hair off his broad shoulders.

"Yes. Have you seen him?" she replied, smoothing her rumpled skirts.

Fletcher lifted his chin. "Over there."

Jo looked up at the platform. Zeb was down on one

knee, the tail of his long black coat laid out behind him, his top hat tilting rakishly. His attention was fully upon the young man standing in the front row, looking up at him and talking. It was Leo.

A flash memory of the night in the barn filled Jo with burning panic. She saw the unmistakable eyes that peered out from holes in a black hood while she'd watched everything from a shadowy stall, knowing she would die if she showed herself.

Jo knew she must show herself now and retrieve Leo if she was to make a difference this time. She squared her shoulders and took a step forward, but Fletcher stopped her.

"Wait, I'll take you. There are a lot of men wanting to be first." He donned his hat and guided her toward the platform steps, his hand on the small of her back.

With a poise and composure Jo fought to maintain, she moved through the crowd that willingly moved aside for the new marshal. Oddly enough, and despite the camaraderie she'd just seen between him and Zeb, she was glad he was here to escort her to the front. His touch and his presence made her feel less alone, less powerless as she made her way to face Zeb.

She picked up her skirts to climb the steps, her movements slow and controlled. She could hear her heart drumming in her ears, voices from the crowd distant and muffled. Each stride took her closer to her enemy until she was standing behind him, looking down at his clean black coat stretched tight across his back, hearing his laughter as he spoke to her son.

"Zeb, there's someone here to see you," Fletcher said. Jo put on her most captivating smile.

Zeb tousled Leo's hair and idly rose to his feet. He turned to face Jo. "Why, Mrs. O'Malley, I saw you in the crowd. It is a sincere pleasure, indeed, to see you again. It has been too long.''

Jo answered in a light tone that masked what she truly felt—nauseous from being so near to him. She held out her hand and he shook it. ''Congratulations on your campaign for mayor.''

He focused his steely gaze upon her. ''I understand you were wounded the other night. How is your injury?''

His question caught her off guard, and she had to remind herself of the role she was playing. ''It's much better, thank you.''

Zeb rested his hand on Fletcher's shoulder. ''I have every confidence that this man's presence will discourage such crimes in the future. It's why I brought him here in the first place.''

Fletcher responded in good humor. ''And I thought it was because my sister missed me.''

Elizabeth approached from behind. ''Oh, but it was, dear brother. You have no idea how I hounded my husband about it. He had no choice but to finally give in.''

Fletcher walked to the edge of the platform. ''Leo, come and meet my sister.'' The boy ran around to the stairs while Fletcher began the introductions. ''Mrs. O'Malley, this is my sister, Elizabeth Stone.''

Too much was happening at once. Jo had not wanted any of this. She had only wanted to get her bag out of the privy floor and return home again. How had she ended up here, shaking hands with the woman she had tried to make a widow? ''It's a pleasure, Mrs. Stone.''

''No, it's *my* pleasure, Mrs. O'Malley. My brother has spoken of you, and let me assure you he plans to do everything in his power to apprehend the man who shot you. I was beside myself thinking of it. You, my brother and my husband, all nearly killed in one shoot-out.''

Jo found it increasingly difficult to look into this woman's kind eyes. She seemed so different from Zeb. How had she ended up as his wife? She could not possibly know the truth.

Fletcher affectionately rested his hand on Leo's shoulder and introduced him to Elizabeth. They shook hands, then Elizabeth turned to Jo.

''Will you come for tea sometime? I'm starting an embroidery club on Tuesday evenings if you would like to join us. Tonight we're meeting at the Presbyterian church on Central Avenue at seven o'clock.''

Scrambling for a polite reply, Jo smiled. ''I shouldn't commit myself. Things are busy on the ranch this time of year and so much has fallen upon my shoulders....''

An awkward silence ensued until Leo offered a need-less explanation. ''My pa died last winter.''

Elizabeth nodded serenely. ''Yes, I know. I'm very sorry about that. Unfortunately, I know what it is to lose someone you love.'' She directed her gaze at Jo, who felt shaken. ''Will you at least stop by for tea when you are in town next?''

After a long pause, Jo gave in. ''Yes, of course.'' She felt Zeb's inquisitive stare.

Elizabeth kissed her brother on the cheek. ''We'll see you at supper, Fletcher? We missed you last night.'' Smiling, she headed for the stairs. ''I must go and speak to Mrs. Jennings about this evening. Excuse me. It was a pleasure meeting you both.'' She descended from the platform and met an older woman at the bottom. Jo watched them converse, envious of such a simple existence where the greatest concern was in acquiring the proper color thread.

She glanced back at Leo. "We must be getting home. There's work to do." She turned to go, hoping the departure would not be difficult.

"But wait," Leo called after her. She halted, closing her eyes with sinking hopes. "I need to talk to Mr. Stone."

Jo turned around, feeling the impatient crowd all listening and staring directly at her, waiting for her response. "I'm sure he's very busy, Leo. Perhaps another time."

She stood tall and silent, willing Leo with her eyes to follow, but knowing she would have to remain and control the damage to come.

"What is it, son?" Zeb asked, resting his hand on Leo's shoulder. The intimate gesture made Jo's skin prickle.

Leo looked up at him hopefully. "The men who killed my father were never caught. Now that you're going to be mayor, I thought you might be able to do something about it."

Revealing nothing, he replied, "Like what?"

"You could spread word around. Marshal Collins said he'd help, and if he becomes sheriff, then—"

Zeb's eyes darted suspiciously at his brother-in-law. Jo saw the subtle annoyance and knew she had to interrupt. "Leo, you have to let it go. Those men left no trail."

Zeb's left eyebrow rose a fraction while he looked down at her curiously. "How do you know there were more than one?"

Jo tried not to let her rising panic show. "I don't. I was just guessing."

Zeb continued to stare at her, saying nothing, and Jo made the mistake of trying to fill the unbearable silence with an explanation. "There must have been more than one because of the tracks I saw."

"But as I recall, you told the marshal you saw *no* tracks. You said they'd been covered by snowfall." He stared down at her and she knew he could see the truth in her eyes. "Perhaps you saw more than you lead people to believe."

Jo tried to backtrack. "They were very clever to have gotten away without being seen."

"How clever do you have to be to hang someone?" Leo asked.

The retort shocked everyone into silence. Jo knew nothing she could say would improve this situation.

Fletcher knelt down. "If it means that much to you, Leo, why don't we go on over to the jailhouse now, if it's okay with your ma, and look up the reports. I'll tell you what was done about your father's death."

Zeb's jaw clenched visibly, but he said nothing.

Jo couldn't believe what she was hearing or seeing. There were no reassuring looks between Fletcher and Zeb, no winks or nudges. Only Zeb's uneasiness and the marshal's sincere interest in seeing the report.

Whatever suspicions Jo had held about Fletcher Collins dissolved right there. She was certain that, for all he knew, her husband *had been* murdered by horse thieves.

Not that any of that mattered. Zeb knew the truth now. That was obvious. And she was in grave danger.

Fletcher rose to his feet. "Is that all right with you, Mrs. O'Malley?"

Jo knew the answer had to be yes, but she felt suddenly ill equipped to see what was written about Edwyn's death. She barely remembered the things she had said to the old marshal about it; she had been in a state of shock, shaking and winded after the midnight ride through the snow all alone. So much of that night was a blur to her now.

"Mrs. O'Malley? Would it be all right?" Fletcher's voice startled her, and she realized suddenly that she had been staring blankly at him. His eyes were intense with concern for her and she found she wanted to leave with him now. It didn't matter where they went, she just wanted him to take her away.

She cleared her throat, feeling Zeb studying her. "That would be fine. I'll come along, of course."

"Zeb, I'll see you later," Fletcher said.

They descended the steps. Jo could not resist the temptation to take one last look back at Zeb. He stood watching, his eyes shaded by the dark brim of his hat. He glared with brows drawn together, eyes so dark it sent chills skittering across her skin.

For the first time, she was glad she and Leo were with the marshal.

Fletcher followed Leo and Mrs. O'Malley around the back of the two-story city clerk's office, noticing that she checked over her shoulder every few seconds. She seemed nervous. He wondered if it was because her husband's killers were never caught. Maybe by checking into it, he would find something that would change that, and help her move on with her life.

He was not completely comfortable with how much he wanted her to move on—to be free from the tragedy that seemed to haunt her so intensely, to look at him and see more than just his badge.

They climbed the back stairs on the outside of the building to the second floor that served as city offices and police court. Fletcher removed his hat, trying to struggle free of the invisible web of attraction he was caught in, trying to focus on his job instead of wishing his potential witness was ready for him to take her into his arms and make her feel safe again.

He hung his hat on a hook by the door, and raked his fingers through his hair. He went around the back of the largest desk and unlocked the top drawer to retrieve a second set of keys that jingled between his fingers. Mrs. O'Malley stood quietly by the door—seemingly unaware of how much her presence affected him—while Leo walked around the room, looking at the "Wanted" posters nailed to the walls.

"Is it true what Zeb said?" Mrs. O'Malley asked curiously. "That you plan to run for sheriff?"

Half laughing, he replied, "No. I reckon Zeb was just trying to make up for what happened the other night, to give folks something new to talk about." He set down the report he was looking at and added, "I'm not the political type, nor am I interested in anything that permanent."

"But it's a very prestigious position."

"Doesn't much matter to me. I don't plan on stayin' in Dodge forever. I'm only going to hang around long enough to establish some law around here and clean up the town's reputation."

"But your sister...I thought you came here to be closer to her."

"Only for a while. Until I know she's okay."

"Why wouldn't she be? She's married to the future mayor." Mrs. O'Malley stared into his eyes with a scrutiny he didn't understand but wished he did. She seemed to be searching for something, waiting for him to say something....

He studied her eyes in return until she grew uncomfortable for some reason and turned away, joining Leo, who was still reading the posters.

Fletcher took a moment to clear his desk, then changed the subject. "I know this can't be easy for either of you—" he crossed the room to a tall cabinet and unlocked it "—but I'll need to know the exact date your husband was killed, Mrs. O'Malley."

"It was the night of February 26," she replied, turning to face him. She clutched her small reticule in both hands in front of her. "Twenty minutes past ten."

Fletcher hesitated at her exactness, feeling his mood grow suddenly somber, and reached for the police court dockets. He flipped through the papers, but didn't find what he was searching for. "February 26 of *this* year?"

"Yes," Jo answered.

He closed the drawer and opened another. "The report must have been misfiled. Has anyone looked at it recently?"

Leo eyed his mother, questioningly.

"Not that I know of." She didn't seem at all disturbed by this.

Fletcher closed the last drawer and walked to his desk. He searched for the report there but found nothing. "You're sure that was the day?"

Mrs. O'Malley tilted her head at him.

"Of course it was. Forgive me," he said gently, hating himself for being so insensitive. All he wanted from this was to give her some peace of mind, not *add* to her woes.

Leo's voice filled with panic. "You mean you can't find it? The evidence is gone?"

"There was no evidence, Leo, that's the point," Jo said. "There was only the information I gave to the marshal that night about what I saw."

Fletcher sat down. "Was that Marshal Samson?"

"Yes. He was only here a few months, and left town shortly after Edwyn died."

"I know. This city seems to have trouble keeping their lawmen. Care to tell the story again, Mrs. O'Malley? Leo gave me the rundown, but you were the one who found your husband."

To his distress, he realized he wanted her to tell him what had happened so that he could feel closer to her.

"I didn't witness anything," she blurted out, then she glanced at Leo's hopeful gaze and her face softened. "I'll try to tell you what happened."

"Why don't you sit down." Fletcher gestured to the chair on the opposite side of his desk, knowing this wouldn't be easy for her.

Hesitantly, Jo sat. "Thank you, Marshal."

"Please call me Fletcher."

Leo stood behind her and rested his hand on her shoulder. "It's okay, Ma. You can do it."

She cleared her throat and began, but her tone was surprisingly dry and emotionless. Fletcher wasn't sure what to make of it.

"Edwyn was in the barn late that night because one of the horses was delivering a foal. I had been reading in the parlor when I heard hoofbeats and went to the window to look. It was very dark and I didn't see anyone, but for some reason I felt concern—call it a woman's instinct—and decided to go out to check on Edwyn. I put on my overcoat and went to the barn. My husband was dead when I got there. They'd hanged him."

Fletcher leaned straight back in the chair, imagining her that night and wishing for her sake that it had never happened. Heavy silence weighed down on all three of them.

Fletcher was silent for a minute. "I'm very sorry, Mrs. O'Malley. I wish I had been here then. Maybe I could have—"

He stopped himself. *Could have what? Held her? Comforted her?*

Mrs. O'Malley only nodded.

"And they took horses?" he asked, trying to focus on the crime and not easing the heart of the beautiful, grieving widow across from him.

"Yes, they took two, I discovered. I ran back into the house to awaken Matilda and tell her what had happened, then I saddled a horse and rode straight here without thinking."

Leo interrupted. "Ma told me the next morning."

Fletcher nodded compassionately. "And what was done about it, Mrs. O'Malley?"

"A posse went after them at dawn, but a heavy snowfall covered the trail. The posse came back two days later with nothing. The horses were never recovered or seen again. No one even had any idea which direction the gang had gone."

"Do you feel confident that everything that could have been done for you was done?"

Mrs. O'Malley considered the question for a long time, then answered, "With the information I provided that night about the events? Yes."

He studied her a moment, and he knew she was holding back. But then again, he always seemed to know that. Always seemed to want her to give him something more.

"Did the marshal examine the barn for evidence?" he asked.

"Yes, but he didn't find anything."

Fletcher stared intently at her. Where was the desperate tone? The hope for justice that he had expected to see in her eyes? He saw it only in Leo's.

Fletcher couldn't help probing a little further. "And there's nothing else you can tell me? Nothing for me to look into?"

Mrs. O'Malley seemed frozen in her chair, the question hanging between them on a thread. What was she hiding?

Leo touched her shoulder again. "Are you all right, Ma?"

She covered his hand with hers. "Yes, I'm fine, but we've done all we can do today. We really must be going."

Abruptly she stood and held out her gloved hand. Fletcher shook it, surprised at the intensity in her eyes, the purposeful way she looked at him.

And that she did not let go of his hand right away.

A few minutes later, feeling shaken by her touch, Fletcher said goodbye to Mrs. O'Malley and Leo. He stood at the second-floor window watching them walk across Front Street. Mrs. O'Malley kept looking over her shoulder. She tried to hold Leo's arm a few times, and each time, he pulled away from the protective gesture, like any boy his age would do.

When they disappeared into Wright's store, Fletcher leaned his head against the window frame. Why was he so drawn to this woman who obviously didn't want anyone to get close to her? And was he interested in this case just as a way of being around her?

No, he thought, telling himself he was still in control.

Something about that murder case was niggling at him. The fact that Mrs. O'Malley hadn't seen much of anything didn't bother him so much as the look she gave him when he asked if the marshal had done everything he could at the time to catch the thieves. It was almost a challenge. A plea for him to see the truth through her eyes, to hear more than what she was saying.

With the information I provided that night about the events...

Was there something else she hadn't told anyone? Maybe something she later remembered? And why were the misfiled papers bothering him so much? Was it the fact that Mrs. O'Malley hadn't seemed surprised they were missing?

Fletcher went to the cabinet to lock it, then dropped the key into his desk drawer and locked it, too. He shouldn't be thinking about a six-month-old murder case when everybody in town was expecting the speedy capture of the notorious Six-Shooter Hank. But he couldn't help it. He couldn't keep his mind off anything that had to do with Mrs. O'Malley.

Ironically, she was the only potential lead he had to Six-Shooter Hank at the moment anyway—a good excuse to go out to her ranch again tonight.

Well, so be it. Perhaps some unexpected tidbit of information would fall into his lap. With any luck, it would be Mrs. O'Malley.

Chapter Eleven

Shortly after dinner, Zeb walked out of the house to find himself a poker game and some good whisky. He climbed into his shiny black carriage, which was waiting for him just outside the door, and cracked the whip to get the animals moving.

As the horses' hooves clattered down his stone driveway, he thought about the best way to eliminate both the widow O'Malley and her meddlesome son without creating any suspicious gossip. He wondered with amused curiosity how she'd managed to keep herself hidden that night in her barn, what she'd seen exactly, and how the blazes she had been so dim-witted to let it slip this afternoon. More proof that you couldn't trust a woman to control a tongue that was, by nature, created to flap.

Zeb supposed it didn't matter what she'd seen or if she had any proof of it. He simply couldn't afford gossip with the election coming up. He would have to discuss a solution with MacGregor, his hired man, pay him a little extra to see that the ''solution'' was carried out properly. This time, there would be no mistakes.

* * *

How many ways were there, exactly, to kill a man? Jo wondered uneasily. She felt sick about the things she was thinking. Over the past five hours, she had considered poison, strangulation and a house fire. She'd even fantasized about a public stoning, but nothing seemed as quick and reliable as her Colt .45.

She only wished it didn't have to be so violent. The last time she'd attempted this, she'd discovered she was not the killer she thought she was. Oh, yes, she'd spent countless nights imagining pulling the trigger, but when it came right down to it, she couldn't go through with it.

Now, standing in front of her bedroom mirror and staring at the fugitive known only as Six-Shooter Hank, she told herself she would not think of her morals. After what had happened with Zeb today, her life depended upon it.

At least she had managed to convince Leo and Matilda to get on the evening train out of Dodge City. It hadn't been easy, but she had told Leo that Matilda needed some time away from the ranch, that she was in need of rest, and Leo had believed the story and was eager to take care of Matilda in her time of need. Jo only hoped Leo didn't tell Matilda that.

Reaching for Edwyn's brown hat, Jo pulled it down snugly over her knotted hair and tied the red bandanna around the back of her neck. Edwyn's old trousers and shirt were a perfect disguise, and the long slicker she'd worn the other night conveniently covered her feminine curves. She was unrecognizable.

The only things missing were her holster and guns.

She turned around. There they lay on her bed—the place Leo was conceived. A disturbing thought at this moment.

Jo fought against the sickening lump forming in her stomach as she picked up her weapons. She buckled the brown leather belt around her hips. Slowly she withdrew one pistol and squeezed the smooth walnut handle. She sat on the edge of the bed and clicked open the cylinder to check it one more time.

Five bullets. The sixth chamber she left empty for the hammer to rest against in case of accidental discharge in the holster. She clicked the cylinder closed and thumbed back the hammer. The cylinder rotated; the trigger was set and in working order. She reset the hammer to rest on an empty chamber again and slid the gun back into the brown leather casing.

After repeating the inspection with the second weapon, Jo stood by the bed and took one last look in the mirror. Six-Shooter Hank gazed back at her from beneath the wide brim of his hat. He was turning out to be a useful character. When Zeb's body was discovered, everyone and their dog would be searching for the elusive gunman, and Jo would be sitting assuredly back at home in her tight corset and blue gingham day dress. She only hoped she would be able to live with herself.

She inhaled a deep breath and walked out of the room. Dressed like a man, it felt natural to walk like one, to stomp down the stairs instead of float down, to grip and squeeze the railing instead of skimming her delicate gloved hand over it. Down the stairs she went, full of purpose and conviction, and determined—this time—to crush her conscience if it threatened to intervene.

She straightened Edwyn's portrait in the front hall and glanced at the clock on the mantel in the parlor. Seven-thirty. Time to go. She'd worked out every detail of her plan right down to the minute, sending all the ranch hands on errands to each of the cow camps, so that no one would see her leave the house.

Swaying back and forth in the creaky leather saddle and listening to the ghostly sounds of cows lowing in the distance, Fletcher walked his horse up the last gentle rise on the way to the O'Malley ranch. Phoebes and mockers made short sweeps across the fields, skimming the ground and chirping into the dusk. The sun had dipped behind a field dotted with cattle, and the long shadows of twilight were fast disappearing.

Fletcher tugged down on his Stetson and then at the collar of his long coat, and tried to shrug away the evening chill. At least there was no wind, and with any luck, Matilda would offer him a cup of hot coffee.

When he reached the crest of the hill, he gently pulled on the reins. The horse paused, snorting, then lowered his head to munch on some buffalo grass at the roadside.

Fletcher crossed his wrists over the saddle horn and sighed. He could see the ranch now, tucked cozily in the small valley. There was a puzzlelike pattern to the corral fences, and the windmill was spinning sleepily, silhouetted against the darkening sky. The buildings seemed so grand in the middle of this vast, empty prairie.

Was this the right thing to do? he wondered nervously. Ride down there and pretend to ask more questions about the shooting, when he knew darn well it was all just an excuse to see Mrs. O'Malley again—to learn more about why she'd looked so desperate in the city clerk's office today.

He sat there another moment, considering it, then leaned back in the saddle and considered some more.

But instead of a clearheaded deliberation about his duties as a lawman, all he wanted to think about was the lovely widow. He imagined her standing on her covered porch, smiling lightheartedly at him as he rode up.

Smiling lightheartedly. It was not something Fletcher had seen her do before. He supposed that wasn't surprising, given her grief over her husband.

But damn, how he wanted to see her eyes twinkle with joy, just for him.

Her smile needed to be rescued, he decided, and despite common sense, despite his resolve to avoid a commitment, he wanted to be the one to do it.

Tarnation, what was happening to him? If he knew what was good for him, he'd turn around now and go back to town.

Shaking his head at the decision not to—so contrary to every instinct, every other decision he'd made since his father died—Fletcher tapped his heels against Prince and started off down the hill in anticipation. Mrs. O'Malley—just the idea of her—was pulling him like a magnet. He couldn't wait to look into those big blue eyes, full of childlike innocence, to see if he could get her to smile. Where it would go from there, he had no idea, and it scared the dust right off his boots.

At the bottom of the hill though, Fletcher's senses shook at the sight of a man walking boldly out of the widow's house and pounding down the porch steps. Fletcher stopped again. Prince nickered while Fletcher watched the man mount an awaiting horse.

His heart suddenly pounded with dread. The man had no facial hair like the other ranch hands. Was this Mrs. O'Malley's lover? he wondered in shock. It was a startling realization that left him feeling ridiculously wounded. Was this the man she had told him about the night she was shot? Had she been telling the truth about that after all? No, he couldn't believe it.

For a moment, his arms and legs went numb with disappointment, until a closer look at the man made him sit up straighter in the saddle. He reached for the rifle from his saddle scabbard.

This man was no lover. He was Six-Shooter Hank.

With a surprising ease and swiftness, Jo pinned her foot into the stirrup and mounted her horse, Mogie. Everything was so much easier without her corset to restrict her movements.

She pulled on her husband's brown leather gloves and reached for the reins, then kicked her heels into Mogie's firm belly. He broke into a trot. With a plan to cut across the fields rather than risk meeting someone on the road, Jo steered her gelding toward the north pasture.

About ten minutes later, as she rode Mogie along a fence, a gunshot shattered the stillness. The noise echoed off the sky and spooked Mogie, who reared up on his hind legs and forced Jo to grab on to the horn for dear life, the muscles in her legs tightening around the frightened animal. Her wounded shoulder throbbed painfully with the sudden strain. Mogie skittered sideways, then bolted across the field.

Another shot rang out. Jo turned quickly to see where the gunfire was coming from, and a mere glance from the corner of her eye told her. She recognized the slicker sailing on the wind and the shoulder-length hair spilling out from beneath the tan-colored hat pressed forward on his head. It was Fletcher.

Shock choked her as she shifted in the saddle, joining

Mogie in his flight of terror and kicking in her heels.
"Go! Go!"

She could hear hooves thundering behind her, then
Fletcher's angry voice. "Stop! You're under arrest!"

What was he doing here?

They raced across the open fields, the sharp wind
stinging Jo's cheeks and threatening to sweep her hat
off her head. There was nowhere to go, nowhere to hide,
and Mogie was breathing hard; he wouldn't last much
longer. She was ruined.

Fletcher was gaining. The drumming hooves were
getting louder and louder, pounding in Jo's ears. Was
there no way out of this?

He fired the rifle again. Was he shooting at her? She
hadn't thought he'd ever killed a man. Would she be
his first?

Heart racing with desperation, she knew there was no
escape. Mogie wouldn't make it and she had to do
something. Her life and Leo's safety depended on it.
With a muttered oath and hands that shook uncontrollably inside her loose gloves, she pulled her bandanna
up over her face and drew her weapon.

Racing across the darkening fields after searching
Mrs. O'Malley's house and finding no one there,
Fletcher cursed the outlaw trying to outrun him. What
had he been doing at the O'Malley ranch and where
was Josephine? If that gunman so much as plucked one
hair from her head, Fletcher swore he would track him
to the ends of the earth.

Fletcher kicked in his heels, but Prince was winded.
Damn, he couldn't lose now.

The outlaw drew his gun, turned in the saddle and
took aim. Fletcher steered Prince in an arc, attempting

to become a faster-moving target, but it gave the gun-man the advantage of speed. The distance between them grew, and Fletcher knew the time for firing at the sky was over. If the rider wanted a gunfight, he was going to get one.

Fletcher reined Prince to a skidding stop, raised his Winchester, shut one eye to take aim, but hesitated. The gunman had lowered his weapon.

Confused, Fletcher watched the rider grow more distant. Hell, if he was going to stop the man from getting away, he'd have to do it with a bullet and do it now. He shut one eye, focusing...*don't miss, don't miss.*

But the rider suddenly dropped out of Fletcher's sights. The fool had fallen off his horse!

"Yah!" Fletcher yelled, dropping his rifle back into his scabbard and breaking into a gallop. The outlaw's horse was idly trotting away and the man lay motionless on the ground. Fletcher had seen men take spills at that speed and most of them didn't come out of it too happily, if at all. He trotted up to the gunman's lifeless form and dismounted.

Slowly, cautiously, he approached. The man was sprawled on his back, the red bandanna covering his face, the hat pressed down over his eyes. Fletcher was finally going to get a look at the kid who'd destroyed his reputation. He couldn't wait to drag Six-Shooter Hank to the jailhouse and lock him up where he belonged.

"Hold it!" the outlaw yelled, whipping a gun out from under his coat and pointing it straight at Fletcher's nose.

Fletcher drew his Peacemaker before he even realized he'd thought about it. "Here we are again."

The kid—he was just a kid, damn it!—didn't reply.

He slowly rose to his feet, never taking his aim off Fletcher. They stood under the moonlight, a few feet apart, weapons aimed.

Fletcher's hand was steady. Hank's hand trembled.

"I didn't appreciate that leg wound," Fletcher said. "It still smarts."

The gunman nodded.

"Before this gets ugly, I'd like to know what you were doing at the O'Malley ranch."

The kid's voice was strained, as if he was trying too hard to sound older than he really was. "Drop your gun."

Fletcher couldn't help laughing.

"I said drop it."

"Not a chance."

A few more seconds passed. Fletcher rubbed the pad of his index finger over the trigger, ready to fire if he had to, but only if he had to.

"Listen kid, it ain't worth it. You're gonna get caught sooner or later. Better to give yourself up now and save yourself a murder charge."

The kid frantically shook his head.

"It wasn't a suggestion. You're coming with me, conscious or not. Take off the scarf."

Without warning, Fletcher's horse stepped sideways and took his attention for one vital moment. The kid came at him, swinging his gun.

Fletcher knew the move all too well and wasn't about to get knocked out cold, not by this kid, of all people. Quick as a shot, he raised his arm in defense and swiped the weapon out of Hank's hand.

Next thing he knew, Hank was coming at him in a tackle. Fletcher maintained his footing against the kid's surprisingly light weight, but felt a second gun at his hip, so he did the only thing that made sense. He hauled back and punched the kid in the nose.

The squeal nearly struck Fletcher senseless.

While the kid staggered and held his nose, Fletcher swung a boot back and swept him off his feet, onto his back again with a *thump*. Before the kid had a chance to realize he was staring at the stars, Fletcher was on top of him, pinning him down and ripping the second gun from the holster.

Fletcher checked the weapon for bullets, then pointed it into Hank's face, right between the eyes. "You gonna cooperate now?"

Hank nodded and Fletcher couldn't wait to get his hands on that scarf. He reached for it, but Hank bit into the fabric and held it in place with his teeth. He was grunting and shaking his head until Fletcher tired of the game and finally yanked with all his might.

The bandanna came loose, Fletcher blinked a few times, then his blood ran cold.

Her nose throbbing unbearably, Jo lay on her back staring up at Fletcher's stunned expression. Her fear shifted course to unmitigated anger.

"What the hell's going on?" he asked incredulously, swiping her hat off her head.

Figuring she owed it to him, she balled up a fist and walloped him in the nose. Fletcher fell onto his backside, leaning up on one hand while he cupped his nose with the other. Blood seeped between his fingers.

Jo scrambled to her feet. She examined her own hand for blood and found her glove stained crimson. "I'm bleeding."

"So am *I*." Fletcher gently pinched the bridge of his nose. "Hell, you broke it."

For a moment, they both sat suffering with their own wounds, until Fletcher looked up at her. "Jeez, look what I did. If I'd known it was *you*…" He rose to his feet and tried to take her hand away from her face to assess the damage, but she elbowed him in the ribs.

"Just let me look," he said, clutching his side. "It doesn't look broken, thank God."

At the sight of Fletcher's bloody nose, which now looked a little crooked, Jo's fury began to die a little. "Oh dear. I didn't mean to do that to you, either."

She touched his face; he touched hers, and they stared for a moment at each other, saying nothing.

"Does it hurt terribly much?" Jo asked.

"Yeah. But I had it coming."

"You were just doing your job."

"It isn't my job to hit women."

"Not even if they're trying to shoot you?"

He shook his head in disbelief. "What in tarnation were you *doing?*"

She'd known that question was coming, should have been prepared for it, but still hadn't the foggiest idea how to reply. Jo pinched her nose and tipped her head back. "You wouldn't understand."

"Try me." He tipped his head back, too.

How was she to tell this man that if he hadn't caught her just now, she would be out killing his brother-in-law? She could barely believe it herself.

Feeling suddenly cold in the evening chill, she flopped onto the ground and sat on her knees.

Fletcher approached and handed the bandanna to her. "Wipe your nose with this."

Thankful for his caring, she took it and wiped the blood off her face.

Fletcher knelt down in front of her. "Was it you that night? In Zeb's store?"

She could feel tears pooling in eyes that had been dry for many months, and she knew exactly the reason why. This man's presence was shining an unwelcome light on what she had nearly become—a cold-blooded killer with a future full of remorse. Sadly she nodded.

"Why?"

"I had a reason. I just can't tell you what it is."

"You're putting me in a difficult position."

"I know. Why do you think I tried so hard to outrun you?" The sharp, steely blade of shame stabbed at her, its sting made worse by the fact that it was Fletcher wielding it.

He stared at her for another few seconds, as if contemplating her answer, then rose to his feet. She could feel his gaze boring into the top of her head and knew with hopeless dread what was coming.

"Get up, please, Mrs. O'Malley." His voice was cold and exact.

Not surprised, but unwilling to believe what was happening, Jo looked up and saw the color drain from Fletcher's face. Heaven help her, she could not bear to think of him despising her so deeply. He was a man who valued integrity above all else and she respected him for that, more than he could ever know. It was precisely why it killed her inside to have strayed so far from his ideals, ideals that had once been her own. Her heart sank with shame and regret and a desperate need to explain herself even though she knew it was hopeless.

"You're under arrest for the night in Zeb's store," he said scathingly. "It was attempted robbery and attempted murder. Of both Zeb Stone...and me."

Chapter Twelve

Jo rose to her feet to face Fletcher, her skin prickling with horror. "You can't do this. You don't understand."

"That's because you won't tell me."

He wrapped his hand around her upper arm. She began to struggle impossibly against his grip, to pry his iron fingers away, but they would not budge. He dragged her toward his horse, then reached for his handcuffs while she twisted frantically so that her back was to him while she tried to squirm away.

"Please, Jo," Fletcher said, straining. "Don't make this more difficult than it already is." He held her around the waist to keep her from slipping free.

Bending and struggling in her husband's loose clothing only served to make Jo more aware of Fletcher's hard body, pressed tight against her backside.

"Fletcher, please, listen."

"You know I can't let you go."

Jo continued to squirm in his hold. The more she struggled, the tighter he held her—until she let out a sob.

Suddenly his hold loosened and her body relaxed.

Then he was hugging her, his warm breath tickling the back of her neck. She closed her eyes, wanting to turn around to face him, to hold him and touch him and beg for his help and forgiveness.

"Jo," he whispered hotly in her ear, sending goose-flesh to the farthest reaches of her body.

She turned her face to feel his stubbled cheek press against hers. Her whole existence became lost in the impossible waiting, then his lips grazed the side of her mouth.

"Please, Fletcher..." She wasn't sure what she was asking for, drowning in the feel of his body so snugly behind her.

Reaching around, she buried her fingers into the hair at his nape, pulling him closer, tipping her face up to the sky as he dropped wet kisses onto her tingling neck.

"Jo, I'm sorry, but it's my job."

She looked up at the starry sky and felt reality crash down upon her mounting desires. What good would it do, to have feelings for this man who had lost all respect for her—and rightly so—the moment he knew the truth about her infernal soul? She had seen the disappointment in his eyes, heard it in his voice and it had crushed her heart to dust. Oh, how she wished she didn't care what he thought of her. Why did it have to matter so much?

Jo broke away from his hold. She felt the urge to sob again but bit it back. She had to talk to him, to make him understand. It was her only hope. "It's not like it seems."

He stood motionless, not making a move to handcuff her at least. "I'm listening."

She tried to find the right way to say this—there was

so much riding upon her explanation—but there was no right way to talk of murder.

She licked her parched, throbbing lips. ''I...I wasn't trying to rob Zeb's store. It was much more complicated than that.''

''Continue.''

Jo's ribs were squeezing around her heart. ''I was there that night because I had no other choice left to me. I had to protect myself. And Leo.''

''You're not making sense.''

''I know. Just give me a chance. The problems began long before the night I walked into Zeb's store. I...I lied about what I saw the night Edwyn was murdered.''

Fletcher stared at her for a moment, then his eyes softened and he helped her to sit down in the grass, away from the horses. She felt the weight of his anger lift a little and prayed it would continue in that vein.

''I knew something was wrong today when you came to the clerk's office,'' he said. ''I knew you were scared and alone and I really wanted to help you.''

''You knew?''

She worked hard to keep her voice steady as he sat down beside her. When had anyone seen the fear she fought to hide, and known she had needed help? Matilda hadn't seen it. Leo had seen a change, but he'd not understood it.

She pulled off her glove and took Fletcher's hand, knowing with surprising certainty that it was time to tell this story to someone. To *him.*

''I didn't find Edwyn murdered, Fletcher. I...I saw it happen.''

''God, Jo, I'm so sorry.''

He pulled her close and she let her forehead rest on his strong shoulder, remembering the horror of what had happened that night and realizing only now that by keeping this secret bottled up tight inside, she had not let herself express all of her grief for Edwyn. It was such a liberating comfort to do so now.

"What happened?" he asked.

"We were *both* in the barn late one night, waiting for a mare to deliver. There was some commotion outside, and Edwyn went out to see what was going on. I could hear him yelling and then it was just a lot of angry voices. I backed into a stall, not sure what was happening. Then the barn door swung open and three men wearing hoods walked in dragging Edwyn, who was weak and staggering. They must have beaten him."

She began to feel sick recalling the horrid details. She paused a moment, searching for strength. "They tossed a rope over a beam, forced Edwyn onto a chair and into the noose, and without a second's hesitation, kicked the chair out from under him. It happened very quickly and I watched everything."

Fletcher stroked the hair away from her eyes and kissed the top of her head. Heavy silence weighed down upon them as a cloud floated in front of the moon.

"The men stayed to watch until Edwyn stopped struggling, and I knew if I tried to stop it, I'd be dead too, and I had to stay alive for Leo. I couldn't move, I was so terrified. By the time they left, it was too late. Edwyn was…gone, and I'd done nothing to stop it."

"I'm sorry, Jo."

She pressed her face into his coat, feeling a single tear soak into the thick fabric. "Why couldn't I have done something?"

"Believe me, you did the right thing. You were outnumbered. Anyone in your position would have done the same. You can't blame yourself."

"But I do, *I do.*"

A deep well of tears she had not known existed overflowed. To her utter dismay, she realized that where she thought she had been winning the battle against them, she had only been postponing them while they multiplied inside her. "I want to be strong, for Leo," she cried. "He's all I have left and I love him so much."

"I know that. I can see it. Everything's going to be okay."

"How?" she asked hopelessly, sniffling and gazing up at him with tearstained cheeks.

"Did you get a look at the men?"

This was the difficult part—the truth about that night. Would Fletcher believe her? If he didn't, there was no hope for her life or for Leo's. She sat back, wiped her eyes and whispered, "Yes."

Fletcher's astonishment showed on his face, and Jo knew he was connecting these events to the ones that had brought them both here. He was remembering the night in the store, when they'd first met and when Jo had shot him in the leg. He stared speechless at her, then shook his head in disbelief. "Jo, you don't think that Zeb—"

He stopped midsentence and laughed skeptically, but it was void of humor.

"I saw it happen, Fletcher."

"But you said they were wearing hoods. How can you be sure it was him?"

Jo looked down at her hands in her lap. "I know. I heard his voice, saw the way he moved. It was him."

Fletcher stood up and raked his fingers through his hair. "Zeb Stone is my sister's husband, a respected, prominent citizen. You can't make accusations like that without some kind of proof."

"I realize that. That's why I'm not making accusations."

Fletcher turned away, staring across the dark prairie, the fast wind lifting his hair. "You can't do that, Jo. I won't let you. It's not right."

"Not right?" Jo stood up and pulled him to face her. "You dare talk to me about what's right? My husband dangled from a rope and struggled for his life, and all I could do was watch. Zeb forced me to choose between my husband and my son and I made that choice, but not without a lot of pain. I've not slept a full night since. I've felt so much hate and anger and guilt…I'll never be the woman I was. Six months ago, I never would have even considered taking a man's life, but now, I just can't see any other way to protect my family, even if it destroys me inside. So don't tell me about what's right."

Jo let out a breath. The realization hit hard—she'd been surrounding her heart with ice just to hide the pain and escape her conscience, and this was the first time the ice had broken. The truth was out. Finally someone knew what she had suffered and what sinful, shameful impulses now lived within her ill-fated heart.

Fletcher stared down at her. She waited with dread for him to say something, but there were no words. He took a step forward and gathered her into his arms. "I'm sorry that happened to you, Jo. I know what it's like."

Surprised, she pressed her cheek into the warmth of his chest. "Your father…"

"Yes, and there was nothing I could do. Just like you, I was too late."

"That's why I have to do this *now*."

Fletcher gently pushed her back a step so that he could see her face. "No, you don't."

"Zeb is a dangerous man. He'll kill anyone who gets in his way. I've kept my secret all this time, knowing he would never let me live if he knew what I'd seen. But he knows now, Fletcher. Leo and I are in danger."

She saw panic flicker across his face. "What do you mean?"

"Today, I saw it in his eyes that he knew."

"Saw it in his eyes! You can't base decisions on something as subjective as that!" He waved an arm in frustration. "What if you're wrong? What if it was someone else who just sounded like Zeb? He's a wealthy man with everything going for him. Why would he kill your husband and steal your horses?"

"I don't know, and there's no way to find out without him getting suspicious. I have no other choice."

"Jo, you're being driven by guilt. You're trying to do now what you couldn't do that night in the barn."

His quick, concise and all too certain summary of the matter caught her off guard and left her reeling. Was he right? she wondered, saying nothing while she mentally squirmed to understand her emotions.

"Did you ever try to have Zeb investigated?"

"A few tried before, and they ended up dead. I won't let that happen to Leo and me."

"You're saying you think Zeb has killed others? Jo, I need proof before I can believe something like that."

"I know, I know. Proof. The impossible."

"It's not impossible."

"It is. Zeb's too smart."

There was no sign of surrender in his eyes when he replied. "I can't just accept all this. Even if it's true, it still doesn't excuse you. You tried to kill an innocent man—"

"He's not innocent!"

"He is, in the eyes of the law, and that's how I see things. Through the eyes of the law. I'll take your suspicions about Zeb into consideration, but for now, the only person I know for sure is guilty is *you*. I'm sorry about this Jo, but I took an oath as a lawman. I have to take you as my prisoner."

All the explaining in the world, it seemed, wasn't going to change his mind. He did not understand, nor did he want to, and that fact alone made her heart ache.

"Please come with me willingly. I don't want to hurt you," he said gently, closing his eyes for a moment. She could see that he was struggling with himself, but it didn't ease her pain.

The thought to escape and disappear with Leo filled her mind—as it had on many occasions before—but she knew she could not outsmart or outmaneuver Fletcher. He would find them. He would never give up. He had never in his career let any outlaw go free.

And so, she asked something else of him. "Just promise, if anything happens to me, you'll look out for Leo. There's really no one else I can ask."

He looked stricken by the request and after a moment's deliberation, only nodded. Then he took her by the hand and led her toward his horse. She went without a fight, but not without hope. There was still one possibility—one more thing she could say—and it just might be the thing to get through to him.

Chapter Thirteen

Jo offered her bared wrists to Fletcher and he clicked the cuffs around them. "Is that too tight?"

With no effort at all, she slipped them off her tiny wrists.

"I guess not," he said softly.

For a moment she thought she might be spared the humiliation of being cuffed, until he reached into his saddlebag and pulled out a small rope.

"I guess this'll have to do." He wrapped the prickly rope around her wrists and tied it in a knot, then whistled to Jo's horse. "Can I help you into the saddle?"

"I'm not going to fly up there."

He bent forward, weaving his fingers together for Jo to step into his palms. He lifted her slowly and she managed to grab on to the horn and swing her leg over the other side, and then, before she knew it, she was sitting high in the creaky leather saddle with her wrists bound together, trying to hold on to some shred of dignity when all she felt was morose, painful regret.

Fletcher rested his warm hand on her thigh, a shockingly inappropriate gesture if she imagined herself in her skirts. She stared into his shadowed eyes and saw agony and confusion, felt the same things herself, but what did it matter? she thought miserably. They were adversaries and always would be once he put her in jail.

Fletcher's brows drew together, the muscles in his forehead tensing. "Do you know how hard this is for me? You've been through so much and I felt—I wish you had told me all this sooner."

"I didn't know if I could trust you. I still don't."

"I'm just trying to do the right thing, Jo, and the right thing for *me* is very...what's the word... circumscribed. If I was a different man, I would let you go."

He rubbed his hand over her leg and went on. "I was coming out to your ranch tonight because I wanted to see you. I had thought maybe we could—" He stopped short, his face bleak.

She wished he hadn't stopped. She wanted desperately to know what he was going to say.

Then at last he did say it. "I was going to invite you to join me for dinner some evening."

Jo smiled, but sadly, knowing the opportunity for something between them was lost forever. "I would have liked that" was her only reply.

He gazed up at her for another moment, as if exploring in his mind all the possibilities of the relationship that would never be, then he withdrew his hand from her leg. The place where it had rested felt suddenly cold.

Fletcher gathered the guns they'd dropped during their struggle. He stuffed them into his leather saddlebag, buckled it and yanked it tight, then reached for her horse's reins. He mounted, and they started off across the dark pasture with only the moon lighting their way.

Jo rode in silence behind Fletcher for a mile or so,

until she felt the time had come to try at her last prospect. She cleared her throat and spoke up. "Is there nothing about Zeb that makes you uncomfortable?"

He didn't look back. "Being rich and upper-class doesn't make someone a murderer."

"Does Elizabeth seem okay?"

Fletcher stopped the horses and turned around. He fingered the brim of his hat. "What are you suggesting?"

Jo shrugged. "If *my* sister was married to Zeb Stone, I'd be concerned."

"My sister can take care of herself."

"So could Edwyn."

Fletcher's horse grew restless and took a few steps sideways. "You're trying to manipulate me, Jo."

"No, I'm just trying to give you more reason to look into this. Is there anything that makes you worry about Elizabeth? A gut feeling?"

"Gut feelings aren't enough for me." Fletcher faced front and continued toward town in a cold silence. Jo's last hope for his support shattered into a thousand irretrievable pieces.

Feeling shaken by Jo's suggestions about Elizabeth, Fletcher shifted in the smooth leather saddle. Elizabeth hadn't exactly been herself since she came to Dodge. There was a time she was more rebellious and free-spirited than she was now, living in Zeb's big stone house on the hill. But Fletcher had assumed she was still mourning the death of their parents and maybe needed some time to adjust to married life, as any woman would in her circumstances.

The problem here was Jo. She could see through him as clearly as he could see through her, and she was dead right about the gut feeling. Hell, tracking outlaws over the years, he'd learned to use his instincts like a compass.

But why couldn't he have told her that back there when she brought it up? He supposed he didn't want to give her any false hopes that might make all this more difficult in the end. For her *and* for him.

Prince nickered softly and twitched his ears. There were still a few awkward miles to go, more time for Fletcher to sit and suffer with a throbbing broken nose, beating himself up about this impossible situation.

Again, for some reason, his thoughts floated back to Elizabeth and how strange it was to see her in silk and satin on a daily basis when she'd always preferred cool muslin, and had made a noisy fuss the one and only time their mother had suggested she wear ornamental combs in her hair.

Not that that was any reason to suspect her husband of murder, of course.

Fletcher shook his head. All that aside, he wondered if he didn't owe it to Jo to uncover the truth. Must he be so hardheaded about arresting her right now, this very minute?

But if he didn't, she would make another attempt on Zeb's life, he knew, and Fletcher couldn't let her become a murderer. No matter how much her grief and guilt tortured her, she did not possess the heart of a killer, that much was clear to him. He'd seen it in her eyes the night in Zeb's store.

Struck suddenly by the memory, Fletcher stopped his horse and turned around. "If you weren't shot by a stray bullet outside the privy that night, who shot you?"

She raised her bound wrists to push a loose lock of hair away from her eyes. "You didn't see Zeb pull out his gun and you were unconscious when he fired. I meant to defend myself, but I panicked and missed, shooting you, instead. That's when he shot me.''

Fletcher hadn't thought to ask Zeb if he'd fired his gun at the outlaw that night, and for reasons that were becoming clearer, Zeb hadn't volunteered the information.

"So there was never any lover," Fletcher added, realizing uncomfortably that this was the information he'd been after all along.

"It seemed like a good alibi at the time, especially with my reputation in town. It was the only thing I could come up with. I just wanted to distract you from the truth."

"You didn't shoot me on purpose, then."

"No," she replied with a subtle smile he hadn't expected. "I only punched you in the nose on purpose. And that particular business I do *not* regret."

He saw humor in her eyes and heard it in her voice. Lord, she was one brave lady.

The sentiment made him stare through the darkness at her, her beautiful golden hair hidden beneath a man's hat, her woman's body cloaked by the long brown slicker. He had not felt a corset when she'd struggled in his arms earlier. Was there nothing beneath the man's shirt she wore? Nothing but her bare breasts against the lightweight fabric?

For the first time, a hot ache began to grow inside of him. Damn, he just couldn't keep his eyes to himself, could he? He wanted to leap off his horse and pull her down into the grass, convince her she was not a killer, then reach under those clothes and feel her soft, warm skin against his. To become the lover he'd imagined her with that night. To do all the things he'd imagined they'd done.

Instead, he bit back the urge and gazed forlornly across the flat, dark plains. The chilly night wind hissed through the grass and brushed over his cheeks. He pulled his collar up around his neck and readjusted the reins in his grip, his urges twisting like a knife inside him.

Fletcher walked his horse up next to Jo's. Maybe, with the question he was about to ask, he was going somewhere he shouldn't be going, but he had to know. He fought hard to stay in control as he asked, "Who are these other people you think Zeb murdered?"

Jo sat back in the saddle, wanting to let out a deep sigh of relief. Whatever his reasons, Fletcher was willing to listen.

"It happened a few months before Edwyn died. A man named Hennigar was killed by horse thieves, and when his wife reported everything to the marshal, she told him that one of the killers looked like Zeb Stone. The marshal questioned Zeb, who of course had an alibi, but a few days later, Mrs. Hennigar was found dead at the bottom of her stairs. People thought she'd been so devastated by her husband's death, she'd taken her own life. Then the marshal who had questioned Zeb was killed in the line of duty. Zeb had an alibi again, and mostly, people were sympathetic toward him, thinking he was wrongly suspected. I'm surprised you haven't heard about it. Hadn't Elizabeth mentioned it?"

Fletcher removed his hat and raked his fingers through his wavy hair. "All that happened before she came here. Maybe she doesn't know."

"Most people have forgotten about it, I guess."

"But *you* haven't."

"No, *I* haven't."

He gazed away from her, his face turned into the wind so that his hair blew off his shoulders, and seemed to be thinking about things. "I can understand how you need to blame someone for your husband's murder, but maybe you're making connections where there are none. If Zeb had an alibi, he may be innocent."

Jo rubbed a finger along her irritated wrist beneath the rope. "It was Zeb, I tell you. Even under the hood, I knew it was him."

Jo's heart pounded wildly while Fletcher considered her story. He had to believe her, he just had to....

After a few minutes, he looked into her eyes. "There's not enough here to arrest him, and certainly nothing even close to what you'd need to convict."

Fletcher put his hat back on his head. "We'd need more proof before anything could be done. A motive at the very least."

We. "Would you be willing to help me find that proof?"

"I'd be interested in the motive first of all. Why would Zeb want your husband dead?"

"I wish I knew."

"What about Hennigar? Did he know your husband?"

"All the ranchers know one another."

Fletcher crossed his wrists over the saddle horn. "Hennigar was a rancher, too?" Jo nodded and Fletcher sat back, shaking his head. "That's at least one connection between the murders, but I don't see how it leads us to Zeb. He has no interests in ranching. He's a little too *civilized* for that."

Jo rubbed her wrists again with her middle finger.

"Is that too tight?" Fletcher asked.

"A little."

He leaned across and untied the rope, then turned her palms up and looked at them. Her wrists were raw and chafed. "Why didn't you say something?"

"There were more important things to say."

He blew on the sensitive surface of her wounds. Jo stared transfixed at his beautiful face in the moonlight, his eyes closed, his cool breath easing the rope burns. For a moment, she was tempted to lean in and press her lips to his, but the expression in his eyes sobered her intentions.

"This doesn't change anything, Jo," he said, his voice rippling with regret.

She pulled her hand away, reminding herself of his sworn duty and fighting to stay true to hers.

He leaned back in his saddle and the wind grew suddenly colder. "I reckon there's something more than horse theft going on here, but that doesn't mean I'm going to set you free. You're still charged with attempted murder, Jo, no matter what happens, and I'm going to have to lock you up when we get to town."

"What about the investigation?"

"That's *my* job, not yours. Give me your hands." He wrapped the rope around her wrists again. "I'll try not to tie it so tight this time."

By the time Fletcher led Jo into town on her horse, the nightly celebrations were in full swing. Music and singing from the vaudeville act in the Comique echoed in the street, and cowboys staggered around in the dust, laughing and hooting and dancing. Fletcher's watchful gaze always went to their gun belts to ensure they hadn't forgotten the city ordinance about carrying firearms in town, but usually they were merely swinging half-empty whisky bottles.

He led Jo around the back of the jailhouse, past the barred window that did not mask the sound of a raspy cough and someone spitting tobacco inside. Feeling more than a little uncomfortable about this, Fletcher dismounted, deciding he would crowd all the men into one cell and give Jo the other cell to herself.

When he helped her down from her horse, he saw that her face was drawn and pale. "Fletcher, if I'm locked up, I'm a fixed target. I have no way to protect myself."

"Deputy Anderson will stand watch. You'll be fine."

"Take me with you."

"I can't do that. I have work to do."

"But isn't it your job to protect people? I'm in danger. I can feel it." Her voice was growing more and more desperate to the point of panic.

"You'll be safe in the jailhouse." He led her around to the front, but he wasn't too comfortable with the idea of leaving her alone.

"Please, Fletcher. I can't trust anyone."

He made a move to go inside but hesitated at the door, his hand barely touching the latch. It was that need to protect her niggling at him again. He certainly didn't want to admit it was personal, not to himself or to her, so he made up some foolish, incomprehensible excuse: "If anyone sees you in this disguise, the story will spread like wildfire and I won't be able to investigate." He turned to face her. "So there you have it— I changed my mind. Come upstairs with me."

She looked so relieved he thought she was going to throw her arms around his neck and kiss him a hundred times, all over his face to thank him. As much as he would have enjoyed her gratitude in a place more conducive to such expressions, he certainly didn't want her—in *those* clothes—to do it here, when his reputation was already in shambles because of the unfortunate fainting thing. So, for the sake of his reputation, he grabbed her collar in his fist and dragged her along behind him.

They climbed the stairs and went into the office, which was dark and empty. Fletcher lit a lamp, carried it across the room and set it on top of the tall cabinet. He forced himself to focus on business, and it sure as hell wasn't easy now that he had her alone in a dimly lit room with a door that could be locked behind them if he was so inclined. He stood facing her flushed cheeks and full lips and thoroughly grateful gaze, and managed to utter, "Do you know the exact date Hennigar was murdered?"

He wasn't at all happy about the fact that he was flustered.

"It was just after the new year, the third or fourth of January."

Fletcher flipped through the files, squinting through the dim, flickering light, pulling papers out one by one, but he found nothing for either of those days. "Are you sure?"

"Yes, but you can't find the report, can you?"

"Just give me a minute. It might have been—"

"Misfiled. I don't think so." She sat down at one of the desks.

Fletcher soon gave up and closed the heavy drawer. "Okay, there's definitely something going on here, but you don't have me convinced that Zeb has anything to do with it."

"So what are you going to do?"

Fletcher paced the room and considered the situation, then began to untie Jo's hands. "I'll agree with you on one point. If Mrs. Hennigar *was* killed because she witnessed her husband's murder, you might be the killer's next matter of business once this investigation gets going. It's my job to see that you're safe. Come with me."

Fletcher held out his hand and she slipped hers into it. Judging by the intense shudder he felt as he closed his fingers around hers and held them tightly, he would have to dig deep tonight for the strength to stay true to his principles.

Chapter Fourteen

Fighting nervousness, Jo watched Fletcher walk confidently around his paper-strewn desk. "Keep your head down," he said to her, "don't make eye contact with anyone. I'll walk behind you about ten paces, keeping watch, and I promise I won't let anything happen to you." He cupped her chin in his hand. "You look pale."

"I *feel* pale." But was it because she had to walk through town in this disguise, or was it a reaction to the sudden change in her alliance with Fletcher? She was suddenly knee-deep in the full emotional impact of her need for him as her protector.

"Don't worry, you'll be fine."

They stared wordlessly at each other as his thumb feathered across her cheek. "It's time to get going. Walk straight to Jensen's Boardinghouse and don't look back."

"Will I have to get a room? The Jensens know who I am."

He placed a cold key into her palm. "Go straight to room number twenty-three on the second floor and let yourself in."

"Is that where you live? At the boardinghouse?"

Fletcher lowered the wick in the lamp and the room went black. "You sound surprised."

"It just seems so temporary."

"I'm a temporary kind of man."

She thought about what she knew of his past—the life he'd lived before his father was killed, the ranch, the home, the family, and now the desire to be near his sister—and she couldn't hold back her reply. "No, you're not. You just try to be."

Fletcher stiffened noticeably and Jo closed her coat around her, pleased that her comment had unnerved him but wishing it didn't matter to her.

"It's time to go," he said, his voice cool and authoritative.

"What about the horses?"

"I'll lead yours to the stable behind the boardinghouse. It's dark. Hopefully nobody will look too close to see he isn't mine. Get going."

"You'll be right behind me?"

"Of course."

She passed him in the doorway, her body brushing lightly against his, then she quickly descended the stairs on the outside of the building, stopping at the bottom when she heard Fletcher whisper, "Not so fast. You don't want to look like you just robbed the livery."

The keys jingled as he locked the door behind him. Jo couldn't stop herself from looking up at his dark, imposing figure on the stairs. Above his head, in the night sky, clouds changed shape and dissolved like smoke from a chimney.

"You're wasting time," he said, dropping the keys with a clink into his vest pocket.

Jo realized with some irritation that she had to haul

her deeply rapt gaze away from him. Quickly turning on her heel, she buried her hands in her pockets and, with the moon lighting her way, crossed over the railroad tracks and headed west on Front Street. Cowboys and businessmen lined the boardwalks in front of Hoover's saloon and the Long Branch. Alert and listening for the sound of Zeb's voice somewhere in one of the small crowds, Jo had to remind herself to move calmly and leisurely.

She walked past the post office and saddle shop, keeping to the middle of the street, but once she turned up Third Avenue, she couldn't help but quicken her pace. By the time she arrived at the boardinghouse, her pulse was racing. Head down, she went inside.

When the door closed behind her, the sound of muffled conversation from an upstairs room seeped into her hazy consciousness. She took two steps at a time to the second floor, glancing quickly at the brass numbers on each of the dark-painted doors. Room number twenty-three was at the very end of the narrow, dimly lit hall.

Jo reached the door, her fingers trembling as she tried to insert the long key into the keyhole. Finally it slid in, and with a turn, the lock clicked and the door creaked open. Wasting not a second, she went inside, shut the door behind her and leaned against it, unable to see anything through the darkness.

Just then, a knock sounded, and Jo nearly leaped out of her skin. She cleared her throat to lower her voice. "Who is it?"

"It's Fletcher. Open up."

Relieved, Jo let him in, then closed the door again.

"You made it in one piece," he said.

"Yes. Now what?"

He crossed the room and closed the curtains. "We get some light in here."

Jo removed her coat and looked around the room while Fletcher replaced a blackened glass chimney onto the kerosene lamp next to the bed.

"Don't you own anything?" she asked, seeing empty surfaces everywhere she looked.

"My clothes are in the drawers. Other than that, I travel light. Makes it easier to do what I have to do."

"And what's that?"

"Be a lawman. I can't get bogged down with stuff. Makes it too hard to leave a place, and I like to go where I'm needed."

She wandered around the room, still looking. "If it weren't for Zeb Stone, we wouldn't have so much *need* for new lawmen."

Fletcher set the matches down on the bedside table then, without warning, moved swiftly and purposefully toward Jo. Startled by his fast approach, she backed up against the wall until she couldn't back up any farther and he was standing mere inches from her, grabbing her wrists and pinning them against the wall on either side of her head.

"What are you doing?" she asked. He was so close she could feel his breath on her face.

He whirled Jo around and set her onto the bed so quickly she didn't have a chance to object. Then he straddled her hips, at the same time pulling her arms over her head and pinning her legs down with his strapping knee. "Get off me!" she hollered, feeling thoroughly and miserably trapped. "What in God's name do you think you're doing? You're supposed to be protecting me...ouch! That hurts!"

"Sorry," he said, distracted by what he was doing,

and when she tried to discern what, exactly, it was, she realized he was reaching down. His hand was maneuvering about, fooling around down low as if he was unbuttoning his trousers! Outraged, Jo tried to struggle, but under his hard, heavy weight, it was difficult to even breathe. "I said get off me!"

"You're not helping things any. Just relax." He pinned her tighter to the bed.

"I will *not* relax!"

The next thing she knew, a rope was twisting around her sore wrists and weaving through the steel bed frame. "I can't trust you to stay put," he said matter-of-factly.

Jo immediately went still, realizing only then what his intentions had been and feeling ridiculously foolish for having thought anything else.

"I can't risk you making another attempt on Zeb's life until I know what's going on."

"You're going to leave me here?"

He pulled the knots tight at her wrists and leaned over her. "It's the only place I know you'll be safe. I'm sorry, Jo." Then he gazed tenderly into her eyes and caressed her face with the back of his hand.

Jo wet her lips, knowing it was unwise to appreciate his kindness when it was accompanied by such a betrayal, but the feel of his warm, gentle fingers upon her cheek and the weight of his firm body covering hers made it impossible. How long had it been since she had been loved and touched affectionately? Edwyn, in the *early* years of their marriage, had come to her in the night, but not often after Leo was born. They had later moved to separate beds because of Edwyn's snoring. At least that was their excuse.

Even so, had she ever wanted Edwyn's husbandly advances the way she wanted Fletcher's now? And would she ever not feel guilty about that...about wanting another man?

She tried to focus her thoughts on the matter at hand. "I'll forgive you if you find something on Zeb."

"I'll try, but...now that I've got you here like this, it's not so easy to leave."

The words barely made it through her dizzied senses. Stunned, Jo stared up at his slightly parted lips, realizing all at once that he was feeling the same pull of attraction she was feeling, as his breath whispered across her face.

Nothing good could come of this, she thought miserably, then despite her mental warnings and her firm emotional objections, found herself responding to his overture. "Don't leave, then."

He considered it a moment, his gaze raking over her face, then his hand slipped slowly into her coat.

Jo's skin began to tingle at the feel of his fingers moving over her clothing. He ran his hand along her hip, then lowered his mouth to hers.

A passionate fluttering passed through her and settled somewhere inside her belly as she realized she'd never in all her life been kissed like this. It was slow and seductive and deeply arousing, and threatened to brand her his forever. She felt the heady sensation of his hot, hungry mouth upon hers like a soul-reaching redemption.

"Fletcher, this is wrong," she whispered, turning her cheek, barely able to get the words out. "We shouldn't be doing this."

"If you tell me to stop, I will."

His lips covered hers again, the kiss velvety and probing. She wiggled sensually on the bed, her wrists still bound above her head, restricted, and all she wanted was to be free of the rough bindings to touch this man everywhere.

"Untie me," she pleaded, wanting to hold him, to feel the whole length of his body upon hers.

He went still and she thought for a moment he had heard something outside, but when she looked at his face, she saw the conflict of his emotions, and it had nothing to do with anything outside this room. Pulling back, he rested on all fours above her and she knew wretchedly what he thought. "I can't untie you."

He backed away and stood, closing her coat over her, yet at the same time, leaving her feeling cold and alone on the bed.

"Why?"

"I can't free you, Jo."

She squirmed and her wrists burned painfully under the coarse rope. "You don't have to *free* me. Just untie me. Temporarily."

Fletcher shook his head. "No, you're my prisoner. It wouldn't be right." He looked around the room, the lines on his forehead deep with frustration.

"What's the matter?" Jo asked, finally lying still.

"The problem with not having any belongings is that you don't have extra rope around when you need it."

Jo ground out a grumble, her body still tingling from the feel of his hands and lips upon her. "Trust me, I'm not going anywhere. These knots are as good as steel." Once again, she tugged at them, releasing some of her own frustration, but it only served to chafe her tender skin even more. She decided to relax and surrender to an uncomfortable night in Fletcher's bed. Alone.

"What are you going to do?" she asked.

He pulled on his long brown coat and settled his hat on his head. "I'm going to talk to Zeb."

"Oh, that's smart. You're just going to walk up to him and ask him if he's a murderer."

"Whatever it takes. Try to get some sleep."

Jo watched him leave the room and close the door behind him. She stared up at the unpainted plank ceiling with the beams exposed, and knew it was going to be a dreadfully long night.

Standing just inside the door of the smoky Long Branch saloon, surveying the crowd of cattlemen and gamblers listening to the five-piece orchestra, Fletcher wondered if he should have dunked himself in the water trough before coming in here. He had work to do, he had to stay focused, but he was irritatingly distracted by Jo's scent still lingering in his memory.

Kissing her had been a big mistake.

He cleared his throat and walked to the white-paneled bar, leaned on the dark mahogany countertop and shouted over the music. "Zeb here tonight?" he asked the bartender, who was standing on a chair, straightening the ornamental rack of horns above the mirror.

"In the back room as usual."

Fletcher thanked the man and walked toward the back, past the billiard table and coal stove, then pushed open the door to the private gambling room. Zeb and three other men sat around a table under a hanging lantern, their money floating in a pile in the center, their cards close to their chests and their chips stacked like small buildings in front of them. Smoke from the tips of their cigars snaked in serpentine streaks toward the ceiling.

"Well, well, well," Zeb greeted, looking up from his hand. He set his cards facedown on the table and slid his chair back. The half-empty whisky bottle in front of him teetered. "Did you come to join us, or to dance to the magnificent orchestral arrangements only the Long Branch can provide?"

"Didn't think they allowed dancing in here," one of the men blurted out, as if he'd been missing out on something.

Zeb glared at him. "It was a joke, my dear man. Now lay down your cards, all of you, and go get yourselves some drinks. I want to talk to my brother-in-law."

All three of the cowboys rose from the table without argument. When they closed the door behind them, Fletcher sat down. "They all friends of yours?"

Zeb tossed back a shot of whisky. "Just a few transient fools willing to part with their hard-earned money." He dragged on his cigar so the tip flared red. "Do you know they only make thirty dollars a month on a drive? Imbeciles."

"Maybe they can't do any better. Don't know the right people."

Zeb eyed him speculatively, then nodded. "You're absolutely right. It's all about who you know, isn't it? What happened to your nose?"

Fletcher touched it lightly, felt that it was still swollen and a little crooked. "Saloon brawl."

"I hope the other gentleman looks worse than you do. Did you bruise his head?"

"I gave it a tap."

"Good for you." They stared intently at each other for a moment, then Zeb reached for the whisky bottle in front of him and poured Fletcher a drink. When he slid it across the table, Fletcher accepted it and raised it before swallowing a bitter mouthful.

"I came to talk about something."

Zeb leaned back in his chair and crossed one leg over

the other. "The sheriff's office. You want to settle in Dodge."

"How did you guess?"

"Never let it be said that women are the only intuitive creatures God put on this beautiful earth." Zeb flicked cigar ashes into a dish. "Before we get down to that bit of business, where were you tonight? I wanted to talk to you."

Fletcher relaxed back in his chair, wondering how to answer that, then made something up. "I went to meet a fellow who said he knew something about the shooting the other night."

"Indeed. Was he helpful?"

Fletcher thought carefully before he answered. "He didn't show."

"No? That's suspicious. Must be hiding something. Perhaps he knows the identity of our enigmatic Six-Shooter Hank." Zeb's speech was slurred.

"Maybe."

"Or better yet, perhaps he *is* Six-Shooter Hank." He laughed at his drunken wittiness. "It could be anyone, you know. The night he came into the store, he was well covered up."

"Any ideas? I'm all out of suspects."

"I'd be willing to wager it's someone right under our noses, yours being the bigger one this evening."

Fletcher humored Zeb, who was drunker than a lord. "And what makes you say that?"

"My punctilious instinct. What I'd do without it, I cannot bear to imagine." Zeb raised his glass and downed the whole of it, as if celebrating something. "Instinct aside, you really have to apprehend *someone* if we're going to get you into the sheriff's office."

Fletcher managed a devious smile. "Anyone will do?"

Zeb laughed. "Now you're starting to sound like a man who's going places. Elizabeth will be pleased to hear you're thinking of settling here. What changed your mind?"

"I figure my prospects are good, with family around."

"Yes, yes, yes. Family loyalty is important. You can always be sure of it. Having said that, if you're going to stay, I'd like to set you up more comfortably. You won't get far on seventy-five a month. Your salary is pathetic. How does an additional hundred sound?"

Fletcher wondered if Zeb would be saying this if he were sober. "Sounds good to me, but you might have trouble convincing the city council."

"I'm not talking about city funds. I'd put you on *my* payroll."

Raising his hands, Fletcher laughed. "No offense, but I never saw myself in the mercantile business."

"Rest assured, I don't see you there, either. You have talents that we could put to better use than counting bags of flour."

Fletcher leaned forward. "What business are we talking about?"

Zeb seemed to consider his reply. After a long pause, he blinked his bloodshot eyes. "The business of being family, of course. Elizabeth wants you to stay here, and if more money will keep you, then that's what you'll get. For now."

For now. Fletcher knew there was something more to this than just being family. Unfortunately, Zeb wasn't ready to trust him with it yet.

"I like to earn what I make."

"Be patient. You will."

Someone rapped at the door, then one of the cowboys peered in. "You want to finish the game, boss? 'Cause Billy wants to meet a lady across the street."

"Tell him if he wants to back out, he'll have to pay me what he owes me."

The cowboy disappeared briefly, then returned. "He said his money's on the table, but only if you say it's okay for him to go."

Zeb shook his head at Fletcher. "Sheep," he whispered, then turned to the cowboy. "Tell him to go meet his lady friend and you can go, too, but don't forget you have a job to do."

"Yes, sir!" The cowboy closed the door and Fletcher heard them hoot as they left the saloon.

"What's this *job* all about?" he asked.

Zeb stared blankly, then spread his arms wide. "The job of getting the whores into bed, of course!"

Trying not to reveal his aversion for the distasteful answer, Fletcher stood and walked around the table to help Zeb up, and the future mayor wobbled to and fro as he gathered up his cash and stuffed it into both his breast pockets. "You'll be by for supper tomorrow evening?"

If Fletcher was going to gain Zeb's trust and find out what was really going on with this so-called family business, he had best accept the invitation. Even if it meant tying Jo to his bed again for another night.

"I'll be there," he answered, then he walked Zeb all the way home, just to make sure he made it back to Elizabeth in one piece.

Chapter Fifteen

It was nearly three-thirty in the morning when Fletcher returned to the boardinghouse and led his horse into the small stable. He'd spent the night on duty, asking casual questions about the Hennigar murder Jo had told him about, to anyone who seemed willing to talk. He learned nothing that Jo hadn't already told him, and discovered that Zeb Stone had held the town's sympathy back then—a man wrongly accused.

Perhaps he was. Perhaps he wasn't. Fletcher had wrestled with the idea all night long, wondering what kind of work Zeb had planned for him, now that he was on his so-called payroll.

Fletcher was beginning to see that Jo was right to be suspicious of Zeb about something, considering the shady characters that were calling him "boss," but with the information Fletcher had gathered so far, he wasn't ready to arrest Zeb for murder.

Exhausted, he fed and watered the horses, then dragged himself up the boardinghouse steps. With any luck, Jo had managed to sleep a little. He thought about what lay ahead for them, and he still couldn't consider making an official arrest and locking her up in the city jail. People would want to know why, and if he told them, he would thwart his own investigation.

He just hoped he could convince Jo to cooperate. If he was going to uncover the truth, she had to go on with her life as if nothing were out of the ordinary; otherwise, Zeb would suspect something. At the same time, Fletcher had to keep her safe from a potential murderer—whoever that might be—and safe from becoming one herself.

He unlocked the door and went inside, relieved to find Jo still secure on his bed, her body limp with sleep. Trying not to wake her, he removed his coat and draped it over the foot of the bed, then unbuckled his gun belt and laid it gently on the chest of drawers. How she managed to sleep with her wrists bound over her head, he could not imagine. She must have been dog-tired.

Needing sleep himself, he carefully moved closer, but paused by the side of the bed when he caught sight of Jo's face, illuminated by the moonlight from the window.

Good Lord, she had a black eye. What had he done?

Wanting to kick himself clear across town, he sat on the bed beside her, trying not to create a stir while he let his fingers hover in the air above her bruised eye. Better not to touch it, he reasoned, when she was so peacefully asleep. He'd done her enough harm already.

He considered the gentlemanly thing—curling up on the floor, but when he thought of what he and Jo had been through together so far, propriety seemed far beyond repair.

Or maybe he was just telling himself that. He might as well admit that what he really wanted was to be close to her. What damage could it do at this point?

Fletcher lowered his weary body down, on his side

with his back intentionally to Jo. Feeling her warmth even through his clothing, he considered the floor again, thinking he might in fact sleep better there, but when his eyes fell closed, there was no hope in getting them open again.

Jo awakened from her deep slumber when she tried to turn over onto her side, only to discover her arms were stretched over her head and her wrists were still bound tightly to the steel bed frame.

Flat on her back in the darkness, feeling the muscles in her shoulders cramping into corkscrews, she wiggled uncomfortably on the lumpy mattress. Her hip struck something and her groggy mind suddenly cleared. Fletcher was sleeping soundly beside her, his head resting in his hands, his backside connecting with her hip.

How, she wondered with senses now buzzing to life, had this situation spun so impossibly out of control?

Through fading hope, Jo looked toward the window to estimate the time, and hearing meadowlarks chirping a full symphony, she guessed it must be between four and five in the morning. It wouldn't be long before her ranch hands awakened and came looking for their breakfast. What would they do when they found the house empty?

Fletcher breathed deeply and rolled into her. He stirred and opened his eyes as if her anchored presence in his bed was the most common thing in the world. "You're awake."

"Yes, no thanks to these ropes. My arms have fallen asleep and it feels like a hundred thousand pins and needles."

He sat up and began to tug at the knots. "I guess I

can untie you for now. You're not going anywhere while I'm here.''

''Guess not.'' Finally she could rub her sleeping arms and hands and scratch all the places that itched. ''What happened last night? Did you talk to Zeb?''

Fletcher sat up on the edge of the bed and lit the lamp. ''Yes.''

''Well? What did you say? What did *he* say?''

The room flickered with a dim, golden light, and Fletcher's large shadow loomed against the wall as he stood. ''Nothing to suggest he killed anyone, though I didn't exactly ask him.''

''Couldn't you have hinted at something?''

''You know as well as I do that Zeb is an intelligent man. I don't want him to know I'm checking into his affairs. It's best if he trusts me. That way, he might let down his guard.''

''So you *do* suspect him?''

Fletcher settled back against the wall, one ankle crossed casually over the other. ''I didn't say that, but he's got something going on that he's being vague about. Some kind of business. I'd like to know what it is, considering I'm an employee.''

''An employee?''

''Yeah. If he even remembers saying it, that is. He was a little inebriated. He told me he'd put me on his 'payroll,' calling it a 'family thing.' He's going to pay me to stick around for Elizabeth's sake. Maybe that's all it is, but—''

''He's trying to make you feel you owe him something. To trap you.''

Fletcher watched her in an intent way, and she felt as if he was forming judgments about her in his mind. She wished she knew what they were.

He took his time to reply. "I'm not jumping to any conclusions, but I'm not ruling anything out, either." He pushed his disheveled hair away from his face. "Did you get enough sleep? How's your nose?"

"My nose is fine, and sleeping's not my first concern right now. I'm worried about my ranch hands, what they'll do when they discover I'm missing."

Fletcher went to the window and looked outside, the faint light gracing the smooth lines of his sculpted shoulders and arms. "That's a good point. They'll probably go looking for you, or worse, report your disappearance to the deputy." He reached for his gun belt on the chest of drawers and buckled it around his waist. "What about Leo and Matilda? They might have already noticed."

"I sent them away last night. They went to Newton and the house is empty."

Assuming she and Fletcher would be leaving soon, Jo crawled off the bed and went to look in the small mirror on the wall over the washstand. "Good heavens, look at my eye!" It was puffy and ugly, her shirt was wrinkled and coming untucked, and her hair, still in a bun, looked like a great big hornet's nest.

Fletcher moved toward her, his voice soft and apologetic. "If I'd known it was you last night…"

"Just forget about it," she said despondently.

She tucked one tangled strand of hair here, another there. "So what are you going to do with me? If it doesn't make any difference to you, I'd like to stay out of sight—Zeb's in particular."

"Zeb's at home with Elizabeth till noon every day and I imagine he'll be sleeping extra late this morning."

"You're not listening to me. I'm in danger."

He strode toward her and pulled a hairpin from her

hair, letting the whole mess fall onto her shoulders. She shivered at the silky play of his fingers around her neck. "I *am* listening. I said I wasn't ruling anything out. That means I'll keep you safe. You need to fix your hair."

Unmoving, Jo stared up at him. "I asked you what you were going to do with me."

He stroked her cheek with his thumb. "Take you home."

"I won't be safe there."

"You will be, if I'm watching over you."

She tried not to acknowledge the one teasing finger that traced the outline of her ear. "And just how do you plan to investigate Zeb from my front parlor?"

"I'm only taking you back to avoid a panic and a search. You'll fix breakfast for the men just like always, while I look at some of Edwyn's things. I might be able to find something that will shed light on all this. You can make up some excuse to be away from the house for the day. I don't want anything to seem out of the ordinary until I can get some answers."

"You're not going to lock me up?"

Fletcher wet his mouth and gazed down at hers.

Rattled, worrying that he was going to kiss her again, Jo tried to quench the fire that was snapping and sparking inside her belly.

"Not today," he answered.

A stress-induced daze wiggled into her brain as she looked up at him, waiting. Then a muscle quivered at his jaw and he seemed to awaken from some kind of trance. He turned his back on her, pulled out his gun and checked it for bullets, and the clicking sound was like a bucket of cold water on Jo's frazzled emotions.

He dropped the weapon into its holster and strode to

the door. "Put your hair up and get your hat on, Jo. We have to get you home before sunrise."

The prairie grass glistened like diamonds with morning dew, reflecting the first gleam of dawn. Warm beneath her coat, Jo could see Mogie's panting breath coming in little puffs like steam from a train as she urged him to trot over the last rise. She and Fletcher had decided to circle the long way around the corral to avoid waking anyone in the bunkhouse. They would hide his horse in the chicken coop where the cowhands never ventured.

Fletcher reached the top of the hill first, stopping on the road when Prince grew skittish.

"What is it?" Jo asked. "What's the matter?"

"I thought you said the house was empty."

She caught up to him and reined in her mount. "I did say that."

"Then what's that light in your parlor?"

Jo stood up in the stirrups, squinting through the hazy dawn. Her bones went limp at the sight. "I don't know."

"I'd better go down there. You wait here." Fletcher reached for his gun.

"I'm coming with you."

"No, you're not. It's too dangerous."

"I know, that's why I have to go. You might need me."

He glared at her as if considering all options, then reached into his saddlebag. "Take this, then." He moved closer and handed her her weapon. She checked the chamber for bullets.

"You're giving a loaded gun to a prisoner?"

His eyes told her he trusted her, and she couldn't

deny being pleased about it. "Just come on. Stay behind me and wait outside while I check the house."

They trotted down the hill, but as they grew closer, Jo noticed the light in the parlor window growing brighter. She stopped. "Wait a minute."

Fletcher stopped, too.

"That's no lantern light," she said.

"You're right. It's a fire!"

Jo and Fletcher kicked in their heels and galloped to the house just as the lace curtains went up in flames.

"Fire!" she screamed, leaping off Mogie.

Five men from the bunkhouse ran outside looking flustered and sleepy, some wearing their clothes, some wearing only their undershirts and drawers. It took only seconds for all of them to bolt to the barn in their bare feet and grab buckets.

Fletcher hopped down from the saddle, ripped off his coat and dunked it in the water barrel by the bunkhouse. He was the first to enter the house, slapping at flames in the window with his wet slicker. Jo followed his lead, dunking her coat, running inside and striking the fire that was consuming the sofa.

Smoke burned her eyes and stung her throat. She covered her mouth with one sleeve, coughing, while she whipped her coat mercilessly through the smoke-filled air.

The ranch hands all ran in with buckets of sloshing water, dousing the flames that were eating the rugs and walls. Jo could see her wedding picture simmering on the mantel, and the fact that she made no move to rescue it sat for a while in her brain as if waiting to be comprehended, until she forced her attention to stay with more urgent matters, like saving her home.

While Fletcher ripped down the curtain rod and

smothered the flames it carried, she slapped ruthlessly at the hot blazes that were nipping perilously close to the bottom of his trousers.

Men ran in and out, tossing water through the air in long silver streaks. Jo coughed and sputtered. Her lungs felt tight as she gasped for breath. Fletcher turned and grabbed her arm, dragging her toward the front door. "You have to get out of here!"

"No!" She shook his hand away.

They stood in the front hall. The bright fire crackled and hissed behind him. "Just go outside and breathe a minute, or you'll suffocate!"

"What about you?"

"I'll be fine!" He ran back into the parlor and fought the flames that were devouring Jo's rocking chair and mantel. Jo ran outside and dunked her coat in the barrel again. She sucked in a few essential breaths, then ran back toward the house with her dripping cargo.

John, her foreman, ran past her in his scarlet knit drawers and matching undershirt, carrying two buckets. He met her at the door and halted. "Mrs. O'Malley! Your eye!"

She didn't stop to explain. "Hurry, John! Help Fletcher!"

He hesitated a moment, then ran in with his two buckets and threw water onto the flames at the mantel. Fletcher was wheezing, covering his face with a sleeve while he battered the fire. Three men came in at once and a torrent of water covered the floor and walls. The blaze winced and recoiled, gasping its last breath in one fatal hissing sizzle.

Coughing, Jo looked at Fletcher, who began to stagger. She ran to his side as he collapsed his heavy frame onto her tiny one. She struggled to stay upright, grab-

bing his arm and pulling it around her sore shoulder to
support him.

"Somebody help me!" she shouted.

John came running. On each side of Fletcher, they
helped him through the front hall and down the porch
steps. He dropped to his knees in the dirt, fighting for
breath. Jo dropped down beside him with her hand on
his back. "Are you all right? John, get him a glass of
water!"

John ran back to the house.

Fletcher drew in one long, deep breath that sounded
hideously thin. "Is the fire out?"

"Yes. It's out." She looked back at the house. "Are
you men all right in there?"

One came out, waving. "We're okay. Just making
sure it ain't gonna start up again."

She turned her attention back to Fletcher, who was
rubbing his eyes. "You were lucky," he said.

"I know. We caught it just in time."

"No, I mean you were lucky, because that fire was
set to get rid of *you*."

Jo sat back on her heels in disbelief. "How can you
be sure?"

He leaned forward, coughed a few times, then tried
to clear his throat. "Because the curtains were doused
in kerosene. I could smell it, and the can was tossed
into the fireplace. A shoddy job, really."

She'd expected something like this, but the reality of
it infuriated her far beyond any imagining. A stranger—
no doubt one of Zeb's hired men—had found his way
onto her land and into her home. She looked all around,
then rose to her feet. "We have to go after Zeb."

"Oh, no, we don't."

"He's not getting away with this!"

She walked to Mogie, who was grazing by the fence, and took the dangling reins. Before she could lift her foot into the stirrup, she felt a hand on her shoulder.

"You're not going anywhere."

"Let me go, Fletcher."

"Not on your life."

"I said let me go!" She tried to struggle free of him, but he held her tight around the waist.

Growing more angry by the second, Jo elbowed Fletcher in the ribs.

Then, in an instant, her feet were swept out from under her and she landed hard on the ground with a thump. The cool handle of a Colt .45 came down to rest gently on her forehead, its light pressure a clear message not to move. She blinked up at Fletcher's irate gaze.

"I don't want to knock you out, Jo, but I will if I have to."

Relaxing the back of her head on the ground, she let out an exasperated sigh, then noticed John's bare feet in the dirt beside her. He was holding the glass of water she had asked for.

"What the hell's going on here?" he demanded. He glared at Fletcher. "Did *you* give Mrs. O'Malley that black eye?"

Jo tried to get up. "John, you don't understand."

His gaze moved up and down her manly attire and settled on her eye again. "I think I do, ma'am. I know the house was empty last night, and seeing how you're riding up so early with the marshal..."

John gave the glass of water to Jo and balled his hands into fists. "What kind of lily-livered vermin are you, hitting a woman like that? If you can dish it out, Marshal Collins, you sure as hell better be ready to take it."

Chapter Sixteen

Barely able to get a full breath into his tight lungs, Fletcher dropped his gun into his holster. He took in John's snug-fitting red underwear and bare toes. "Now, listen here..."

"Don't you *now listen here* me! I'm about as savage as a meat ax over what you did!"

"It's not what it looks like," Jo said.

"You stay out of this, Mrs. O'Malley."

"It's *my* business, not yours!"

Before Fletcher had a chance to explain anything, a tight fist came hurling through the air, straight for his nose. "No, wait!"

The crack of bone against bone cleared Fletcher's lungs in a hurry. His cheekbones vibrated with agonizing spasms of pain that shot straight to his brain until his whole head hammered. "Ah, hell! Not again!" He cupped his throbbing nose, feeling blood drain onto his lips.

"John! Stop it!" Jo yelled, trying to take hold of him. The other ranch hands emerged from the house and gathered on the covered porch to watch.

John pounced away like an amateur boxer. With both

fists drawn, he bobbed up and down on the balls of his bare feet. "Face me like a man, Marshal."

"Let's talk about this," Fletcher said.

"What's there to talk about? Somebody's gotta stand up for the lady."

Furious, Jo ripped off her hat and threw it on the ground. "I can take care of myself!"

"No lady should have to take care of herself against men like him," John said. "Preying on this lonely widow—listening to the gossip about her, no doubt! You're a disgrace to your badge."

Fletcher bent forward, still holding his nose. "Jeez, what next?"

"If you weren't such a bastard, I'd force you to marry her."

"Marry her?"

"Marry me!" Jo echoed.

Not sure what to say, Fletcher tried to stand straight. He wiped his bloody nose on his sleeve. John bounced like a March Hare toward him and threw another punch. Fletcher dodged it.

"But you ain't good enough for someone like her. So if you ain't gonna honor her by proposing, I will!"

Another punch flew past Fletcher's ear. He wiped more blood off his throbbing nose, his nerves just about at the breaking point. "Nobody's marrying anybody."

John bounced around the barnyard, then made one more lunge toward Fletcher. "Oh yeah? We'll see about that!"

Enough was enough. Fletcher went for his gun.

The very next second, John was flat on his back, blinking up at the sky and rubbing his bruised noggin. Fletcher dropped his gun back into the holster.

"Damn, that was fast," John mumbled.

Jo set the glass of water down on the ground and knelt beside him. "Are you all right?"

"I think so."

She helped him sit up.

"I feel a little dizzy, though."

Jo gave Fletcher an irritated glare.

"What—he was going to punch me again!" Fletcher insisted.

"You didn't have to hit him so hard."

"I wasn't about to get my nose broken a third time."

Jo parted John's hair to examine his head. "I don't see any blood."

"Plenty of blood over here," Fletcher pointed out, feeling around the bridge of his nose.

Jo ignored him. "John, why don't you go get dressed. We'll talk later."

He rose to his feet and Fletcher had to strain to hear what John whispered to her: "I meant it about marrying you, Mrs. O'Malley. If that's what you need, I'm your man."

Jo only nodded and tapped him a few times on the arm. The sheepish foreman made his way awkwardly to the bunkhouse, rubbing the top of his head.

Jo turned to the others on the porch, all staring in silence. "Thank you for your help, gentlemen, but you can get to work now. Breakfast will be a little late this morning."

A general murmur of acknowledgment floated down the steps with them as they moved past, all glaring irately at Fletcher. "You okay, Mrs. O'Malley?" one of them asked. "You want someone to stick around?"

"I'm fine, thank you. This is all a misunderstanding."

When they were gone, Fletcher tipped his head back to stop the blood from dripping onto his boots.

"I'm sorry about that," Jo said swiftly, picking up the glass and rising.

"Yeah? You don't look sorry to me."

"What's that supposed to mean?"

Fletcher hobbled to the house and up the porch steps, hearing Jo pick up her hat and follow behind him. "You just got yourself a marriage proposal."

"As if I wanted it! I don't want to marry *him*. Or *you*, for that matter!"

"No?"

"No!" Face-to-face on the covered porch, breathing in the scent of singed carpet, they glared angrily at each other. Jo slammed her hat onto her head and Fletcher could feel all his pent-up frustrations exploding at once.

"Well, I don't want to marry you, either," he said, holding his painful, swollen, crooked nose.

"So you said already."

"No, I didn't."

"Yes, you did! You said, 'nobody's marrying anybody.'"

He stood quietly, trying to remember what, exactly, he had said, then he gave up on it and tipped his head back again to stop the blood that was dripping onto the porch floor. Throat burning, he coughed dryly. "I need a drink of water."

"Here!" Jo threw the water she held straight into his face.

Feeling the cold slap against his dry, sooty skin, Fletcher shut his eyes. He kept them shut a moment, trying to rid himself of the shock before he opened them to meet Jo's surprised gaze.

She covered her mouth with her hand. "I can't believe I just did that."

Fletcher wiped a hand over his wet face and flicked the water into the air. "Feel better?"

"As a matter of fact, I do," she replied, the rage all gone from her voice now.

He wished *he* felt better, but since he didn't have a glass of water to pour over her head, all he could do was keep on struggling against the impossible cravings that had been torturing him ever since he'd made the mistake of touching her on the bed last night.

Feeling hot all of a sudden, he stared down at her blushing cheeks and full lips and noticed a spot of soot smeared across her chin. Her golden hair was falling in stray tendrils onto her dust-covered shoulders; the hat she wore was wrinkled and rakishly askew, and she hardly seemed aware she still held an empty drinking glass in her hand.

Without thinking, Fletcher grabbed her by the wrist and dragged her into the house. "Come in here."

"Why? What are you—"

Once inside, he slammed the door behind them, pushed her up against it and smothered her next words with his mouth.

Jo dropped her hat and the glass onto the floor. Fletcher barely heard the smash as it shattered into tiny pieces. All he could comprehend was the sound of his own breathing, deep and labored. Her tiny moan of pleasure made his body ache for the rest of her. She wrapped her arms around his shoulders and opened her moist lips to his kiss.

"I want to take you upstairs," he whispered against her neck as he nibbled the soft flesh.

"No, we can't, not with the men just outside." Her

leg came up to wrap around his hips, and he thrust against her, wishing their clothing wasn't stopping him from what he really wanted to do to her, here against the heavy oak door. "They'll be looking for their breakfast," she mumbled in a drawn-out whisper.

"Let them eat the roasted curtains."

Jo threw her head back and he kissed the skin just beneath her collar.

"Maybe you should lock the door," she whispered.

Eyes closed, he clumsily felt around for the key in the lock, found it and turned it. "No one's getting in."

Just then, someone knocked upon it.

Fletcher stopped kissing her.

Jo's eyes opened. "Who is it?" she asked in a melodic voice.

"It's John. Do you need any help with breakfast, Mrs. O'Malley?"

Her face paled as she squeezed Fletcher's shoulders. Fletcher raised his forefinger to his lips to keep her from sounding as if anything was out of the ordinary—he certainly didn't want his nose broken again—then he nodded for her to reply.

"No, thank you, John." Her voice seemed strained, out of breath. "I'm fine."

Silence swelled on the porch. Then John asked, "You okay in there?"

"Yes. I'll ring the bell when everything's ready." Still, they did not hear any departing footsteps.

Growing impatient while staring down at Jo's wide-eyed gaze, breathing in the distinct orange flower water scent he had grown to associate with her, and her alone, Fletcher kissed the top of her head. His body throbbed with need, and he could not stop himself from pressing his lips to hers again, slowly, gently, as quietly as possible, letting his tongue drift inside her mouth.

Jo's little moan of pleasure soon made Fletcher forget about John, even as he heard the footsteps tapping down the porch stairs.

Quieter now, they finished what they'd so hastily begun—a chain of kisses as long as the Santa Fe Trail, each one melting hotly into the next. Before long, Jo buried her face into Fletcher's neck, clutched at his shoulders, and told him in whispered words, "Take me upstairs."

Damn, how he wanted to hear her cry out as he knew she would if he made love to her. The idea alone made his blood race until he could hardly make sense of anything. He had to mentally shake himself to see reason.

He continued to hold her, to kiss her neck and collarbone, trying to think of a way to make himself refuse what she was offering. He took her trembling hand in his and pressed the soft, warm palm to his lips.

"I can't do that, Jo," he said softly.

He felt the weight of her stare and saw her expression change from heated arousal to insulted disbelief. "*You* can't do it?"

"I didn't mean to—"

She yanked her hand away and he closed his eyes in defeat. Sometimes he could be so unimaginably *stupid*.

"You're not the only one who's risking something here!" she burst out. "I have reasons to stay away from you, too, and let me tell you, they're infinite."

"Jo, let's not do this."

"No, I think we should. If not now, when? I'll be in jail before long, so we won't be able to have much of a conversation there."

"Jo, don't—"

"Why not? I am still your prisoner, am I not? And I wasn't kissing you to get you to change your mind about arresting me."

"I didn't think that."

"It sounded like you did."

"I didn't mean it the way it sounded."

"How *did* you mean it? No, never mind. There's no point discussing it. When I suggested we go upstairs...well, that was rash of me. I've been confused about a lot of things lately, but I wasn't trying to trick you."

She was rambling now, and Fletcher had the feeling it was her pride talking; she was trying to hold on to her dignity. "Look, I don't usually analyze these things. I wanted you, too," he told her, just to be sure she didn't think he wasn't interested. Nothing could have been further from the truth. "It was as simple as that."

"That's right, I forgot. You're a temporary man. These things would have to be simple, wouldn't they?"

"That's not fair."

She bent down and picked her hat up off the floor. "None of this is fair. You're going to drag me off to jail as soon as you've solved the murders and upheld your precious law. That's the only reason you haven't put me in shackles already—because you need me to act like nothing's happening in order to close this case."

"Jo, it's more complicated than that."

"Complicated. I thought you said it was simple."

"It is simple...the other part of it, I mean."

He backed away and sat on the bottom stair, resting his forehead in his hands, feeling more confused now than ever. For a long moment, he just sat there.

"I don't understand," Jo said despondently.

He looked up at her, his eyes burning and bloodshot.

He didn't want to talk about this now, or tell her how he felt about her, but with things the way they were, he probably owed her at least that before he locked her up and called in the judge.

"The fact that I *want* you is simple enough," he said after a great deal of painful deliberation. "It's the way I *feel* about you that's complicated."

Jo sank down to sit on the floor, her legs stretched out in a V in front of her.

"This isn't at all how I'd planned things," he went on, "and I *always* plan things." He moved forward to kneel between her legs, and found himself revealing more than he'd intended to.

"When John told me he would marry you if I didn't, I wanted to flatten him."

"You *did,*" she reminded him with a hint of a smile that eased him, but only a bit.

Fletcher grinned, too. "I guess I did."

"John's a kind man, but I'm not going to marry him."

"I know it's none of my business, but I'm glad." He took her hand in his. "I'm sorry for all this, Jo, I really am. I do care about you—*more* than care—but you know *I* can never marry you. I'm a lawman and I don't plan on changing the way I live."

Jo stood up, catching him off guard, and glared down at him. "I never asked you to marry me."

She moved around him on her way to the stairs, but stopped to straighten Edwyn's portrait on the wall. A mixture of fatigue and sadness passed over her features and, watching her, Fletcher felt a heaviness center in his chest.

"Now, if you'll excuse me," Jo said, forcing all emotion from her voice and telling him in no uncertain terms that she was shutting him out, "I have work to do. And I believe you do, too."

When she turned her back on him and started up the stairs, he dropped his head into his hands, and wished that he could somehow change the man he had become.

Chapter Seventeen

Fletcher rose to his feet in the front hall and touched the tender bridge of his nose, still throbbing painfully. Right now, his whole body was aching, but mostly from the icy tone in Jo's voice when she'd turned away from him.

He had to admit, though, she was right. They'd become too damn close, and her shutting him out was the best thing for both of them.

What had he been thinking, anyway, kissing her again like that? He'd taken advantage of her, that was certain, in her very own house after it nearly burned to the ground, up against her front door and under the watchful gaze of her dead husband's crooked, smoke-stained portrait. It was a stupidly selfish thing to do.

Feeling guilty and more out of touch than ever with the part of himself that was supposed to be a lawman, Fletcher looked up the long, empty staircase and heard the floorboards creaking under Jo's angry footsteps.

Her harsh tone reverberated inside his head. *I never asked you to marry me....*

What had possessed him to bring up marriage? It was the furthest thing from his mind—with any woman—

and Mrs. O'Malley was hardly ready for marriage...
hell, the way she constantly straightened that darn picture.

Fletcher went to the kitchen, found a rag and managed to wet it under the forceful flow of cold water from the indoor pump. As he wiped the dried blood from under his nose and pressed the cool cloth to his burning eyelids, he struggled to remember who—and what—he was. A lawman. The sooner he took Jo to jail and left her there for someone else to deal with, the sooner he'd be back in control of his senses and better able to do his job.

He winced when he touched the cloth to his nose.

Returning to the front hall, he decided it was time to find the men who had killed Jo's husband and finish this investigation. That was the only way to be free of her and her effect on him. It was time he looked more closely into her affairs.

He glanced once more up the staircase and, hearing nothing, he decided to take a look around. He walked down the hall toward the back of the large ranch house, and let himself into what, as luck would have it, appeared to be Edwyn's den.

The room was small and plain, painted green with chairs upholstered in a slightly darker green leather. A collection of rifles hung in a balanced display on the wall opposite the gray stone fireplace.

Fletcher glanced at the floor-to-ceiling bookcases with the books organized by author, but was more interested in the black walnut rolltop desk under the window. He closed the door behind him and strode across the room, his footsteps muted over the dark red Oriental carpet.

Taking a seat in the oak chair, he rolled up the bowed

desktop. The contents were neatly arranged—the ledger and account book standing in one corner, ink jar and pens set back in the other, and correspondence stuffed tightly into a small cedar box on the desk shelf.

Beginning with the account book, Fletcher flipped through the pages to check the postings, but found no amounts out of the ordinary, nor any of the account names suspicious. Reaching for the ledger next, Fletcher pulled out the thick black book and opened it. The silvery light of morning shone through the window and onto the long pages, which revealed typical journal entries—a debit to cash here, a credit to revenue there. All the amounts seemed reasonable for an outfit this size.

The only thing that made him stop and stare was the change in penmanship.

Sometime in February, the entries went from a small, dull scribble to a larger, more graceful, right-slanting script. Fletcher knew it was Jo's handwriting, for it matched her style—smooth and elegant, yet clear and strong—no fancy, curly swirls and loops in her letters.

He ran his finger over it. Tragic, that she'd put this ink to the page only weeks after her husband's death. How hard it must have been for her to look at his script, a personal mark of his existence still living inside the book. She had probably run her dainty fingers over it, too, just like Fletcher was doing now, and what a task, he thought soberly, to undertake her husband's role as master of this ranch while the grief was still so fresh. He wished she would talk to him about it.

Realizing he was sliding off the track of his duty again, Fletcher slammed the book shut and looked out the window at the rolling pasture, at rest beneath the white, overcast sky. He had to stay focused.

Setting the ledger back in place, he reached for the cedar box of letters on the small shelf and began reading. Unfortunately, all the letters were dated over the past six months, personal correspondence addressed to Jo from various friends or relations. Fletcher found nothing suspicious, just a lot of continuing condolences about Edwyn's death...*how lonely you must be,* a hundred times over.

Reminded again of Jo's recent sorrow—her problems, her vast responsibilities, her heartbreak over losing the man she loved—Fletcher tried to shake away the jealousy he didn't want to feel and the regret about what had just happened between them. He stuffed the last letter back into the box, steepled his fingers together and rested his forehead on them.

Concentrate. If this was Jo's workplace now, where were Edwyn's business papers and correspondence?

Swiveling in the chair, he glanced around the small room. On the floor beside the bookcase, he spotted a small oak sea chest.

He crossed the room and knelt before it, but found it locked tighter than a bank safe. It was just as heavy, he discovered, upon trying to move it away from the wall. What in God's name could weigh so much?

He jiggled the lock a bit, but nothing budged. He jiggled it a little harder, but froze when the door to the den suddenly swung open.

Fletcher rose to his feet to face John's skeptical gaze.

"What are you doing in here, Marshal?"

Hell, he couldn't tell John he was investigating Edwyn's murder. He couldn't tell anyone. So what, exactly, *was* he doing in here?

At Fletcher's hesitation, John's eyes narrowed. "Where's Mrs. O'Malley?"

"She's upstairs."

"Nonsense. I'm right here." Wearing a white cotton apron over a yellow calico bodice and skirt, Jo walked in and stood beside John. "What seems to be the problem?"

"Marshal Collins weaseled his way in here, ma'am. I found him lurking around like a bandit."

Jo cupped her hands in front of her. "Well, of course he's in here. Where else is he to wait for breakfast? In the burned parlor?"

"But I saw him jiggling the lock on Mr. O'Malley's private box right there."

"I was just admiring it," Fletcher said. "I like old sea chests."

Jo cleared her throat, looking shaken. "John, if you'll wait for me in the kitchen, I'd like to speak with you. I'll be along directly."

"Sure thing, ma'am." He glared at Fletcher before backing out of the room.

Jo moved into the room, her skirts whipping between her fast footsteps. "Here's what you're looking for."

Impatiently, she rose up on her toes and retrieved a brass key from the highest shelf over the chest. Her tone had never been so cold, and Fletcher felt the chill clear down to his boots. "Though I don't know what you're after," she went on. "It's just full of Edwyn's personal letters from Ireland. They're old, they were written before he even came to America. He was sentimental and brought them with him."

Fletcher's finger touched hers as he took the key from her, and she immediately jerked her hand away. Trying not to let it bother him as much as it did, he knelt down and turned the key in the old lock. The rusty hinges squeaked as he opened the chest.

"Yep. Letters, and lots of them." He flipped through a few.

"I wouldn't lie about it." There was something odd in her tone. Something that struck him.

"I didn't think you would." Fletcher closed the box and stood. "But is there something you're not telling me? Something about these letters?"

"I assure you, they're just personal. So what *were* you looking for?" Jo asked, returning the key to its hiding place, and seeming anxious to change the subject.

"Edwyn's business papers and correspondence. I didn't find anything in the desk."

"You searched my desk?"

"I thought we agreed I'd look through Edwyn's belongings. It seemed like a wise place to start."

Jo moved to the collection of rifles on the wall and pulled another key from behind the Winchester on the mantel. "You'll find everything over there." Pointing to another larger chest covered by a green plaid blanket, Jo handed the key to him. "I've looked through it all and didn't find anything unusual, but you have a go at it. Shall I bring your breakfast on a tray?"

He took the key. "It would get me out of here faster."

Jo lifted her chin. "Yes, of course. You don't like to stay in one place for too long, do you?" She turned to leave.

Too late, Fletcher realized how insensitive his words had sounded. "Jo…"

But in a whisper of petticoats, she was already out the door.

Jo walked down the wide hall, her hand on her stomach. She paused at the bottom of the staircase, her other hand resting on the carved oak of the bottom post. The parlor to her left was blackened and smelling of scorched fabric, kerosene and smoke. Someone was trying to kill her, and Fletcher was itching to take her to prison.

Why, oh why, then, was she fantasizing about kissing him again, about making love to him, all problems forgotten? Why was she so completely heartsick and tormented by the fact that that would never happen?

She took a breath, trying to find the heart to move. Ridiculous, that she could be falling for such an unfeeling, soulless man. A man with no devotion to anything, land or people, no ability to love anything deeply enough to stay in one place longer than it took to arrest a few criminals, including someone he admitted he cared about—her.

How could Fletcher tell her he cared, knowing he would toss her in jail the first chance he got? And why was she letting herself care for him when she knew the kind of man he was?

As she considered it more, she found herself remembering the things he had said to her on the dark prairie, how he had reacted when she'd confessed her sins and secrets—that she had lied about what she saw the night Edwyn was killed and, after that, had taken the law into her own hands. Of course, Fletcher did what his duty demanded of him—he'd arrested her—but at the same time, he had listened and understood and consoled her. He'd told her that Edwyn's death was not her fault, that she had done the right thing, staying hidden. He did not condemn her for the thing that mattered most in her heart—the thing she believed was her greatest sin.

How then, could he be soulless? How could a man

with no heart manage to touch hers, when she thought she'd cloaked it in ice?

It was all so frustrating. She could no longer deny how desperately she wanted and desired the man beneath the badge, the man she knew existed but could not have.

She supposed that if her heart was to be broken, she had only herself to blame for confiding in him, for entrusting her life to him, and for letting him kiss her and touch her the way he had.

It would not happen again.

Dropping her hands to her sides and forcing herself to stand tall, she glanced toward the kitchen where John was waiting—after having offered to marry her in front of everyone—and she dreaded talking to him about this. She hoped it would not be too awkward.

Working hard to focus on what had to be done, she squared her shoulders and walked with purpose into the kitchen. There he sat, hands clasped together in front of him, full of hope when he knew nothing about all of Jo's reprehensible sins and failings. He stood as soon as he saw her, and she felt a twinge of guilt.

"Good morning, John. Thank you for waiting. Please sit down."

Jo sat across from him. Unable to meet his gaze, she let hers fall to his rough, callused hands. "I...I want to thank you for what you tried to do this morning, after the fire was put out. I know you were just concerned for my well-being."

"Yes, ma'am. I am concerned."

She tried to smile. "There's really no need to be. I'm quite capable of taking care of myself."

Before she had a chance to finish, John was leaping out of his chair and dropping to his knees before her, clasping her hands in his. "Mrs. O'Malley, that man in Mr. O'Malley's den is no good for you, no good at all."

"John, let me—"

"No, please, let me talk first. I reckon I can guess what he did to you, why your eye looks like that, but I promise not to ever mention it again if you'll just let me and the boys throw him out of here."

"John, this is all a misunderstanding." She hated herself for keeping the truth from him.

"No need to make up stories for me, ma'am. I'm just glad to see you popped him one in return."

"It's nothing like that, John—"

"I'm glad I popped him one, too."

Her head throbbing with frustration, Jo pulled her hands from John's and stood up. She walked to the sideboard and leaned against it. "Fletcher did not intentionally hurt me. It was an accident."

"Then why'd you hit him back?"

"That was an accident, too."

John hesitated, his forehead crinkling. "I sure hope you're not going to marry him."

"Of course I'm not, and I would appreciate it if you would not speak of it again."

John's chest heaved with a deep breath. He stood and approached her. "Then my offer still stands, ma'am. I don't know what happened between you two last night, and I'm willing to forget about it. I won't mention it again if you'll just consider my offer."

"John…"

"Please listen first." He knelt down on one knee and held her hand. "I know you've had a rough year. We all have, after what happened to Mr. O'Malley. He was a good man and a fair boss, but you shouldn't have to

be all alone and run things by yourself. Folks are talkin'
about you living out here with all of us—''

"I know that, John, and I really don't care what
they're saying."

"Maybe you don't love me, but you might in time.
I'm a nice enough fellow, I'd always treat you decent,
never raise a hand to you or Leo. I ain't like that."

Jo didn't know what to say. His words were echoing
inside her head. She had a million reasons not to marry
him, but the only one that seemed to reveal itself to her
now was a witless infatuation for a man who cared only
for the steel badge he wore on his vest. "John…"

"It would be sort of like one of them marriages of
conven—conven—''

"Convenience," she finished for him.

"Yeah, yeah, one a' them. You'd get your reputation
back and I'd get a ranch out of it."

Jo slowly pulled her hand away. "A *ranch*…?"

"Yes, ma'am. And a darn good one. Is something
wrong?"

"Uh, John, to be frank, you don't know the first thing
about me. If you did, your feelings might be different."

"Ma'am, a ranch is a ranch."

Turning her back on him, she cupped her pounding
forehead in her hand. *Oh, dear, sweet, simple Edwyn.
Nothing was ever this complicated with you.*

"Maybe we should talk about this later," Jo suggested, setting aside the sharp edge to her voice and
replacing it with a gentler one that took significant efforts to produce. "The men are waiting for their breakfast."

He stood in silence behind her. She could hear him
breathing hard and it made her uneasy, so she faced
him squarely. "Wait outside, John."

Finally his boots thumped across the floor and she heard the front door creak open and slam shut behind him.

Good God, was there no one she could trust?

Feeling angry and disillusioned, she collapsed into the chair and wondered how in all the world her life had plunged to such a depth of misfortune, and how she would ever claw her way out of it.

Chapter Eighteen

While the ranch hands burrowed into their breakfast plates in the dining room, Jo stood at the stove in the kitchen, serving up a large helping of fried eggs and bacon for Fletcher.

Perspiring over the hot stove, she reached for two slices of corn bread that Matilda had made before she left, dropped them onto the plate and set the heavy cast-iron frying pan aside. She reached for a jar of molasses to set on Fletcher's tray, wondering why she was taking such pains with his food. It wasn't as if her cooking was so stupendous it would convince him to let her go.

She poured a cup of black coffee for him and arranged everything on the tray. Untying the strings on her apron, she draped it over the kitchen chair, picked up the heavy breakfast tray and walked down the hall toward the den with caution on her mind. When she set eyes on Fletcher, she would not—absolutely not—let herself think about the kissing. She would focus on her purpose: to ensure her family's safety and see Zeb pay for what he did.

With that and only that in mind, she pushed open the door to the den and entered.

Fletcher sat in one of the leather upholstered chairs reading a letter. Both his eyes were black from being punched in the nose so many times, and Jo felt a twinge of guilt about that fact. She stared at his focused expression, then at his capable, masculine hands, and a flurry of disloyal butterflies created a disturbing breeze within her belly. Why wasn't her body listening to what her head was telling it?

Standing like a dazed ninny in the doorway, Jo tried to concentrate on moving her feet, one in front of the other, and somehow she managed to fully enter the room. She set the tray on the center table, brushed her hair back from her perspiration-dampened forehead and looked toward the window, all in a determined attempt to fight the memories that would not retreat from her mind. She thought of Fletcher giving her back her weapon that morning, of the way his eyes told her he trusted her with it; she remembered how he had courageously fought the fire and how he'd insisted she leave the smoke-filled parlor to go outside and breathe some clean air. He did those things not because it was his job, but because he sincerely and genuinely wanted to protect her. That's just the kind of man he was.

It was such a nice feeling, she realized, to have someone care about her like that when she'd had only herself to rely on for so long.

Fletcher lowered the page he was reading and the sound startled her out of her thoughts.

"Did you know that Edwyn reported cattle theft to the city council more than once?" he mentioned with interest.

So, for him, it was business as usual. It would be that way for her, too, she decided, then she moved to stand behind the chair and look over Fletcher's shoulder at what he was reading. "Yes, I've seen that letter, but I never thought much about it. Most of the ranchers have lost head to rustlers."

"Seems like there's been a lot of rustling in these parts lately." He rose from the chair and moved to the old ledgers lying open on a corner table. "I just compared the losses Edwyn reported at year-end with the losses from previous years. I know ranching," he added, "and these numbers seem high to me."

Jo followed him and looked at Edwyn's year-end adjustments in the ledger. "It was a hard winter. We lost quite a few head to the early storms. Maybe that's why he was adjusting the accounts."

"No, no, he was a very meticulous bookkeeper. There's a year-end entry over here for winter losses, and a separate entry over here for unexplained disappearances—most likely theft. It's this number that doesn't compare to other years. Look at the difference." He lifted up the ledger and pulled out the one from the year before.

Jo examined the two books. After Edwyn's death, she'd pored over the year-end statements and thought she'd gained a thorough understanding of the bookkeeping. Why hadn't she thought to study the previous years?

She stared at the ledgers in disbelief. Had Edwyn been murdered because he knew something about the cattle rustling around Dodge? How could she have missed this?

Fletcher walked toward the breakfast tray. "Looks like we may have found something."

Jo turned. "No, *you* found it."

"Don't be too hard on yourself. I only found it because I'm used to following tracks. Hoofprints or a trail of paper, it's all the same to me.'' He pulled a chair across the rug toward the table and sat down to eat.

Jo paced back and forth behind him, remembering the night Edwyn was killed and all the times she'd seen Zeb Stone, before and after. She'd never connected him with the business of ranching. Even Fletcher had called him too civilized to meddle in it.

Unable to come up with any answers herself, she sat down in the leather chair across from Fletcher and watched him eat. ''How much do you know about the cattle thefts around Dodge?''

He didn't look up as he cut his eggs. ''Not a whole lot. You've been my chief concern since I got here. You and Six-Shooter Hank, that is.''

She tried not to let him make her feel guilty. ''I apologize for that. Perhaps I can make it up to you by filling you in on some of the local crime. I do read the papers, and there's at least one herd with missing cattle reported each week. Different ranchers, small outfits and large ones, Texas-based herds driving up the trail. They start out with a certain-sized herd, then arrive in Dodge with a much smaller one, and the cowboys can't explain it.''

''And you think you can?''

''Just give me a chance to explain what I think. Maybe Zeb is running a cattle-rustling ring and that's why he was so vague last night about what he hired you to do. Maybe Zeb killed Edwyn because of the letters he sent to the city council.''

''How long has this cattle rustling been going on?''

''You saw the books. A few years, perhaps. It seems normal to most people now.''

Fletcher took a sip of coffee and nodded his head, still without looking up. ''A few years, you say. If this has been going on for a few years, **don**'t you think it's possible that you might be the teeniest bit mistaken about Zeb? After all, he's only been in these parts for two.''

Feeling as if her theory had been quashed, Jo tried to prevent the inevitable loss of color to her cheeks. ''Where was he before that?''

''Chicago. Meeting my sister for the first time.''

Jo shifted in her chair and cleared her throat, her hopes sinking at this supposed alibi. ''Are you sure?''

''Elizabeth told me she met him briefly in her first year of college—the year his family died and left him all his money—then he courted her and proposed to her during her third and final year.''

''But he could have been back and forth that first year.''

''He opened his dry goods store exactly two years ago, and before that, he was burying his parents in Chicago. It was only after he inherited his money that he decided to invest it out here, in the West.''

Jo twisted her wedding ring around on her finger. ''Perhaps, with your resources as city marshal, you could look into it. His past may very well be a fabrication.''

''And my sister imagined meeting him in Chicago three years ago?''

Jo squeezed the smooth arm of the chair. She had held a loaded gun to Zeb's head and very nearly pulled the trigger. She would not have done that without the strongest of convictions about his murderous heart. ''Perhaps Zeb became involved with whoever started this cattle-rustling ring after he came here.'' Proud of herself for that little suggestion, she raised her chin.

Fletcher set down his coffee cup and wiped his hands on the linen napkin. ''Your theories are all well and

good, Jo, but you know I need real evidence. I'm willing to look into these cattle thefts, but I don't know
how to do it without locking you up.''

''But Fletcher—''

''There's no other way to keep you safe and in cus-
tody at the same time.''

''But I won't be safe in jail. I can't trust anyone, not
even your deputies. Zeb might own them already, and
you said yourself that if people find out why you arrested me, you won't be able to investigate without—''

''What do you suggest we do, then?'' Fletcher rose
from the chair and threw his napkin on the tray. ''I can't
let you off and I can't take you with me. That would
look just as suspicious. If I believe you that I can't trust
my deputies to help me—''

He paced the room for a few minutes while Jo just
sat there, watching him.

''Unless…'' he said, not looking at her, his thoughts
only on his job, it seemed, and the best way to do it.

''What's your idea?''

Fletcher rested his hands on his hips. ''This may
sound strange, but we should get engaged.''

Despite the sleep she badly needed, Jo was instantly
wide-awake. ''You can't be serious.''

''I know it sounds ridiculous, but it would just be an
act to distract people, of course. If you were my fiancée,
we could be seen constantly together without raising
suspicion. There'd be all kinds of gossip and no one
would question what was really going on. Look, I'm
between a rock and a hard place. I want nothing more
than to solve this murder and to…''

She knew what he was going to say. *To get away
from you.*

''I'd only be doing it to keep watch over you without

raising suspicions, and to solve this case at the same time, as quickly as possible. If there's any truth to what you say about Zeb, this will rattle his cage for sure.''

He paced the carpet, never making eye contact. ''And you'd only be doing it to help find the men who killed your husband,'' he added. ''Maybe lighten your sentence a bit, if the judge is sympathetic.''

''What a perfectly romantic marriage proposal, Fletcher,'' Jo said, trying to keep her voice clear of emotion. ''But if it means Zeb will get what's coming to him, I'm willing to go along with it. Just don't expect me to play the lovesick fool. I have more important things to accomplish.''

That last little bit was her pride talking and she suspected that he knew it.

He sat down and leaned back in his chair, staring into her eyes as she struggled to force away any sorrow or regret she might have felt, realizing uneasily that she was in for a hard battle.

It was nearly noon by the time Zeb forced himself to roll over and slide out of his mahogany four-poster bed. His bare toes touched the cold floor, and he cursed the maid for not making his house more comfortable, especially when he paid her far more than her pathetic, stubby fingers were worth.

Only then did he realize, with another irritated curse, that he'd worn his blue silk nightshirt to bed inside out.

Squeezing his hammering temples, he swallowed against the dry, detestable taste in his mouth. He was glad Elizabeth had risen early, as was her usual habit, for if she were here, just the sound of her high-pitched, chattery voice would have driven him insane.

Zeb rang for Matthews, who assisted him in dressing

and shaving, then he made his way downstairs, trying not to move too quickly. He was on his way to the library for a medicinal shot of brandy when he heard Elizabeth's heels clicking across the polished floor behind him, and he had to fight the urge to whip around and silence her with a slap as he had silenced her last night. "What is it, Elizabeth? And don't ask me how I slept."

She stopped in the center of the wide hall and cleared her throat. "I...I'm sorry to disturb you, Zeb, but Fletcher is in the drawing room. He has some news, but he wanted to wait for you before he said anything. I believe it's about Mrs. O'Malley."

Ah. Fletcher had come, no doubt, to deliver bad news about a fire and a dead widow—news that would cure this headache just as effectively as a glass of brandy, Zeb thought with some complacency. He guided Elizabeth back toward the drawing room. "Nothing wrong with the woman, I hope."

"I don't know. He's been exceedingly secretive about it."

"Well, we shall find out soon enough."

Fletcher stood in the drawing room at the window, his gaze following Zeb's tree-lined driveway, his worries drifting to Jo. He hoped she was still sitting in the church confessional where he'd left her. He felt bad about tying her to the bench leg, especially after she'd protested, but he still couldn't be sure she wouldn't try to escape and he wanted to deliver this news on his own, without distraction. And Jo pretending to be his fiancée would definitely have been a distraction.

He turned when he heard Elizabeth and Zeb enter the room. Watching them together—her slender arm looped through his, both of them richly dressed in the finest attire Dodge had to offer—Fletcher felt his heart darken with regret.

Maybe Jo was wrong about Zeb. He was Elizabeth's husband, after all. The man she had chosen above all others, the future she had embraced when she'd married him.

Fletcher wondered uneasily if he was prepared to kick it all out from under her.

Zeb stopped in the doorway. "Good heavens, you look exhausted. What has happened?"

"I am a little tired. I was up most of the night."

Zeb moved fully into the room. "Busy, were you? Please sit down and tell us all about it."

Fletcher studied Zeb's eyes, hoping he would not see what he'd come here to find. "Truthfully, I wasn't busy. I was up all night, just thinking."

Zeb sat silently, staring. "About what?"

"About marriage."

Elizabeth glided closer, her cheeks flushing, her eyes regaining some of the radiance Fletcher all of a sudden noticed had been missing lately. "Marriage? Fletcher, what do you mean?"

"You, Liz, of all people, should know what I mean. Can't you tell by looking at me?" He had to swallow the bitter realization that he'd never lied to his sister before now.

Zeb continued to stare at Fletcher, dumbfounded, and Fletcher stared right back at him, searching.

"Oh, do say it, Fletcher! Is it what I think?"

He would come clean soon enough, he told himself, trying to ease some of the guilt. Just as soon as all this nasty business of murder and cattle rustling was cleared up.

"You said you had bad news about Mrs. O'Malley," Zeb interrupted, his tone heavy.

"I never said it was bad, but you can judge that for yourself." Fletcher's gut wrenched at Zeb's slipup, but he tried to hide it as the lie spilled from his lips. "Mrs. O'Malley and I are going to be…married."

"Ohh!" Elizabeth squealed, but Fletcher was watching Zeb, who cupped his head and winced with pain at his wife's jolly outcry.

She hurried to sit beside Fletcher and throw her arms around his neck. "I'm so happy!"

"Me, too," he replied, still digesting Zeb's words.

"But you've only known her a few days! She must be wonderfully special. I thought her so when I met her. She and I will be like sisters, I know it."

Fletcher watched Zeb, who rose and dutifully offered his hand. "I suppose congratulations are in order."

"Thank you, Zeb." Fletcher stood and shook his brother-in-law's hand.

"You've asked her, I presume."

"Of course."

"When? You must have ridden out there very early this morning," he commented, his tone brimming over with impatient curiosity.

Fletcher thought carefully about how he should answer that loaded observation. Was it best to let Zeb believe, for a little longer, that Jo might be dead, if that was in fact why he was asking?

Or was it worth the risk to see his face when he found out she was still among the living?

"I asked her this morning," Fletcher replied matter-of-factly. Then he paused to await Zeb's reaction.

The tall man's jaw twitched.

"She came into town to buy some things for her

house," Fletcher continued, laying down more information for Zeb to take in. "There was a fire in her parlor."

"What a shame," Zeb replied, his eyes void of any sentiment.

Elizabeth covered her mouth with her hand. "No one was hurt, I hope."

"No. It was a small fire. Clumsily started, I think."

"No doubt," Zeb said, his mood dark.

"Will you bring her for supper this evening?" Elizabeth asked. "We could celebrate."

Fletcher glanced at his sister, so lighthearted and smiling, and he wanted to sink through the floor at the thought of capsizing her new life. He glanced at Zeb, saw the annoyance hovering in his eyes, and Fletcher felt his instincts begin to boil. He had no definite proof of anything, but he knew something was up with Zeb, and it was his duty to find out what it was.

He supposed it was time to surrender to the one thing he'd wanted to avoid—a social evening with Zeb and Jo together.

Chapter Nineteen

Jo stood inside the city clerk's office while Fletcher dug into his pocket for keys.

"I'm curious what the city council did about your husband's letters," he said, unlocking and opening a drawer in the large desk under the window. "Were they publicized at all?"

"Not that I know of. I never heard another word about it after he sent them."

"He didn't send them to the newspaper or anything like that?"

"No, definitely not. Edwyn didn't like to bring attention to himself."

Fletcher nodded his understanding. "He took the time to make copies of the letters, so he must have been serious about the situation." Fletcher pulled a large hard-covered book out of the drawer and set it on the desk. He began to flip through the pages. "I'm looking for the city council minutes of last July. That's when he sent the first letter."

Jo leaned forward over Fletcher's shoulder, trying to ignore the subtle scent of leather from his gun belt as she watched his sun-bronzed hands turn page after page of the ruled paper. "Here it is—council meeting on July 23. Look for your husband's name."

They both read over the minutes, but Edwyn's letters were never mentioned.

"Are you sure the first letter was dated in July?" she asked, refusing to give up hope that they would find something.

"Positive. I'll check August. Maybe he sent it late."

They searched through the records, page after page, every month in the whole year.

"There's nothing," Fletcher said grimly. "No mention of either of Edwyn's letters or any cattle-theft problem." He set the book back in the drawer and leaned against the desk, the heel of his palm braced upon the top while he rubbed his forehead with the other hand.

Jo stood before him, watching the stress lines deepen around his eyes. "Zeb got rid of those letters. He must be involved in the cattle-rustling ring and that's why he came after Edwyn and why he destroyed the police records about Edwyn's death."

"We can't be certain of that yet."

"But Zeb has the power and the access to these records."

"So do a lot of other people."

"But I know it was Zeb that night. This only confirms it. Why can't you at least say it's possible? Give me that much?"

She saw an apology in his eyes and wanted to shake him for something more than that. "I'd like to believe you, Jo, but we'll have to keep looking."

Jo watched Fletcher lock the desk and retrieve his hat from the hook by the door. She began to worry that he'd change his mind about not locking her up.

"I want to know more about this cattle-rustling problem," he said, pressing the hat onto his head.

Frustrated and feeling stuck, Jo followed Fletcher outside into the bright sunlight and shaded her eyes with her gloved hand. "Shouldn't we be focusing on Zeb's affairs?"

"I'm not investigating Zeb, I'm investigating your husband's murder. If what I find leads to Zeb, then I'll look there. Until then—"

"Fletcher, this isn't fair."

"What's not fair?" He locked the door behind them and began to descend the steps ahead of her.

"You're supposed to be doing your job, the thing you say matters most to you, but the way it looks to me, you're not willing to see past your sister. You don't want to spoil things for her and it's influencing your judgment."

He paused at the bottom of the stairs, then turned to look up at Jo, his bruised eyes shadowed beneath the brim of his hat. "Nothing is influencing my judgment. I'm just trying to do my job right. Hurry up, I want to get to the stockyard before the train comes in."

Picking up her skirts in one gloved hand, Jo glided down the stairs and followed him over the tracks toward Front Street. "Fletcher, stop and listen to me. Please. I swear, Zeb could steal the badge off your vest, right under your nose, and you still wouldn't see it. You're protecting him so Elizabeth won't get hurt."

"I'm not protecting him. I just need to be sure. I need solid proof."

Walking fast to keep up, she tried to lower her voice so that no one would hear. "Can't you see you're doing exactly what your father did? You're trying to protect your kin. You don't want Elizabeth to suffer so you're resisting me and what I'm telling you.''

He looked straight into her eyes and spoke with a surprising rigidity. ''It's not my *kin* I'm trying to protect right now. Trust me on that.''

She stopped in the middle of the street. A noisy buckboard rattled by behind her, blowing dust onto her yellow skirt. Standing there, she felt her confused emotions peak. ''If you're going to bend the rules for someone you care about, why can't you bend them for me? Do I mean that little to you?''

A few feet ahead of her, Fletcher stopped. She watched his broad back, could see his shoulders fall slightly, and she wanted to kick herself for revealing so much.

Fletcher slowly turned around. Jo stared at him, feeling desperate for his touch and hating herself for that weakness. He was not a person she could turn to, no matter how badly she needed him.

He walked toward her, his strides long and deliberate. ''Firstly, I'm not bending the rules for anyone. I need proof, and in the eyes of the law, your word and what we've found so far just isn't enough. Let me do my job. If what you say about Zeb is true, I'll find what we need to convict him. And I *will* convict him, Jo, whether he's my brother-in-law or not.''

He stood before her, staring into her eyes, as if looking to find something there. She met his gaze without flinching.

''And secondly?'' she asked, trying to break the angry tension blazing between them.

''Secondly...secondly, the way I do my job has nothing to do with how I feel about *you,* and I wish you could stop reminding me about what's been happening

between us.'' He glanced toward the boardwalk in front
of the butcher shop where a couple of older women
were standing in the shade watching, twirling their parasols. He lowered his voice to an angry whisper. ''*You*
were the one to say all the kissing we did was a mistake.''

She squared her shoulders. ''I said it was rash. I don't
remember calling it a mistake. I hope you don't twist
my words in court.''

Fletcher ripped off his hat and raked his fingers
through his wavy hair. He made no effort to hide his
frustration as he glanced back at the women on the
boardwalk. ''Whether you called it a mistake or not,
that's what you meant, and don't try to deny it.''

''I'm not...I...'' She heard her voice break and hated
herself for it. Then, the very next second, she found
herself rambling like a fool about her feelings and con-
fessing the most intimate details to him, yet again.
''Fletcher, this is too hard. I want to be with you and
know you and talk to you about things that have nothing
to do with Zeb or cattle theft, and it makes no sense
because I know you're going to arrest me. God, I should
hate you, not feel as if I'm falling in love with you.''

The words flooded out before she had a chance to
stop them, and when she saw the agony in Fletcher's
eyes—oh, how she wished she could take them back.

Fletcher sighed deeply, his brow creasing with what
looked like regret. Jo wanted to disappear into the
ground.

When he finally responded, his voice was quiet and
tender. ''Am I the first man you've kissed since Edwyn
died?''

The question caught her off guard. ''Yes, but that has
nothing to do with—''

"Maybe you should think about that."

"No, Fletcher, I—"

"Hear me out, Jo. You've been telling me a lot of personal things about the night he was killed and I'm the first person to offer any comfort or understanding about that, and I reckon you're confusing me with the general onslaught of emotions you must be feeling.

"And even though you're my prisoner, there's been an element of..." He paused a moment, as if searching for just the right word. "An element of intimacy between us. We've been together almost constantly the past few days and now we're pretending to be engaged. Maybe that wasn't such a good idea."

"Wait a minute," she said harshly, holding up her hand. "I can handle this."

"I'm sure you can. It's just that...it's hard for me, too."

She stared at him, dumbfounded, realizing she was overjoyed to hear him say that.

Until he finished what he meant to say.

"But we can't let ourselves get caught up in the way we've been feeling. We have no future together, Jo. I'm the law and you're my prisoner, and even if you weren't, this wouldn't be right. You're not over your husband yet. I see how you're always straightening that picture of him and staring at it. You need time to grieve and get over him."

There was so much about her relationship with Edwyn that Fletcher did not know, but it was not something she wished to discuss with him now, not here in the street.

"Besides that," he went on, "I'm not the marrying kind. I never stay in one place very long and you're the opposite. You deserve better—a man who'll stick around and be a father to Leo.''

Not wanting him to see in her eyes that her heart was breaking, she dropped her sad gaze to the ground. ''Fletcher, I only know how I feel.''

A moment of silence lingered between them, then without warning, he wrapped his large hands around her waist, pulled her close and pressed his lips to hers right there for all the world to see.

For an instant she was paralyzed with shock, until she felt his strong arms embrace her. All she could do was arch her back into him and relax her burning lips, taste the manly flavor of his mouth. Eyes falling closed, she wondered what in heaven's name she would do when this moment ended, if she had the strength to even stand.

Jo had not the faintest idea how long the kiss lasted, only that it was hot and intoxicating, and when those lips pulled away from hers, her knees felt weaker than watered-down whisky. She tried to open her eyes and realized numbly that she was being supported in Fletcher's arms in the middle of the street with every last cowboy looking on, her feet barely touching the ground.

''Why did you do that?'' she asked, her voice a light whisper.

''Because I wanted to. And because those ladies over there are looking for something to gossip about, and it ain't gonna be what we're investigating.''

Instantly sobered by his answer, and annoyed at herself for thinking he could forget about his job while she was laying her heart out on her sleeve, Jo stepped back and wiped her mouth with the back of her hand. ''Of course. Always thinking with that badge.''

His eyes colored with a shade of contrition that surprised her. "Not always, Jo."

She recognized the tenderness in his tone but did not want to acknowledge it. If she did, she'd be done for...back in his arms whether those ladies were watching or not.

"You were right," she said, covering what she truly felt. "There they go into the bakery to spread the news. Our engagement will distract the entire town. I just hope it works on Zeb. Now can we get going? I don't like standing here in the middle of the street."

Glancing over her shoulder, she picked up her skirts and walked off toward the stockyards, her body still trembling from his kiss. She knew she had to concentrate on sweeping it from her heart and mind, no matter how much it hurt. She had to focus on finding something—anything—that would lead them to Zeb before he found a way to keep her quiet forever, and kissing Fletcher Collins would only make it harder.

Fletcher and Jo approached the cattle-loading pens, packed tight with Texas longhorns shrieking and snorting and clacking their horns together while they awaited the train that would take them east to a Chicago slaughterhouse.

Fletcher guided Jo past the station depot, not knowing what to say about what had happened between them in the street. All he knew was that there was a lump in his gut the size of a watermelon; he could feel his brows pulling together, the muscles in his forehead tight with a tension that just wouldn't quit.

God, he wanted her too much. He cared too much. He wanted to talk to her about her life and her marriage and her son; he wanted to be the shoulder she cried on about Edwyn, to help her grieve and put it behind her and feel closer to *him*. He wanted to tell her everything he suspected about Zeb, confide in her with every thought and feeling he had…but how could he? He had to remember his position. She was his prisoner and she wanted her own brand of justice with a passion that was simply too dangerous.

On top of all that—and most importantly—he just couldn't be the man she needed him to be.

They approached a short, stocky cowhand and Fletcher had to work hard to get his mind back on business.

"Mornin'," Fletcher said to the man, who was leaning back against the gate, his dusty brown shirt damp with perspiration under the arms, his face leather-brown from hours spent in the saddle under the scorching western sun. "You responsible for this herd?"

The young man took one look at Fletcher's badge and stepped away from the fence. "Yes, sir. I'm the trail boss, Curly Hays." He glanced at Jo and fingered his hat. "Morning, ma'am."

"Where you from?"

"I come from Montana originally, sir."

Fletcher nodded. "This herd from Texas?"

"Yes, sir. It belongs to Mr. Addison of San Antonio. There a problem, Marshal?"

Fletcher glanced at the branding on one of the steers—the letter A in two places—on the shoulder and back hip.

Jo stepped forward and the young man smiled nervously at her. "Have you lost any head to rustlers, Mr. Hays?" she asked directly.

Fletcher gave her a long, dark stare, wishing she

would remember that she was pretending to be his fiancée, not his deputy.

"As a matter of fact, ma'am, yes. Or at least, that's what we think. They just seem to disappear. Mr. Addison hired extra hands this season, hoping to figure out what was happening, maybe put a stop to it. But the size of the herd keeps getting smaller and smaller as we drive 'em up the trail. It don't make a lick of sense."

"How many have you lost?" Jo asked.

"He ships about fifty thousand head a year, altogether. He probably lost close to five thousand and he ain't too happy about it."

Jo nodded her understanding and gave Fletcher an *I told you so* look.

He squinted across the top of the pen, over the heads of cattle toward the treeless, unbroken horizon. "Do you lose them off the ranch in Texas, Hays, or just along the drive?" Fletcher asked.

"Both, sir. All year round. And it ain't just the Western Trail. I hear they go missing off the Chisolm Trail, too."

Fletcher inclined his head in a way of saying thanks. "You can tell Addison that there's a new marshal in Dodge, and I'll be looking into things for him. I'll do my best to clear up this problem."

"Yes, sir, Marshal Collins. I'll tell him today when I send the wire."

Fletcher placed his hand on the small of Jo's back and directed her toward town. "I'm supposed to be asking the questions," he told her quietly. "You're just supposed to be my fiancée."

"I'm trying to speed things up, that's all."

"Just trust me and let me take care of this."

She said nothing more and he could feel her frustration in the way she moved—the straight set of her shoulders, the sway of her hips. He found himself wanting to explain everything better, to talk openly and reveal how completely torn he felt about all this. Maybe then she would understand his position, not resent him so much.

"Let's go to the bakery for some bread and a pie," he suggested, trying to push that lump farther down in his gut.

"I'm not hungry, thank you."

"Neither am I, but I hear the lady who works there has a nose for gossip."

"It's the widow Harper you're talking about, but I doubt she'd know who's stealing the cattle."

"Maybe not, but we'll need something for our engagement picnic." Sensing her surprise, he took hold of her arm and looped it through his, held it tightly as they walked past the crowd of curious onlookers standing in front of the Dodge House Hotel.

"I wasn't sure when I should mention this," he said, leaning in and taking advantage of the opportunity to smell her hair. "But maybe it's time you removed your wedding ring. Folks might wonder about it otherwise."

And he had to wonder, himself, why—after all his efforts to keep from caring about her—he'd noticed that she still wore the ring and why he was pleased for this excuse to get her to take it off.

Jo stopped, appearing flustered. "Of course." She fumbled to pull off her gloves and fumbled even more to pull the tight gold band off her slim finger. "There." She popped it into her reticule and pulled the drawstring closed.

Fletcher offered his arm again, feeling uneasy. He didn't want to lose this battle with his emotions, but it was becoming more and more difficult with every passing moment.

"I haven't told you this," Fletcher mentioned as he steered Jo's wagon across the toll bridge toward the open plains, "but we've been invited to supper tonight."

Jo held on to the spring seat as they bumped along, her sunbonnet tied tightly under her chin. "Something tells me I shouldn't ask who our dinner companions will be."

"I couldn't very well refuse the offer," he went on apologetically. "I'm supposed to be proud about us getting engaged, and Elizabeth...well, she was just so darn happy."

"Really?" Jo replied, trying not to feel too flattered. Why should it matter that Fletcher's sister had approved of her?

"They're expecting us at seven, but I don't know if it's such a good idea. I don't want you in the same room with Zeb."

"Are you worried about me or him?"

He shook his head with what seemed surprisingly like admiration. "I've never met a woman quite like you before."

"I wasn't trying to impress you," she said, bumping shoulders with him.

"I know. That's what impresses me the most." A subtle grin with a hint of melancholy passed across his lips. Jo had to force herself to look away.

Fletcher steered the wagon off the bridge and over the short grass toward a cowhand, sitting against his bedroll with one knee up while he watched his herd, his horse grazing nearby.

"Howdy," the young man greeted as he rose to stand and brush off his pants.

"Morning. I'm Fletcher Collins, the new marshal."

"I know who you are. What can I do for you?"

Fletcher held the reins loosely. "I'm looking into some missing cattle."

The cowhand removed his black sombrero and brushed the dust off it. "You'll be looking for a while, Marshal. Nobody seems to know where they end up."

"I take it you've lost some head?"

"You take it right, but I can't help you any. It's a mystery."

Fletcher tipped his hat and they drove on, asking every cowhand they came upon if they knew anything, and the answer was always the same.

An hour later, Jo reached for the bread they'd bought at the bakery and tore off a section. "Are you hungry? It must be midday."

She handed Fletcher a thick chunk, which he ate while steering them toward town. The cattle on either side of the road grazed quietly, stopping to raise their heads only when the wagon rolled by.

"This isn't much of an engagement picnic, eating on the road like this," he said.

Jo considered a string of possible replies, but to protect her heart and prevent any more kissing, she settled with, "It's probably best."

He nodded at her, telling her with his eyes that he agreed, then he changed the subject. "When will Leo and Matilda be back?"

"In about a week. I wanted them to be safe. The less they know about what's going on, the better." She swallowed some bread. "Though they'll find out soon enough, I suppose."

Fletcher didn't comment on that. He stared straight ahead and clicked his tongue at the horses. "So your house is empty?"

"What's left of it, yes. The hands sleep in the bunkhouse, of course. Why do you ask?"

He answered her in a calm, indifferent tone. "Just thinking ahead to tonight. It might be a bit of a problem. Being engaged doesn't make it okay for me to spend the night at your house. Especially when the engagement is going to be broken. I don't want to spoil any chances you might have for...well, for moving on."

Jo tried to suppress her hurt. Why did he have to keep reminding her that he was anxious to be finished with her?

She made an attempt to lighten the mood with a joke. "Well, we're not getting married today, if that's what you're thinking."

"It may come as a surprise to you, but there are limits to what I'm willing to do in the name of the law."

"Thank you very much. That was most flattering."

His warm gaze met hers and they shared in the moment of humor, all too brief.

"It still doesn't solve our problem," he said. "I doubt I'll have your husband's killer behind bars by nightfall, and I'm not taking any chances with your safety. You'll need to be in hiding again."

Jo settled back in her seat, considering her options. "Your room won't do, now that everyone thinks we're engaged. That'll be the first place Zeb will look for me if I'm not at home."

She handed him another chunk of bread and they both ate in silence for a few minutes.

"I suppose the only way around this," Jo said, swiping at the crumbs on her skirt and trying to block out all thoughts of Fletcher keeping watch over her bed, "is to prove Zeb's guilt before the sun goes down."

Chapter Twenty

Steering Jo's wagon onto Front Street after a fruitless search for information on the plains, Fletcher watched two gentlemen shuffle out of Zimmerman's Hardware Store. They were carrying a potbellied stove toward their wagon. One of them spotted him and yelled into the street, "Congratulations, Marshal!" and in his excitement, he nearly dropped the heavy stove.

Fletcher tipped his hat and nodded, reminding himself not to feel too proud. This was just a performance.

Jo wiggled in her seat beside him. "I hope we're doing the right thing."

"We are." Fletcher steered the wagon toward the depot again, determined to get his mind off betrothals and back where it belonged—on his job. "I want to ask about the herd loading onto the rail car."

"Wait, stop." Jo touched his arm with her gloved hand. "Deputy Anderson is waving at us. Over there by the barbershop."

Fletcher pulled the wagon to a gentle halt. Anderson walked across the street, one hand in the air to signal them to stop, the other holding a newspaper.

"Where you been, Marshal Collins?" he asked curiously. "I been looking for you all day." He handed the newspaper up to Fletcher. "You sure have a way of making headlines. And what happened to your nose?"

"It's a long story."

Hesitantly, Fletcher unfolded the paper and read the front page, feeling Jo lean over his arm to look on. "Bruiser To Marry Local Widow."

"Oh, don't tell me..." Jo said, taking hold of the corner of the page to read the small print aloud.

"'Marshal Collins, the newest addition to Dodge City's band of lawmen, has decided to take a wife. The lucky lady is the reclusive widow O'Malley, who has squashed the long-held notion that she prefers to keep to herself. Other news, Mr. Garry Owens of Walnut Street has a new overcoat.'"

"Good heavens," Jo said, sitting back in her seat. "Does the editor have nothing better to do?"

"Congratulations to you both," Deputy Anderson said, tipping his hat. "When's the big day?"

Fletcher glanced at Jo, who met his gaze with equal uncertainty. They were getting into this deeper and deeper by the minute. "We thought we'd wait until after the election," he replied, tapping her knee.

"Of course," Anderson said. "The family's busy enough, I reckon."

"Any goings-on this morning?" Fletcher asked, trying to change the subject.

"Nope. But folks are wondering what happened to Six-Shooter Hank and why we haven't caught him yet."

Fletcher flicked the reins. "Tell them I have a lead. We'll get him."

He felt Jo tense beside him and wished he could have answered the deputy differently, but as always he'd been thinking of his reputation, and he quickly realized he wasn't proud of himself for it.

The wagon lurched forward and they started toward the depot, leaving Deputy Anderson to deal with a pig who had wandered into the middle of the street and stopped traffic with its squeal.

"Just wait till the newspapers get wind of what's really going on," Jo said. "You and I will be famous from here to the Panhandle."

"I'll do my best to keep this from turning into a circus."

"I doubt that'll be possible, even for you."

Her sharp tone cut through his resolve and made him wonder if any of this was worth it.

"Come with me," he said, pulling the wagon to a halt behind the depot where he could see cattle being loaded into the rail car, their hooves thumping madly over the wooden ramp, their moos and snorts muted below the hiss of steam from the train. "I don't want to leave you alone."

He climbed down and circled around the front of the team to help Jo down. She rested her hands on his shoulders while he cupped his around her tiny waist, lifting her lightly to the ground. The faint scent of orange flower water drifted on a breeze under his nose and made him all too aware of her womanly presence in his arms. Damn, but it felt good to hold her.

"I hear you two are getting married," a voice said from behind.

Startled, Fletcher dropped his hand to his gun and turned around. He found himself staring at the cowboy who had been gambling with Zeb the night before.

"What's the hurry, Marshal?" he asked. "You only just got here a few days ago. Don't you want to taste what delicacies Dodge has to offer before you settle on beef and potatoes for the rest of your days?'' Glancing down at Jo, he licked his lips.

Fletcher squeezed the handle of his Peacemaker in an effort to keep control, then reached around to touch Jo's arm and urge her directly behind him where this brute wouldn't be able to even look at her. He glared into the man's narrowing eyes, smelled tobacco on his stale breath and noticed a scar through his eyebrow.

"This your herd?" Fletcher demanded.

"Yeah, what's it to ya?"

"You work for George Greer?"

"As far as I'm concerned, there ain't no other outfits in Texas worth the effort."

Fletcher glanced at the large brand that covered almost the entire side of each steer.

"Any of your herd go missing on the drive?"

The trail boss smirked. "If you're talking about the rustling ring that's got everybody in a huff, you're wasting your time with me and my boys. We know how to handle a herd. Greer pays well to make sure he gets the best. And to answer your question, Greer cattle *doesn't* go missing."

Fletcher nodded his head, still resting his hand on his gun. He could feel Jo behind him, and sensing her desire to say something, he figured he'd better move on before she found a chance to open her mouth. Taking her arm as he backed away, he helped her into the wagon, then called to the trail boss, "What's your name?"

"Why? You want to invite me to your weddin'?"

"What's your *name?*"

The man spit on the ground. "MacGregor. Will MacGregor."

Fletcher climbed into the wagon, in a hurry to take this new information with him to the telegraph office. He had some friends in Texas who owed him favors. With any luck, he'd get replies back before he and Jo had to clink champagne glasses with Zeb over his fancy red silk tablecloth.

Jo sat across from Fletcher in the city clerk's office above the jail, tapping her foot while they waited for the telegraph replies to come in. Fletcher had asked the operator to send them over right away, without wasting a minute, but nothing seemed to be happening. No one seemed to be at the other end of the wires.

"What time is it?" Fletcher asked, pacing the floor behind his desk.

Jo took her timepiece out of her bodice pocket. "It's almost six-thirty. I don't think we're going to hear back from anyone before seven. We'll just have to go to Zeb's house for supper."

He stopped pacing, his brows drawing together. "You don't sound too uncomfortable with that."

"Quite frankly, I'm not. We've looked in the streets and on the plains and we've found nothing. I'm after proof to use against Zeb. What better place to find it than his own home?"

Fletcher raised his hand. "Wait a second. I'm not going to let you rifle through his things, and I certainly hope you don't want to shoot him in front of my sister."

Jo's shoulders slumped with a sigh. "Of course not. And I presume he won't try to shoot me in front of her, either. That's why it's the best opportunity I can hope for."

"No."

"Why not? What have you got to lose? You'll be

there to watch over me, and if Zeb is as innocent as you think he is, we'll find nothing and be on our way. If he's guilty..." She stopped at that, not sure what would happen if they discovered something, what Fletcher would do.

What *she* would do.

"At least we'll get a fancy meal out of it," she said, trying to put a tidy finish on her thoughts.

Just then, footsteps thumped up the stairs on the outside of the building and the door opened. Deputy Anderson walked in with a telegraph message.

"What does it say?" Jo asked, standing.

Fletcher took it from Anderson and read it. His mouth became a hard line as he slapped the note against his thigh. "Why hasn't anyone looked into this before?"

Deputy Anderson sheepishly removed his hat. "I guess nobody was suspecting a rancher like George Greer of stealing. He's the richest there is."

Fletcher picked his hat up off the desk and pressed it onto his head. "Rich or not, he doesn't own a square inch of land in Texas."

"Maybe he's just using the free range, like everybody else," Anderson suggested.

"This says he hasn't leased anything from the state. Where's he grazing his herds over the winter? He doesn't even own a headquarters site."

Jo stood, realizing uneasily that George Greer was casting a shadow over Zeb and his reason to kill Edwyn. "Maybe he has a ranch in Colorado or New Mexico."

"Not according to his employees and everyone who's heard of him. But we might as well know for sure." He pointed the telegraph message at Deputy Anderson. "I want you to send a couple of wires to check it out. Then find Greer's trail boss, Will MacGregor, and bring him to see me. He was down at the depot loading a herd not long ago.''

''Sure thing,'' Anderson replied, going out the door.

Fletcher turned to Jo. ''We'll have to cancel our dinner plans.''

She swallowed hard, trying to control her irritation. ''We can't do that.''

''Why not? This is the first lead we've had on your husband's murder and I want to follow it through.''

''Fletcher, I'm a witness. What better lead can you ask for than that? It was Zeb who killed Edwyn, not George Greer, whoever he is.''

''But if the killers were wearing hoods, you're not an *eyewitness,* Jo, and my instincts are telling me that there's something not right about Greer.''

''Why don't you ask Zeb about him?'' she suggested. ''He's a prestigious merchant, soon to be mayor. If anyone knows anything about Greer, surely Zeb would. Maybe he's even done business with him.''

Fletcher eyed her suspiciously. ''You're trying to manipulate me.''

Jo sighed. ''You have to admit I have a point.''

He hesitated, considering it. ''I suppose you do. Zeb supplies the cattlemen all the time. Not to mention that he was gambling with MacGregor last night. Maybe I should talk to him.''

Trying not to show how relieved she was, Jo gathered up her gloves. ''We should go, then. It's almost seven.''

Fletcher stood to face her. ''All right, we'll go, but I don't want you asking questions about any of this. Leave it to me.''

''Can I comment on the wine or is that off-limits, too?''

Fletcher offered his arm. ''Just try and control yourself. Remember the part you're playing. Your only task tonight, Mrs. O'Malley, is to be hopelessly in love with me.''

When Zeb Stone's large front door swung open, Jo stood dumbfounded, staring at the tall butler who stood in the doorway to greet them. A sudden ripple of tension made her body go weak. Could she fool the man who had murdered her husband? Could she even face him?

Without a word, the butler invited them into the wide front hall.

Jo walked into the magnificent house, and staring at Zeb's gilt-framed wedding portrait the size of a window, she felt instantly humbled. Elizabeth sat poised in an armchair while Zeb stood behind her resting his white-gloved hand on her bare shoulder. She looked like a princess in her sheer, lacy veil and white silk gown, the skirt trimmed with enough satin drapery to cover every window in this house. Zeb looked as he always did—impressive and intimidating with his dark brows, dark mustache and expensive black jacket. He was a striking figure in any context.

''Mrs. Stone is waiting for you in the drawing room,'' the butler announced, taking Jo's shawl and Fletcher's hat, and showing them across the shiny floor and past the ornately carved mahogany staircase.

Jo felt underdressed in her plain calico bodice and skirt, but when she glanced at Fletcher, whose spurs were chinking with each step, she thought better of it.

They walked into the drawing room and there was Elizabeth in a pale yellow evening gown with white lace ruffles on the train, standing in front of the fireplace with her back to the door. As soon as the butler announced Jo and Fletcher, she turned gracefully from re-arranging a vase of pink roses on the mantel.

"Fletcher! Mrs. O'Malley!" Elizabeth approached and took Jo's hands. "Congratulations. It seems we will be sisters." She leaned forward and kissed Jo on the cheek.

Jo glanced at Fletcher, who dropped his gaze to the floor.

"Please, call me Jo," she replied.

Elizabeth turned Jo's hands over and looked at them. "No ring yet, I see." She gave Fletcher a lighthearted wink. "I've been waiting all day for this moment."

She moved toward a round table adorned with glass figurines and vases of colorful wildflowers, and picked up a small silver-plated box.

Fletcher's lips parted with recognition. "Elizabeth, that's not necessary. I know how much that means to you."

Jo listened to Fletcher's voice, so full of regret and guilt and anguish at having to lie to his sister this way. Seeing the sisterly love in Elizabeth's eyes as she handed the box to him made Jo realize why Fletcher was so reluctant to accept the truth about Zeb. Why she, too, now wished it was not so.

Fletcher took the small box from Elizabeth and held it in his hand, staring down without saying a word. A vein pulsed at his temple. Jo saw it and touched his arm. "Are you all right?" she asked quietly.

Elizabeth gazed back and forth between the two of them, then spoke to Jo. "It's our mother's wedding ring. She wanted it to be passed down."

Jo had to swallow the guilt-ridden lump forming in the back of her throat. She glanced from Elizabeth to

Fletcher, back to Elizabeth again. "But you should have it," she suggested. "You were her only daughter."

Elizabeth shook her head. "No, Zeb wanted me to have something he picked out himself."

Jo glimpsed down and was not surprised at the large diamond on Elizabeth's finger, meant to impress even the wealthiest Dodge City patrons and voters.

"I don't know, Liz," Fletcher said, still holding the box, turning it over in his strong hand.

"Please, it would break my heart if you didn't accept it. I know Mother would have wanted you to have it. You know how she believed in you, Fletcher. She always wanted you to be happy."

Fletcher walked to the window and stood in front of the drawn velvet curtains, his back to Jo and Elizabeth. Alone, head down, he opened the box and looked at the ring.

Jo stood in the center of the room, unable to tear her gaze away from him as he heaved with a sigh. A cold knot formed in her stomach. How she wanted to go to him. To tell him to call off this charade before they all got hurt.

Elizabeth strolled forward and placed her delicate hand on her brother's broad shoulder. "Take the ring, Fletcher. It's been too long since you've been happy."

He turned slightly and looked at Jo. The pained intensity in his eyes shattered the last remnants of her resolve. She wasn't certain if it was guilt she saw there, or if it was something closer to what she was feeling—a sense of anguish that this engagement was only a game. It would never be real.

What were they doing? How could they pretend like this?

Jo stepped forward. "Elizabeth, I think there's something you should know about Fletcher and me.'' A long silence squeezed around them. Elizabeth cupped her hands in front of her and turned to face Jo.

"This is very difficult, but—''

Fletcher quickly crossed the red Oriental rug that separated them. "Jo, don't say another word. Elizabeth is right. Our mother would have wanted you to wear this.''

Any hope for revealing the truth vanished beneath her surprise. She could barely control her breathing as Fletcher took her hand, raised it to his lips and placed a warm, soft kiss on her knuckles—a kiss so genuine she could have sworn he'd meant what he said.

Did he mean it?

Unable to grasp at words, she gave in to Fletcher's lead and allowed him to remove her glove and slip the ring carved with tiny hearts onto her trembling finger.

"It fits,'' was all he said, staring into her eyes as if he was trying to tell her something. Or was she only hoping he was?

"It must be fate, then,'' Elizabeth said, approaching. "Mother had the most beautiful hands, like yours.''

"Oh, hardly,'' Jo said self-consciously, pulling her hand from Fletcher's and dropping it to her side. "With all the work I do at the ranch.''

"That's what makes them beautiful,'' Elizabeth returned.

Just then, the door of the drawing room swung open and Jo turned, startled, to look into the dark eyes of her husband's killer.

Chapter Twenty-One

"Zeb, you're back," Elizabeth said uneasily, crossing the room to greet him. "I hadn't expected you so soon. I'd instructed Matthews to hold supper for another half hour."

He stood in the wide doorway, staring into Jo's eyes, and bowed at the waist. "Welcome to my home, Mrs. O'Malley."

Elizabeth gave him a nervous smile. "They arrived only a few minutes ago."

"I see that."

He eyed Jo curiously, and she felt her heart wash with fear as she whisked her hands behind her back.

"What's that you're hiding?"

He strode toward her and her stomach flared with dread. She thought she had been prepared for this, but she wasn't. "What do you mean?"

"Oh, come now, you can't hide anything from me." He stood too close, trying to lean around her to see what she had.

Not aware of anything but the reality of facing Zeb in person, close enough to smell the hint of whisky on his breath and take in the extravagant quality of his black suit jacket, Jo had to fight the urge to slam her hands onto his chest and shake him for an explanation as to why he had killed her husband.

Fletcher reached for her hand and laced his fingers through hers. The supportive gesture pulled her abruptly from her fury and reminded her what she had come here to do.

She let her hand relax into Fletcher's, who stood next to her, tall and composed.

"She's hiding a wedding ring she shouldn't be wearing yet," Fletcher said good-naturedly, raising her hand to show off the gold band.

Zeb glanced at it, nodded once in an exaggerated, patronizing manner that suggested to Jo that even if the wedding was real, she would not live to see it.

"Sorry I'm late," he said, changing the subject and stepping back to wave at the butler. "I had some important business to attend to. Get us some brandy, Matthews. No, on second thought, make it champagne. This celebration requires something bubbly."

Seizing the distraction, Jo managed to take a few deep breaths that helped calm her a bit. She reminded herself of her role as Fletcher's fiancée while he and Zeb spoke casually.

The butler returned with a bottle of French champagne and four glasses on a silver tray. He filled each one and made his way around the room with them.

"Here's to family," Zeb toasted, raising his glass. "May we all prosper."

With that, they dutifully sipped the cold, fizzing champagne.

Jo watched Elizabeth, curious what had drawn a woman like her to this man. She could only guess it had something to do with being alone in the world and being naively romantic. It was the only thing that made any sense.

When Fletcher and Zeb began to discuss city matters, Elizabeth invited Jo to join her on the green damask sofa. "I would very much like to see your ranch," she said, setting her glass on the marble-topped table in front of them. "I do so admire you, running it on your own. How big is your herd?"

Odd, to hear Elizabeth, adorned in silk, satin and jewels, ask about cattle. "We drive about ten thousand head up from Texas every year, but we keep seven thousand breeding cows. Edwyn believed the future was in winter feeding, fencing and breeding, and I have to say I agree."

"Yes, I've often thought that—"

"What's this?" Zeb interrupted as he helped himself to another glass of champagne. "Ladies discussing ranching. I believe I've heard it all." He glanced at Fletcher, expecting him to join in laughing, but Fletcher ignored the remark and set his glass down on a table.

Jo hoped her eyes were not conveying the loathing she felt.

Elizabeth fiddled with an earring. "But Mrs. O'Malley is running her husband's—"

"She has cowhands for that, we all know. I hear your foreman, John Cook, is an ambitious man."

"Yes, he is at that," Jo replied, hiding her hostility beneath a polite smile. "But he doesn't make the decisions about land that belongs to *me*."

Zeb strode forward and leaned his elbow on the mantel. "Maybe you should let him make some of the decisions. I hear you're building more fences when any wise businessman knows that cattle can be grazed for almost nothing on the free range in Texas. To dispense large amounts of capital on acres and acres of grass here and to fence it in is simply foolish.''

''I don't believe that building something is ever foolish, Mr. Stone, especially when it can be passed down to future generations and—''

Zeb smirked and raised a brow. ''Why not build your bank account instead and pass that down if you so want to leave something behind. I'd wager your son would prefer a stack of cash over an obligation to break his back making hay.''

Elizabeth spoke to her husband but directed her gaze at Jo. ''Perhaps Mrs. O'Malley has a point. I've heard the open range has been overgrazed to the point of—''

''Don't be silly, Elizabeth. The farmers are starting those rumors. Texas will never be overgrazed. There's enough acreage to feed a—''

''It's not the quantity of land that's the problem,'' Fletcher broke in, and everyone fell silent. ''One of these days, a bad winter is going to wipe out entire herds and folks are starting to think about that. I reckon in the future, more ranchers are going to move toward winter feeding. Like the O'Malleys.'' Fletcher sat in the red upholstered armchair beside Jo and crossed his legs. ''But I didn't know you had an interest in ranching, Zeb.''

''Doesn't everyone?'' he replied haughtily. ''This *is* a cow town.''

Fletcher sat very still, watching Zeb until the door to the drawing room opened and the butler stepped inside. ''There is someone here wishing to see Marshal Collins.''

''Who is it?'' Fletcher asked, still watching Zeb, who moved to sit in the wing chair in front of the fireplace.

"Yes, who is interrupting our intriguing discussion? I hope it's important."

"It's Deputy Anderson, sir."

Fletcher turned in his chair. "Anderson is here?"

"Yes, Marshal Collins, sir. He wishes to speak to you."

Fletcher stood. "Will you be all right?" he asked Jo quietly.

"Of course, she will," Zeb answered. "We'll see that she's properly entertained."

Fletcher hesitated. "I'll just be on the other side of the door. Liz, I'll trust you to make sure this lady doesn't run out on me."

With a teasing smile, Elizabeth touched Jo's arm. "I doubt she'll do that, Fletch."

He swept his hand lightly over Jo's cheek, cupping her chin and gazing into her eyes. "I won't be long."

She nodded. "I'll wait."

Jo anxiously watched the butler close the double doors behind Fletcher. She felt Zeb's dark gaze rake over her and glanced at him. With a subtle, sinister grin, he raised an eyebrow at her.

"What do you mean, he was dead?" Fletcher whispered to Anderson, leading him across the wide hall and into the dining room where the butler wouldn't hear them speak.

"I mean he was dead, Marshal Collins. Laid out cold behind the Long Branch saloon."

"Any bullet wounds?"

"Yep. Straight through the heart. You gonna come and see for yourself?"

As much as he wanted to, Fletcher couldn't leave Jo alone with Zeb, especially not with this new development. "Not right now. I trust you to take care of things. Seal off the area. Ask if anyone saw anything. I'll be by later to have a look."

"Yes, sir." Anderson settled his hat on his head and saluted the butler. "Don't bother yourself. I know the way out. Door's right there."

Fletcher stood in the dining room thinking, then approached Matthews. "Tell everyone I had to step out for a few minutes. I'll be back in time for supper, though. I just want to ask Anderson a few more questions and check something at the jailhouse."

"Shall I get your hat, sir?"

"Not necessary," Fletcher replied, going for the door.

He stepped outside into the twilight, hearing birds chirping in the straight row of trees Zeb had imported to line his driveway.

Fletcher looked all around the yard for witnesses. Seeing only Deputy Anderson on his horse, trotting off the property without looking back, Fletcher ducked down below the windows and circled the outside of the large stone house toward the back.

He knew the servants were busy downstairs preparing supper; Jo, Elizabeth and Zeb were still in the drawing room, and because Zeb had chosen a property on a hill on the edge of town, it was secluded enough to avoid the company and curiosity of neighbors.

Fletcher sneaked around to the back and found an open window, hoping it would take him into a closed room and not a hall or some other visible section of the house. Grabbing hold of the wooden window ledge, he pulled himself up and, with one swift thrust, he was inside.

He straightened his shirt, looked around the dark

room and found himself in Elizabeth's private sitting room. He went to the door and peered into the hall, then quietly walked across and tried the door on the other side. Finding it locked, he retrieved the rusty hairpin he kept on his key ring for moments like these, and gently persuaded the lock to open.

Fletcher walked in and closed the door behind him, straining to hear any sounds from the hall outside as he made his way across the room. He walked to the desk that stood on a round Oriental carpet near the back wall, sat down and grabbed for whatever he could get his hands on—papers, letters, invoices, bank statements. Most letters were addressed to Zeb at Zeb Stone's Dry Goods; the invoices were for store merchandise he brought in from all parts of the country.

Reaching for the bank records, Fletcher checked over the amounts and had to swallow his surprise at the balance carried forward each month. There was enough money in there to stuff the entire county courthouse to the roof.

Fletcher looked for large deposits, but there were only standard amounts from the business, the balance having been deposited when he originally opened the account. Elizabeth's explanation about Zeb inheriting his money seemed legitimate.

Hearing silverware clinking in the dining room, Fletcher decided to get back before Jo had to sit down at Zeb's table on her own.

He left the same way he came in and, within moments, he was walking through the front door of the grand house and smelling roast beef in the downstairs kitchen.

Matthews stood outside the drawing room with his hands clasped behind his back. "They've been waiting for you, sir,'' he said, opening the door to the drawing room.

Fletcher walked in, and there was Jo, sitting where he'd left her, her gaze darting up at him and her eyes shimmering with relief and happiness to see him. He felt himself take in a deep breath of awe at the sight of her sitting there wearing his mother's wedding ring, returning his enamored gaze as if there were no one else in the room but them.

Only the sound of Zeb's voice drew Fletcher out of his stupor. ''You're back, finally. What did the deputy want that couldn't wait until after dinner?''

Fletcher regarded him with an inquisitive gaze. ''He came to report a death.''

''Good heavens,'' Elizabeth said, covering her mouth with a hand. ''Who was it?''

Fletcher didn't take his eyes off Zeb, who sat calmly in the chair revealing nothing. ''No one you would know, Liz. He was a drover who'd just shipped a herd out east.''

''How did he die?'' Zeb asked, leaning back in the chair, his hands relaxed on the armrests.

''Looks like his heart gave out,'' Fletcher replied, not wanting to mention in front of Elizabeth the true circumstances, or that Zeb had played poker with the man the night before.

''What a shame. The fellow must have been working too hard,'' Zeb said.

''I reckon so.''

''Shall we go to the table?'' Zeb asked, his tone light.

Elizabeth nodded serenely and accepted her husband's hand to lead her out of the room. All Fletcher could do was stand and stare at Jo on the sofa staring back at him, her pale cheeks showing her concern. He knew without a doubt that something was going on in this town and Jo was a sitting duck in the middle of it.

"I'm glad you're back," she said, rising.

"Why? Did something happen? If Zeb said or did anything—"

"No, nothing at all. I'm just glad to see you. I was worried about you."

"I was worried about you, too," he replied, trying to keep the emotion from his voice, but it was no use. "I didn't like leaving you."

He offered his arm and she looped hers through it on the way out of the room.

"Then don't do it again," she said.

He wished with all his heart that he could give her that promise.

The ladies' refined presence at the dining table may have kept conversation away from cattle rustling and murder, but it astutely anchored it in far more dangerous territory.

"Perhaps we should set the date," Elizabeth suggested, sipping on red wine from a crystal glass.

Fletcher and Jo looked at each other. "We don't want to rush anything," Jo replied, moving her food around on her plate. "With the election coming..."

"All the more reason to do it now. We could make it a double celebration. I would be happy to help plan things."

"My dear," Zeb said, cutting her off, "you'll have more than enough planning to do for my victory celebration. Perhaps Fletcher and Mrs. O'Malley are wise to wait until afterward."

Elizabeth smiled politely. "Perhaps."

"Are you afraid they'll change their minds?" Zeb eyed them with arrogant humor.

Fletcher took a sip of wine and set it down. "We're not going to change our minds."

More surprised than anything at his definite tone, Jo forced herself to swallow a forkful of the tender roast beef.

"You don't plan to take up ranching, do you?" Zeb asked. "What about your career? The sheriff's office? I hope you haven't forgotten it."

"No, I just think it's time I reevaluated some of the decisions I've made in my life."

Was this part of the act? Jo wondered, astounded as she watched him carry on this uncomfortable conversation with Zeb.

"I think that's very wise of you, Fletcher," Elizabeth said. "Love is the most important thing."

"No, not love," Zeb disagreed. "You cannot depend on it. Family, and the responsibility that goes with it, is what matters most."

"With any luck, I'll have a family soon enough," Fletcher said, refusing to meet Jo's gaze across the table.

Elizabeth wiggled in her chair. "I'm sure you will, Fletcher, in no time at all." Her eyes smiled at Jo, who wanted to crawl under the table and hide until this conversation was over.

"Do you want a large wedding or something more intimate?" Elizabeth asked both of them. "Either way would be lovely. We could hold the celebration here afterward. What a delightful time it would be."

Jo tried not to sound unappreciative. "Please, you don't have to go to all that trouble. We just want to keep things simple."

"It would be no trouble at all. But if you really do prefer a simple ceremony, I wouldn't dream of interfering. Your happiness is what matters most." She smiled warmly at Jo, who could not bring herself to meet Elizabeth's kind gaze.

During the remainder of the meal, Jo was happy to turn the discussion toward the embroidery group that Elizabeth had begun on Tuesday evenings, then to lead the conversation into the poor selection of men's formal wear in town.

After dessert and coffee, when the table was cleared, Elizabeth gathered up her gloves and said to Jo, "Shall we retire to my private sitting room and allow the men a chance to talk business?"

"We really should be going," Fletcher said, sliding back his chair and standing.

Jo stopped him with her hand. "Please, Fletcher, sit down. There's no hurry. Enjoy some time with your brother-in-law. I'll be fine."

His eyes clouded with a warning.

Zeb signaled the footman to bring the cigars and a bottle of brandy. "Yes, do as your future wife tells you, Fletcher. You'll have to start sometime."

Jo breathed deeply to prevent herself from responding to Zeb's comment, then joined Elizabeth on her way out of the dining room. She felt Fletcher's eyes follow her but refused to acknowledge it. She could only hope he would do as much with his opportunity as she intended to do with hers.

Chapter Twenty-Two

"This is so romantic," Elizabeth mused. "It must have been love the very instant you laid eyes upon each other."

Jo tried to grasp for a sensible reply, but supposed with some uneasiness that matters of the heart were never sensible. "You know how these things are."

Elizabeth stood and walked to the window, pulled the heavy brocade curtain aside with one finger and looked out into the darkness. "I envy you, marrying a man like my brother."

"I'm sure most women in Dodge envy you for *your* husband."

Elizabeth let the curtain fall closed. "Thank you for saying that."

"It's the truth. You must be…" Jo could barely get the bitter-tasting words past her lips. "You must be very happy."

Elizabeth sat down again. "We are fortunate in what we have—this house and the business. It's a good life, but you will be fortunate in other ways when you marry my brother. You'll be far happier than most people could ever dream."

Jo pondered that statement and imagined it would be true if this engagement was not a sham.

"May I ask you something, Elizabeth?"

"Of course, you may ask me anything. We're going to be sisters, remember?"

Jo lowered her eyes and forced the words out, knowing she should be concentrating on connecting Zeb to George Greer, but unable to resist this opportunity to ask a question that only Elizabeth could answer. "Do you think Fletcher truly enjoys being a lawman?"

Elizabeth touched Jo's knee. "I knew you were the right woman for him."

"Why do you say that?"

"For someone who hasn't known him very long, you've seen right through him, past his badge."

"I suppose," Jo replied uncertainly.

"Maybe it's because you're cut from the same cloth," Elizabeth continued. "When you said earlier that you wanted to build something, I wanted to weep with joy that you and Fletcher had found each other. Fletcher always used to say the exact thing—those very words. Before he got caught up in the law, of course."

"You don't approve of his career choice?"

"It's not that I don't approve. I'd approve of anything he truly wanted. I just don't think that being a lawman makes him happy. It just keeps him from letting go of something that happened a long time ago. Something he needs to put behind him."

"Your father."

Elizabeth regarded Jo with surprise. "He told you? He must trust you very much."

Jo shrugged. "I just asked him about it, that's all."

"Even so, he usually won't speak of it to anyone. Perhaps there is hope for him after all."

"Hope?"

"Yes—that one day he'll leave the law to someone else and follow his dreams."

"Of owning a ranch," Jo finished for her, remembering John's proposal and feeling a twinge of disappointment.

"No." Elizabeth's blue-eyed gaze intensified. "Dreams of having a family to love, people to call home. That's what he always wanted to build."

At that moment, Jo's decision to keep from loving Fletcher Collins shattered like a sheet of thin ice dropped upon a rock. She realized suddenly that she wanted more than anything to help him find what he was looking for. He needed her, he always had, and she'd tried not to see it—even thought him soulless when all he ever wanted was the very thing she could give him. Or would have been able to, if things were different. She felt a painful lump lodge in her throat.

She looked down at the shiny gold ring she still wore. Had Fletcher truly wished all this was real when he slipped it on her finger and told her that his mother would have wanted her to wear it? Was the love in his eyes genuine, despite the differences that separated them?

Drowning in confusion and remembering suddenly that she had come here to prove Zeb's guilt, not fall in love with Fletcher, Jo removed the snug ring and handed it to Elizabeth. "It's too early for me to be wearing this."

Elizabeth accepted the tiny gold band, closed her fingers tightly around it. "I'll take good care of it until the special day." She stood and placed it in a mother-of-pearl, heart-shaped box on the corner desk.

All Jo wanted to do now was run out of this room

and go to Fletcher, wrap her arms around his neck, tell him she loved him and beg him to love her back. But would he be ready to hear that? she wondered. Jo knew Fletcher cared for her, but she also knew he would have to forgive his father before he'd ever be able to give up his obsession with the law and let himself be close to someone again.

She gazed blankly at Elizabeth, who was setting the ring box up on a shelf behind the fancy rolltop desk. Jo reminded herself that nothing with Fletcher would even come close to being resolved if she didn't find some evidence about Zeb to end this pursuit, because she knew enough about Fletcher to know that he would never let it go unsolved.

Oh, how she wanted him to let it go. She wanted him to let go of *all* of it.

''It's a shame what happened to that man Fletcher mentioned,'' Jo said unsteadily. ''I saw him earlier today. He looked fit as a fiddle loading his herd onto the railcar. I believe he said he worked for George Greer.''

Elizabeth returned to the sofa and sat down. ''It makes you stop and think about how fragile life is, doesn't it? Makes you want to live it to the fullest.''

Jo realized she'd have to be more direct. ''Have you ever met George Greer?''

''No, but someone delivered something here for him once. I had to send it back, all the way to Amarillo.''

Jo was too startled by the comment to feign indifference. ''What was it?''

''I have no idea. It was a small box from a bank and I didn't think it proper to open it.''

''Did you tell your husband about it?''

''Yes, of course. He explained to me later that it must have been a clerical error on the bank's part.''

"The bank?"

"Yes. Zeb also keeps an account in Amarillo."

Feeling her heart begin to pound harder, Jo cleared her throat. "Why would he keep an account there?"

"To diversify his holdings, he tells me. It's a good way to keep his inheritance safe from thieves and vagabonds and banks that fail."

"How very wise of him. Does he keep many? It must be a bookkeeping nightmare."

Elizabeth laughed. "I don't know. That was the only time I've ever seen anything from another bank. Zeb handles those things, of course."

"Of course," Jo replied, understanding. When Edwyn was alive, he had handled them, too. "But goodness, how very rude of me. I don't know who would be more shocked—Zeb or Fletcher—to know I'd been speaking about money with you."

They shared a smile.

"Don't worry," Elizabeth assured her. "You're my future sister-in-law, and from now on, our conversations will always be kept in the strictest confidence."

Jo smiled, but inside, she felt only a hopeless and despairing yearning.

"How very clever of you, Fletcher." Zeb picked up his brandy glass and swirled the amber liquid around. "I was beginning to think you'd lost your mind."

Fletcher smiled and tapped his cigar ashes into the tray. "If folks hear I'm going to hitch my wagon to one of the Dodge City widows, they'll realize I'm here to stay, and the sheriff's office will be a snap."

"Music to my ears."

"I thought you'd like it."

"When do you plan to have the wedding? We've got to manage this in the best possible way."

Fletcher settled back in his chair, carefully contemplating his answer. "The sheriff's election isn't until November. If we move too fast, all the hoopla will be over by the time folks go to vote and I'll be saddled with a wife. I reckon the anticipation of a big wedding—real romantic-like—will be better than the actual thing. If you get my meaning."

Zeb smiled. "I believe I do. You want to plan something marvelous, then after you're elected...a lover's quarrel, perhaps?"

Fletcher took a slow sip of brandy. "Perhaps."

Zeb studied Fletcher as if testing him. "Mmm, no, I don't like it."

"Why not?"

Zeb ran his finger around the top of his glass, thinking. "You don't want to spend the next few months courting a woman like Josephine O'Malley. Besides, Elizabeth will be impossible to live with if she has all that time to plan your nuptials."

"It'll give her something to do."

Zeb considered that. "What will your 'widow' do in the meantime?"

"What she always does. Sit out at her ranch and let the men run things while she's waiting to marry me." He hated saying all this, but it seemed to be working in his favor. It was exactly what Zeb wanted to hear.

He smiled. "And you'll be too busy upholding the law to visit her."

"Most of the time, I reckon that'll be the case."

"*Most of the time.* You won't become infatuated with her, will you? The effect will be lost if you decide to go through with it and push things forward."

"I told you, I'm not the marrying kind."

"But you're married to your job," Zeb commented, his eyes narrowing as he studied Fletcher for a response.

"A man's gotta believe in something."

"Yes, yes, he does." After a pause, Zeb inclined his head with a suggestion. "Have you considered actually going through with it? The O'Malley land is the best around."

Fletcher raised his eyebrows. "And what exactly would I do with a ranch?"

"If we're going to own Dodge, we might as well really *own* it, don't you think?"

Fletcher casually tossed his hair over his shoulder. "Interesting suggestion, but why make me marry her? Why not just buy her out?"

"That widow will never sell. I know for a fact. And she's bequeathing the place to her son, then a whole string of Irish relations who will probably be too sentimental to ever sell."

Fletcher kept his expression deceptively cool. "Thinking about getting into the cattle business?"

"It never hurts to control things."

"But ranching, Zeb? After all that talk about not needing to own land when there's open range to be had?"

"Let's just say my interests are varied. We'll leave it at that for now while you think about all this."

Fletcher *would* think about this. Very carefully.

"So, what about that raise you promised me?" he asked, rising to his feet. "When does that start?"

Laughing, Zeb stood also. "You're a shrewd man, Fletcher. I thank you for bringing it to my attention. What did I promise you? A hundred a week? Two hundred?"

"If I recall correctly, it was an extra hundred a month."

"Gracious, that won't do at all. A hundred a week sounds better, don't you think? I wasn't exactly at my best, was I? Did I thank you for seeing me home?"

"Not yet."

"Well, I'll thank you now with your first installment. How does that sound?"

"Sounds mighty fine, Zeb."

"I thought it would. Use the money to buy yourself some new clothes. Take Elizabeth with you. She has very good taste. We need to tidy up your image if we want things to go our way, and if you can get your hands on that ranch land, things will get even more interesting. I promise you that."

Fletcher spoke with restraint, hiding his suspicions for the time being. "I'm looking forward to finding out what you have in mind, Zeb."

"You'll never believe what I learned from Elizabeth," Jo said to Fletcher as their wagon rattled off Zeb's property and onto the dark, quiet street back to town.

Fletcher pulled at the brim of his hat, seeming distracted. "I'd believe anything right now. My pockets are stuffed with cash and I've committed myself to run for sheriff."

"You have? What did Zeb say about the wedding?"

Fletcher wouldn't look at her. "Don't worry. We're off the hook until November."

"Why November?" Would they have to continue this charade until then, she wondered uneasily, or would all this be over and done with?

"Because that's when the election will be, and no

voter can resist a groom in a big romantic wedding to which they've been invited.''

Jo huffed with disgust. ''That must have been Zeb's idea. I'm not surprised.'' Fletcher said nothing. ''What's the money for?''

''It's my salary from Zeb. He must keep a safe in his office, though I didn't see it when I sneaked in there.''

''You sneaked in? When?''

''After Deputy Anderson came. That's what took me so long.''

Jo turned to look at him, her curiosity impossible to hide. ''Did you find anything on George Greer?''

''No. Just papers relating to the store.''

''Well, if there was nothing in Zeb's study that mentioned Greer, he must have another hiding place, because Elizabeth told me they once received a package for Greer.''

''You asked her about it?''

''Don't worry. I was clever. We were talking about the man who died, and it came up that he worked for Greer. So now do you believe me about Zeb?''

''I believe he's up to something and that he's not the man Elizabeth thinks he is.''

Jo couldn't keep herself from probing further. ''But do you believe that he killed Edwyn?''

For a long time, Fletcher didn't answer. He gazed up at the stars. ''I believe it's possible that he might have been involved,'' he said finally.

Having waited so long to hear those words, Jo exhaled a deep, shaky sigh. She couldn't help leaning in and giving him a hug. She knocked his hat off-kilter.

''What are you doing?'' he asked, half laughing while straightening his hat.

''I just wanted to thank you for helping me.''

"Don't get too excited. I haven't helped you yet. We still need to know more before we can be certain," he added, not surprisingly.

But Jo was happy enough with what he offered. She sat back in her seat. "Where do we go from here?"

He steered the wagon onto Walnut Street. "First we're going to look at a dead body. Then we're going home. To *your* home. And I don't care what folks say about it. I'm going with you and I'm staying. The whole damn night."

Chapter Twenty-Three

After going to see MacGregor's body and finding him just as Deputy Anderson had described—dead from a bullet wound through the heart—Fletcher and Jo drove to the ranch.

The horses led the wagon toward the barn, and even though Fletcher sat beside Jo in the seat, she felt her pulse quicken as it always did at the thought of going inside, of seeing the place where Edwyn had gasped his last breath.

Feeling foolish and not wanting Fletcher to know about this irrational fear of hers, she made some excuse and hopped down from the wagon just before Fletcher drove in. She waited by the door, nervously tapping her foot while he unhitched the team and fed and watered the horses. When he finally walked out with his hand on his gun, she let out a deep breath of relief, rose up on her toes and hugged him.

"What's that for?" he asked, smiling and falling back against the barn wall. "You're awfully affectionate tonight."

She leaned into his warm, muscular frame, looking up at him in the moonlight. "I'm just glad you're here."

"I'm glad, too," he replied, his eyes roaming curiously over her face. She could see that he was studying her and seeing something there, something she'd not wanted him to see.

"Are you all right?" he asked, touching her cheek with his thumb.

"Of course," she replied, still leaning into him.

"But you're trembling."

"It's cold out here."

He shook his head, his gaze still full of scrutiny. "No, that's not it. You're afraid."

Taken aback, Jo rubbed at the chill on her arms. "Well, you have to admit, this whole situation has been—"

"You don't like to go into the barn, do you?"

Jo continued to at least try to hide what she felt. "What makes you think that?"

"A hunch." He took a step forward, away from the wall. "How long has it been since you've been in there?"

Oh, she didn't want to talk about this. "Too long."

"How do you manage to work the ranch without being able to go into the barn?"

"Leo and Matilda and the cowhands look after the chores there. I do other things."

He shook his head, not with disapproval, but with a genuine compassion that made her heart melt. "I'm so sorry you saw it happen, Jo."

Tears threatened; she tried to push them away but couldn't.

"You don't have to be scared anymore," he said. "It's all over."

"No, it's not, not in my mind. I keep seeing it."

He didn't say anything more, he only took her into his arms and held her.

"I just can't go in there," she whispered.

"Yes, you can."

"Please, don't force me, Fletcher. I've tried many times to force myself and it only makes it worse."

"I would never force you to do anything, Jo, but I'm here with you now. You're safe with me. Why don't you let me take you inside and show you that everything's okay?"

Her stomach began to churn with dread. "I know I should, but I don't want to."

"Look, I have my gun." He pulled it out of its holster and cocked it. "Nothing will happen while I'm here."

Her heart was pounding like a drum in her ears, faster and faster. "I don't know, Fletcher."

"Come with me," he gently urged, taking her hand and moving toward the door.

She didn't follow at first until her arm was outstretched and only her fingers were touching his. "Come on, Jo, you can do it. Just stay close to me."

Oh, he had such a way with his voice—that smooth Texas drawl. It always soothed her.

She took an uncertain step forward and he squeezed her hand. "That's it." He led her through the door and her breath came in short gasps and her heart felt as if it was going to burst with fear, until she stepped over the threshold and into the dark central bay.

The smell of moist hay and cows and manure wafted into her nose, bringing back a whole slew of memories which surprisingly were mostly about her childhood. It had been so long since she'd smelled these familiar scents.

Then Fletcher lit the lantern that hung on a post by the door, and the barn became recognizable. She swallowed nervously, her stomach suddenly burning as she looked up at the thick square beam overhead. Images of Edwyn's last helpless moments—his legs kicking and his face ghostly white with terror as he wrestled with the rope around his neck—flashed like sparking embers in her mind. She was breathing hard now, staring upward, seeing things that were not there.

"It's all right to be afraid, Jo," Fletcher said to her, dropping his gun into its holster and taking her hand. "It was a terrible ordeal, what you went through."

Frozen with fear, she could only nod.

She let the memories come, saw it all in her head, remembered huddling in the corner, waiting—God only knows how long—for Zeb and his men to leave, then longer still to be sure they had ridden far, far, away. The rope had creaked back and forth with Edwyn's limp body, clad in his dark wool trousers and wool vest, while Jo had trembled and shivered and cried until she found the courage to finally get up and saddle a horse. There had been no ranch hands around then in the dead of winter so she had ridden off into the night alone to get help, through the snow and over crusty patches of ice, and when she found the city marshal, she had remembered the other dead rancher's wife, and Jo had lied about what she had seen.

She heard Fletcher's voice, speaking to her as if from a great distance away. "What can I do, Jo? How can I help?"

Shakily she let her gaze go to him. "Just hold me."

And then he was hugging her, and the visions of Edwyn disappeared with her fears as she wrapped her arms around Fletcher, rested her cheek on his firm chest and felt him stroke her hair with gentle fingers. "It's over now, Jo. You're going to be okay."

She nodded and wiped away a tear. "Yes, everything's going to be okay."

He continued to hold her for the next few minutes, rubbing his hands over her back and kissing her cheeks until her heart slowed to a normal pace and she was able to look up at the beam and not see Edwyn anymore. She looked around at the hay and horses and saw the door to the tack room and smelled the leather, and what had happened to Edwyn suddenly seemed far away, a horrible tragic nightmare that was now part of her past.

She wiped away another tear and faced Fletcher's caring expression. "Thank you for coming in here with me. I couldn't do it alone."

"You just needed some help. We all need it sometimes."

And you still need me.

"Are you hungry?" she whispered, her muscles relaxing beneath the feel of his hands resting on her hips.

He smiled warmly. "Got any cookies?"

"That's why I keep my cookie jar full. For moments like these. Let's go in the house."

"Sounds good." Fletcher lowered the wick in the lantern and the barn went dark. Hands clasped, they walked quietly out into the yard, their path lit by the full moon, and slowly climbed the porch steps. Jo reached out to open the front door of the house but Fletcher stopped her.

"Let me go first," he said, drawing his Peacemaker and cocking it. "After that fire this morning, I'm not taking any more chances. Stay close."

They walked into the front hall, where the smell of

charred fabric and wood was still heavy in the air, then checked each room for intruders who might have been there or who were still lurking. They found no evidence that anyone had been there since breakfast.

Fletcher holstered his gun and finally turned to face Jo. They stood in the darkness of the front hall, close enough that Jo could feel his breath on her face. When their eyes met, it seemed they both realized at the same time that they were alone together in this dark house and would be until morning.

"Why don't we go into the kitchen?" Jo suggested, feeling suddenly awkward and nervous.

She led the way in and, while Fletcher removed his hat and sat at the table, she lit a lamp and filled a plate with frosted shortbread cookies from the jar beside the window.

Fletcher helped himself while Jo set two small plates out for each of them. "These cookies look great," he said.

"Would you like some coffee?"

"I reckon I'm going to need it tonight."

She knew he planned to stay awake and guard her safety, but where did he plan to do it? From downstairs—or closer to her bed? The idea of him nearby while she slept made her tremble with apprehension. Would she be able to stay out of his arms?

Warily she filled the stove with kindling and lit it, then prepared the coffeepot and set it to boil. She sat down at the table across from Fletcher and reached for a cookie. "Do you think anything will happen tonight? Zeb's already tried once."

"Killer or not, Zeb has a very good reason to keep you healthy for the next few months. He wants a wedding to ensure my election to the sheriff's office."

"Did he say that?"

"Yes, after I convinced him of it."

Jo swallowed the sweet shortbread. "Clever of you, Marshal, but I still wouldn't trust him. If he thinks I might expose him, our wedding will hardly seem important, even if it does get you the job of sheriff."

"Well, there's more to it than that."

He gazed at her uncertainly and her stomach lurched with dread. "I'm not sure I want to know."

Fletcher ran his fingers through his hair. The nagging sensation in her gut refused to be still.

"Tonight I learned that Zeb wants your land," Fletcher said finally. "He knows you won't sell and he wants me to get it by marrying you."

The walls seemed to be closing in around Jo. She was beginning to understand.

"Is that why he killed Edwyn? For the land?"

"I don't know."

A chill grew inside her. "How could he do that? Take a man's life—Edwyn was a father!—just for a piece of land! I don't understand!"

"Jo—"

"If Zeb thinks he can get away with this..." Her thoughts began to race dangerously as she considered the implications of Zeb's intent. "The land is to go to Leo after I'm gone. If anything happens to—"

Fletcher covered her hand with his. "I won't let that happen. You're safe with me and Leo is safe with his uncle, and all this will be cleared up before we let him come home. Trust me."

She stood up. "Maybe I should just sell to Zeb. Get out of here while we can. The land isn't as important as our lives."

"No, Jo. I know what it is to give up your home and

everything you've worked for because something didn't go according to plan. It can change your life forever. I won't let that happen.''

''But Fletcher…''

''I'll keep you and Leo safe, I promise.'' Fletcher's eyes burned with intensity as he looked up at her.

Jo struggled with the anger and fear boiling within her. She dropped her forehead to her hand to suppress the throbbing in her head.

''The thought of ever losing you…'' Fletcher continued. ''It makes me want to destroy him, too.''

Jo's anger cooled at the sound of those words on Fletcher's lips. *He didn't want to lose her?*

Slowly she sat back down. ''So you do believe that he's capable of murder?''

''Yes.''

''What changed your mind?''

''Will MacGregor's murder tonight, for starters. Besides that, I find that I want you to be safe more than anything. Your devotion to your family and your home moves me, Jo.''

Jo covered her face with her hands, her heart breaking from the shame she had for so long been trying to escape. ''Oh, Fletcher, I don't deserve admiration from you. When I walked into Zeb's store to kill him that night, I told you I was doing it for Leo—for our safety, but that's not entirely true. I was doing it for me, too.''

Fletcher leaned across the table and covered her cheek with his warm hand. ''You don't have to say—''

She pulled back. ''I'd dreamed of that moment with more hatred than you can ever imagine. I wanted to watch Zeb plead for his life. I wanted to squeeze the trigger over and over, to watch him die for what he did to my family. Is that what you call *moving?*" Tears found their way down her cheeks.

Fletcher shook his head at her. "Anyone in your position would have had those thoughts. I certainly had them about the men who killed my father. But I didn't kill them and you didn't kill Zeb."

"I would have if you hadn't walked in when you did." She gave in to the sobs that shook her.

"No, you wouldn't have. I saw it in your eyes, and believe me, I've seen enough killers' eyes to know."

"You're wrong. I've been telling myself this was all for Leo and our safety, but I have to accept that I'm not the person I once was. Knowing you has made me see that I'm capable of terrible things and I deserve what's coming to me. I deserve to go to prison." Wiping away tears so she could see, she stood and moved to the stove.

"I don't deserve any favors from you, Fletcher. You saw your father murdered and, still, you wouldn't kill those men. We're different, you and I. You don't have the heart of a killer."

"I would kill to protect you," he said from behind her, placing his hands on her shoulders.

She turned to face him. The honesty and affection she saw in his eyes startled her. Was he blinded by his feelings for her? Or did he understand her more than she understood herself?

Tenderly Fletcher wiped a tear from her cheek. He glanced down at her hand. "You took off the ring."

Jo could barely speak. She was still so shaken by his kindness. How could he be so forgiving? "I gave it back to Elizabeth. I didn't think it appropriate to wear it."

"Because we're not married," Fletcher said matter-of-factly.

Jo nodded, trying to keep her eyes from filling with tears again.

"It looked nice on you."

"Thank you." To hear him speak those words made her long for him, and at the same time made her feel more empty than ever.

He reached down and laced his fingers through hers. "When I told you my mother would have wanted you to wear it, I meant it."

"You don't have to say that."

"It's true."

Jo felt as if her heart was touching his through their joined hands. "Fletcher, I don't know what I would have done these past few days without you."

He kissed her fingertips and her whole body awakened beneath the heat of his lips.

"I'm glad I found you," he said softly. "Not because of what's been happening…just because."

A sense of urgency filled her as he touched her cheek. Her eyes fell closed and she turned her face into his palm.

"I'd really like to kiss you," he whispered.

"I think I'll collapse in a heap if you don't."

Her last words were smothered on her lips as his mouth came down to claim hers. The kiss was velvety and tasted like the sugar cookies. Jo reached up to his shoulders for support, deepening the kiss until her entire body melted into his. She trembled from the overwhelming sensation of love in her heart and her complete and undying trust in this man.

As the coffeepot hissed and steamed and filled the air

with its heady aroma, Jo held Fletcher tighter than she'd ever held anyone.

"Let me stay with you tonight," he whispered into her ear, his hot breath sending gooseflesh down her arms and legs.

"I thought we'd already decided that," she managed to say.

"No, I mean let me stay *with* you. In your bed."

Her senses spun madly for the thing she had so wanted but dared not suggest.

Giving herself to the heat of Fletcher's desire, she nodded, then felt him sweep her off the floor and into his capable arms. She buried her face into the firm wall of his chest and let go of all her fears. She wanted to give him everything, no matter what the future had in store for them. Closing her eyes, she let him carry her up the stairs to her dark bedroom.

Once inside, he kicked the door closed with his boot, carried her to the bed and gently laid her down. She inched back toward the pillow, watching him in the moonlight from the window. He pulled off his vest and draped it on the wing chair in the corner of the large room, then unbuttoned his shirt and crawled onto the bed to lie beside her. His nearness overwhelmed her to the point of trembling.

He held her in his arms, kissing the top of her head. "Are you all right?" he asked gently.

"I'm fine."

"This can't be easy for you. I know this is where you and Edwyn—"

"Fletcher, there's something you should know about Edwyn and me." She sat up to talk to him. "I cared deeply for Edwyn and I respected him. He was a kind man and a good father, and I do miss him, terribly, but we never loved each other, not the way a man and woman ought to.''

"But he was your husband."

"Only on paper. His heart always belonged to someone else."

"Someone else?" She heard the shock in Fletcher's voice. "How could you have respected him so much if he was—"

"No, it's not like that. He was never unfaithful. It was a woman he had loved before me, before he came to America. They were engaged, but she broke it off to marry another man. That's why Edwyn left his home and his country."

"He told you all this?"

"No, I found out after we were married for a few years, after Leo was born. That sea chest in the den, it's filled with the woman's letters and Edwyn's, too. She must have given them back to him. He had told me he kept letters from his family in the chest and I had often wondered why he kept it locked. Then one day, I came across the key while I was cleaning, and I couldn't resist my curiosity. It was wrong of me, I know, but I wanted to understand my husband better and know why he didn't love me."

Fletcher's eyes were melancholy. "I'm sorry, I didn't know."

"It's all right. In all the years we were married, I was never heartbroken about it, and that always surprised me. Now, I understand. It was because I never truly loved him, either. We were friends, that was all. And by the time he died, it had been years since we'd been...intimate."

Fletcher kissed her on the forehead.

"Edwyn's gone, Fletcher. You're here. That's all that

matters now.'' She felt a great weight lift from her heart.

He raised her chin in his fingers and laid a kiss on her lips. ''I don't want you to regret this.''

''I won't. No matter what happens, I...I love you, Fletcher.''

She had hoped he would say something, tell her everything was going to be all right like he always did, but he said nothing as he gently rolled on top of her and leaned on both elbows looking down into her face.

In his eyes, she saw sorrow, and she was devastated by it.

Forcing herself to crush the hurt and think of nothing but finding pleasure in this one night, she wrapped her arms around his neck and kissed him deeply. She couldn't think about the future or all the reasons why he, like Edwyn, couldn't love her. Not now.

''Take this off,'' he whispered, reaching for the buttons on her bodice and unfastening each one. Within a heartbeat, she was sitting up and shrugging out of it while he removed his shirt and kicked off his boots.

She lay back onto the pillows and let him straddle her to unhook her corset in the front. As it came loose and he pulled it out from under her, she took a deep breath, welcoming her body's freedom, but wishing— hopelessly she knew—that he loved her and that he was completely devoted to her as she was to him. But he was not the man he once was—the man Elizabeth described. Jo saw that in his eyes tonight.

''Now this,'' he whispered, pulling her skirt and petticoats down over her ankles. He rolled down her stockings and began to untie her boot laces. ''These, too.''

Wearing only her chemise and cotton drawers, she sat up and pushed him onto his back.

She felt his Peacemaker against her knee. "This will be the first to go," she said in a low voice, then unbuckled his leather belt and pulled it away.

He raised his hips in compliance, but reached for the gun before she tossed the belt onto the floor.

"I'll keep *that*." His large bicep tightened as he slid the weapon beneath his pillow.

He rolled her over onto her back again and there was a flicker of doubt in his eyes. "Are you sure you want to do this when there are no promises?" His gaze locked with hers while he awaited her reply.

"Yes, Fletcher, I want you more than anything, even if it's just for tonight." Her body tingled with unleashed desire as he pulled off her chemise and flicked his tongue over her breasts. He removed his trousers while she wiggled out of her drawers and kicked them off.

They both slid under the covers and finally Fletcher's hot flesh covered Jo's. The explosive sensation of his body moving to rest between her legs made her ache for his touch. "I want you inside me now, Fletcher. Time is too precious."

She gasped as he entered her, his forehead resting upon hers, their bodies beginning to move together. Exhilarating shivers shook her as her arousal grew to a peak. Within minutes, she was soaring to a new height, pulling him deeper inside and holding him there as her body throbbed and quaked with rapture around him and he spilled fiercely into her.

Many moments later, when they were finally catching their breath, he gazed down at her. His green eyes were warm with affection, but nothing had changed.

"You're trembling," she said to him.

"I know. Just give me a minute...." He rested his

forehead on hers, his breaths coming slower now. "I've never felt like this, Jo. It makes it so difficult to—"

She blinked back a tear. "Please, Fletcher, I want to pretend for just one moment that nothing outside this room exists."

He rolled off her, pulled her in to rest her cheek on his shoulder and kissed the top of her head. "It does exist."

Disappointed, she closed her eyes into the warmth of his body.

"Zeb wants you dead, I can feel it, and I think you're right. He's up to something with George Greer, something to do with the cattle rustling, but I have no proof and I don't know how to get it. It's making me crazy."

"Maybe the wires you sent will help us."

"Maybe." But his tone revealed his doubts. He sat up, leaned against the oak headboard and raised a knee under the light sheet. "Maybe you should leave Dodge."

Jo tucked a lock of hair behind her ear and sat up, too. "What are you saying?"

"I'm saying you could pack a bag and ride off. Go to Leo and take him someplace safe, a place no one knows."

"But you'd have to let me go."

He said nothing for a moment, then met her gaze with emotion-filled eyes. "I know."

"But Fletcher, you've never let anyone go in your life."

He gently stroked her hair. "Things have changed."

Stricken, she leaned forward and hugged him, feeling his hair tickle her neck. "I can't let you do it. The law is your life. Besides that, I don't want to leave you."

"I don't want you to leave, either, but I think it would be best."

A feeling of sorrow broke from her heart. "Are you just trying to get rid of me?"

"Of course not. You know that's not true."

"But I'll be a fugitive."

"No one but you and I know what really happened. I've never filed papers."

She shook her head. "I can't let you do that. I wouldn't want you to always think of me as the criminal you let escape from justice. If I have to face a judge for what I did, I'll face him. When this is solved, I'll explain myself and hope for the best. It's the right thing to do, Fletcher, and God knows I haven't chosen the right path lately. But you made me see that it's time I did. I understand if you don't want to marry me. It wouldn't help your reputation any once I'm arrested, certainly wouldn't buy you any votes as sheriff, but at least you'd know I tried to do what was right."

Fletcher's chin shook as he spoke. "I don't want to be sheriff, Jo."

She laughed and sobbed at the same time. "We have to prove Zeb killed Edwyn. The truth has to come out. I just feel sorry for Elizabeth."

"I know my sister. If she's married to a killer, she'll want to know."

Jo hugged him again, and she snuggled down under the sheet to hold him through the rest of the silent, dark night, with the heartbreaking knowledge that it would be the last time.

Chapter Twenty-Four

"If I'm going to find anything to use against Zeb," Fletcher said the next morning, tossing the sheet aside and sitting up on the edge of the bed, "I'm going to need some time. I definitely want you to go and stay with Leo in Newton."

"I don't want to go. I told you, I'm prepared to face the law for what I did." Staring at his bare, muscular back in the pale light of the rainy dawn, Jo waited impatiently for his response.

"I'm not giving you a choice. I can't protect you and investigate Zeb at the same time."

"I can take care of myself. I know how to use those weapons you took from me."

Fletcher picked his trousers up off the floor and shook them before pulling them on. "I don't doubt that at all, but whether you can protect yourself or not isn't the point."

"Then what is the point?"

"The point is I'd be thinking about you. I'd be worrying when I wasn't with you and distracted when I was. Not a good mix for a man in my line of work."

He pulled on his wrinkled cotton shirt but didn't button it.

"What if Zeb catches on to what you're doing? I don't think I could bear…"

Shirt half-open to reveal his smooth, muscular chest and rippled stomach, he crawled onto the bed and cupped her face in his large hands. "Zeb is beginning to trust me. And I promise I'll be careful."

She sat up on her knees, and the sheet that covered her fell away. She rubbed her thumbs over Fletcher's moist mouth. "Do you have to get dressed right now? The men won't be expecting breakfast yet. They're always slow when it rains." Jo pulled him in for another more demanding kiss.

He gently pushed her onto her back and crawled on all fours above her. "I'll stay on one condition."

"What's that?" She hurried to pull his shirt off.

"You promise to leave town."

"But I don't want to go."

"I'm not giving you a choice," he said again, and she knew there was no arguing as he pressed his open mouth to hers and, like a warm blanket, covered her body with his own.

It had just stopped raining when Leo hopped out of his uncle's buggy, splashed into the mud and hurried into the Newton post office. Inside, he removed his hat to discover the brim was holding enough rainwater to fill a bucket, and he accidentally spilled it onto the floor.

He tried to spread the puddle around with his boot so no one would slip, then made his way to the counter. "Anything for Cecil O'Malley?" he asked the postmaster.

The gray-haired, craggy-faced man turned and retrieved a pile of envelopes from the box behind him and, without a word, slapped them onto the unpainted counter. Leo gathered them up and thanked the man, but he'd already turned away to finish sorting the mail.

Once outside, Leo replaced the rain-drenched hat on his head and flipped through the letters. His eyes widened at the sight of the return address on the last one— *Edwyn O'Malley, Dodge City, Kansas.*

Leo spun around and hurried back into the post office. "Where did this letter come from?" he asked the postmaster.

The man faced him and peered over his spectacles at the envelope. "Return address says Dodge City. Maybe it's time you learned to read."

"I *can* read. But this letter's old. Look!"

The postmaster glared at him, then snapped the envelope into his hand and held his spectacles between two fingers to examine it. "Postmarked January 10. You're right. It must have gotten lost for a time. Now if you'll excuse me."

Leo turned and walked out of the building, staring in stunned silence at his father's penmanship on the outside of the damp, tattered envelope. Leo heard the post office door fall closed behind him. He stood beside his uncle's buggy, the letter in his hand making his heart ache with longing. He looked at the familiar writing again and, before he could think, ripped open the flimsy envelope and read what was inside.

After preparing breakfast for the men and seeing them off to work, Jo grudgingly packed a bag and left a note for John on the bunkhouse door, asking him to see to the animals for the next few days and ensure the men were fed from the cookhouse. She didn't explain where she was going, only that she would be gone a while.

She *wasn't* happy about it.

The rain fell mercilessly from the ashen sky as she crossed the muddy yard toward the wagon. Holding her umbrella over her head, she climbed into the wet seat beside Fletcher, who wore his long brown slicker and his hat pulled forward on his head, the brim dripping with rain. She curled her gloved hand around his arm, but he wouldn't look at her as he set them in motion. It was as if, after leaving the sanctuary of her bed, he had all of a sudden decided to close the door in her face.

"We have an hour together," she said, trying to keep her mood light when all she wanted to do was shake him and ask why he refused to let her into his heart. The wagon swished through a deep puddle and she worked hard to keep from letting him see how truly heartbroken she felt. "Enough time for me to get you to change your mind, I hope."

"No, Jo."

"But I want to be with you, and you need me for this."

He was quiet for a minute. "It just can't be like that, Jo. I'm sorry. You should be with Leo. Take him somewhere to keep him safe in case things get dangerous."

She couldn't very well argue with that. When it came to Leo, she would do anything, and Fletcher knew it.

He squeezed her hand with reassurance but nothing else, and she felt the love in her heart swell far beyond what she had once, not so long ago, believed possible.

If only it was not such a painful love. If only Fletcher could open his heart to her as she would open hers if he let her. Lord, if he was willing, she would at this very moment vow to love him for the rest of her life.

"Please, be careful, Fletcher."

"Nothing will happen. I'll find the evidence." He put his arm around her.

They drove through the rain and over the low, sodden hills, crossing mile after mile of weather-beaten landscape, but Jo could not make herself relax. She had a bad feeling about all this.

By the time they reached the railway station, the train was there and waiting with hissing bursts of steam. Jo's clothing was soaked straight through to her petticoats. She was shivering, and her heart was aching at the thought of saying goodbye. What if she left Dodge and something terrible happened to this man she had given all of her heart, soul and body to?

Fletcher ran into the station to purchase her ticket and returned a few minutes later. "I bought a ticket all the way to Topeka, just in case anyone sees you get on and asks where you're going. Change seats along the way— cars if you can—and try to get off without too many folks noticing. Don't tell anyone you're getting off at Newton, and when you get there, take Leo somewhere safe."

Jo nodded as he helped her out of the seat and retrieved her valise from under the canvas in the wagon bed. He led the way to the platform and stepped up onto the train, turning around to take her hand and pull her up.

Carrying her folded, dripping umbrella, Jo entered the train and followed Fletcher down the narrow aisle until he found her a seat to herself at the far end of the car. He set down her bag.

"I guess this is goodbye," Jo said shakily, facing him.

The lady in the seat behind her coughed.

"I guess so. Will you be all right?"

"I'll be fine." Jo fought the crushing urge to throw her arms around him and beg that he come with her and leave all this behind them. "Will *you* be all right?"

"Of course."

And yet, she did not feel reassured.

They stood in the aisle, staring at each other. Jo made no move to sit down; Fletcher made no move to leave. The conductor blew a whistle outside.

Suddenly Fletcher grabbed for Jo's hand and pulled her almost violently through the back door. It slammed behind them and they paused in the small space between two passenger cars.

His mouth came down upon hers. The kiss was urgent and desperate, and it was all Jo could do to keep from falling to her knees and pleading for his safety. She wrapped her arms around his broad shoulders, tears spilling from her eyes; she felt his steel badge pressing against her heaving breast. "I can't leave you," she sobbed, hugging him.

"You have to."

The train began to puff and shudder. "We're starting to move," Jo cried miserably.

"I know. I have to go." He cupped her face in his strong hands and kissed her again. "Remember what I told you. Keep to yourself."

"I will."

He moved down the steps and, looking up at her, held the steel handrail. His eyes were full of sorrow and apologies and Jo's heart sank. She knew what he was going to say next.

For a moment, time seemed to stand still, until he spoke. "Jo, please don't let yourself love me. I can't change who I am."

She stared numbly at him, her heart beginning to tremble with a horrible, debilitating pain. Then, before she knew it, she was yelling. "Can't change who you are! But you don't *know* who you are!"

The train chugged beneath the soles of Jo's boots and she clutched at the wall for balance as the ground seemed to race past the door. She stepped forward just as Fletcher leaped off the moving train and disappeared out of sight.

He was gone, but she had so much more to say.

At that moment, Jo felt as if her heart had been ripped from her body and would never, ever, be returned.

After visiting the telegraph office only to learn there were no reply wires from Texas, Fletcher checked in at the jailhouse and found Deputy Anderson busy with paperwork from the night before.

He walked in and shook his hat off at the door, trying also to shake the pain from his heart. He'd done the right thing, he told himself, ending it with Jo like that. It was the best thing for both of them. He'd had to stop it before their relationship got any more out of hand. Hell, he'd already sacrificed his professional integrity by setting her free and it was eating away at him now, just like she said it would. It was the exact kind of thing his father would have done.

No, it was just too dangerous and confusing, being involved with her during the case, and who knew how long it would be before it was solved?

And anyway, even if the case was closed tomorrow, Fletcher certainly wasn't about to give up the law.

But what had she meant when she said he didn't know who he was? He knew exactly who he was. He was Fletcher Collins. Lawman.

"Any problems last night?" he asked the deputy, struggling to forget about Jo and keep his mind on his job.

"Nope. Only the usual sluggers after midnight at the keno table. Folks were asking about you though. Wondering where you were and if you were still looking for Six-Shooter Hank."

Fletcher hung his hat on the hook by the door and crossed to the desk where Anderson was sitting. He flipped through the pile of affidavits the deputy had written out, reviewing them for anything out of the ordinary. "You can tell people I have a hunch we won't see him again." He shuddered inwardly at the thought. "Any wires delivered here for me?"

"Nope. And I asked around about George Greer like you told me to, real casual-like. No one I talked to ever met him or knew anyone who did. I'm beginning to think the man's a ghost. Hey, you're dripping on my papers."

Fletcher stepped back. "If I was rustling cattle, I'd keep a low profile, too. Let me know if anything comes in today. When you're finished there, go get yourself something to eat. I'll take over as soon as I get back."

"Where are you going?"

Fletcher retrieved his hat from the hook and settled it onto his head. He opened the door and looked out at the curtain of rainwater dripping from the roof. "To talk to someone who knows something."

Fletcher walked past Zeb's store, peered through the window to see him talking to one of the town councilors, and kept right on going. He walked all the way up Railroad Avenue in the pouring rain until he reached Zeb's house, then rapped hard on the door.

Matthews finally came and met him with an unimpressed glare. "Marshal Collins. Do you not own an umbrella?"

Fletcher kicked his muddy boots against the doorstep. "My Stetson does the trick and keeps my hands free. Sorry about the mud."

"I'm sure you are. But I'm afraid Mr. Stone is not at home this morning."

"What about Elizabeth?"

"Mrs. Stone is in the drawing room if you wish to see her."

Fletcher stepped inside and handed his dripping coat and hat to Matthews, who carried them away at arm's length. A moment later, the butler returned. "Mrs. Stone will see you now."

"Thanks a bunch." Fletcher followed him into the drawing room.

Elizabeth rose from the sofa and approached, her hands held out. "Fletcher! What are you doing here?"

"I came to talk to you."

"Would you like some tea?"

"I'd prefer coffee."

She smiled wickedly. "So would I, but Zeb insists I always offer tea first." She gestured to Matthews, who backed out of the room and closed the double doors behind him.

Elizabeth led Fletcher to the sofa. "You're dripping wet. It must be important, whatever you came to talk about." She tried to whisk some water from his hair.

"It is, but I don't know how you're going to react."

Elizabeth's rosy smile faded. "You haven't broken your engagement, have you?"

"No, nothing like that. It's…" He hesitated. "It has to do with Zeb."

"Zeb? He's not in trouble, is he?"

Fletcher stared into his sister's troubled eyes. "Why would you think that?"

Rising from the sofa and turning her back to him, Elizabeth began to rearrange some flowers in a tall vase. "No reason. You just seemed uneasy."

Fletcher watched her slender arms flit around the tall vase, moving a geranium here, replacing another there.

"To tell you the truth," he said, rising to move to the other side of the table where he could see her face, "I need to know if I can trust you."

"Of course you can. I'm surprised you even have to ask."

"Well, this is different. I need you to keep something from Zeb."

The rain beat hard against the large windowpanes. Elizabeth slid the vase to one side so it was no longer between them. "You know I'll do anything for you, Fletcher. Are *you* in trouble? Do you need money?"

He shook his head and took her by the arm. "Come over here and sit with me."

They returned to the sofa. Fletcher held Elizabeth's hands and kept his voice low. "There's been a cattle-rustling problem in Dodge lately. The herds that arrive here are substantially smaller than they were when they started out."

"I've read about it in the papers."

Just then, the drawing room doors opened and Elizabeth jumped. Matthews walked in with a tray. "Set it here, please, Matthews. Then you may go. I'll take care of it.''

"Yes, Mrs. Stone." He peered suspiciously at Fletcher, then left the room.

Elizabeth poured two cups full of the steaming coffee, added cream and sugar to hers and handed Fletcher his, black. "Go on."

"I think I may know who's responsible for the thefts."

"Who?"

"A man named George Greer. Ever hear of him?"

Elizabeth set down her cup. "His name came up last night when Jo and I were talking."

"I know. She told me. That's why I'm here."

"Well, I don't know anything else besides what I told Jo," she said nervously. "We received a package that was meant to go to Greer. That was all."

"And Zeb told you he and Greer had accounts at the same bank in Amarillo?"

"Yes."

"Have you ever heard Greer's name mentioned besides that one time?"

"No, never. But Zeb doesn't usually speak of business matters with me. Do you think he knows Greer?"

Fletcher took another sip of the hot coffee. "Zeb knew Greer's trail boss. The man who died last night."

"I see." Her heart-shaped face went pale. "Have you spoken to Zeb about any of this?"

"No, and I don't want to just yet. This is difficult to say, Elizabeth, but I think Zeb might be involved somehow."

"Do you have any proof?"

Fletcher felt suddenly ill equipped to be having this conversation. He lowered his eyes. "No."

"Something tells me you want my help."

"Yes."

Elizabeth sat back. "He's my husband, Fletcher. You're asking me to go behind his back." The rain continued to course down the window, obscuring the view outside. Elizabeth stared blankly at it.

"What do you need?" she asked finally, meeting his gaze.

"I need to get into his study for another look around."

"*Another* look? Fletcher, don't tell me…"

"Sorry, sis. I was pressed for time."

She shook her head at him. "All right. I'll send Matthews on an errand. I'll ask him to…oh, I'll get him to book the church for your wedding. That should keep him busy. Reverend O'Grady loves to talk."

They both stood. "Thanks, Liz. And is there anywhere else you know of where Zeb keeps papers or correspondence?"

"The store, perhaps. I've only been in the office once and he shooed me out."

"Then that sounds like a good place to try next."

Late in the afternoon, just as the dark clouds began to separate in the sky over Newton, Jo drove toward her brother-in-law's homestead in a buggy she'd hired from the station. She sat next to the quiet driver, her eyes burning from the long train trip across the stormy plains. It had been exhausting, to say the least.

To say the most, it had been heartwrenching. She had sat uncomfortably in her hard seat with her forehead resting against the cool windowpane, watching lightning split the sky in the distance and listening to the deep roar of thunder, but thinking only of Fletcher and all the things she wished she had been able to say.

She wanted to tell him that his obsession with the law was nothing but a cover-up, that he was only trying to prove to himself that he was right and his father was wrong, so that he could continue to be angry with him. She wanted Fletcher to understand that he was running from what he really needed to feel, that he was afraid of missing his father, and because of that, he'd closed himself off to any feelings that might be deep and true. His heart needed something more than a drifter's empty existence, she was sure of it. Fletcher needed a home and a family. That's how he was raised, and until his father's tragic death, it had been what he'd wanted out of life.

But would he ever believe any of that? Sadly, she thought not.

She realized at that moment, as she dug into her reticule to pay the driver, that she had never experienced heartache like this before—not even when Edwyn died. The feelings then had been different. She'd been grievously distressed by it and felt the loss like a great stone in her stomach. She'd been morose and lonesome and desperately afraid of carrying on without him—she still felt that way—but she had never felt *hurt* by him. Even when she discovered his love letters, she had not been shattered. She had only been low-spirited for a time, then quickly recovered to the point of feeling relieved. Relieved to finally know the truth about why her husband did not love her.

There was no relief today. Not even a scrap. Fletcher's words had crushed her.

Knowing it was time to see Leo and not wanting him to know of her pain, she forced a smile and climbed down from the leather buggy seat. She wondered what he would say when she appeared unexpectedly at the door. He would probably think she had come to check up on him. Somehow she would have to convince him that was not the case.

Wishing there had been time to let someone know she was coming, she accepted her valise from the driver, lifted her skirts, which were trimmed with mud at the bottom and walked across the dirt yard to the house. Three chickens clucked and scurried out of her path.

Before she reached the steps, the front door swung open and Matilda walked onto the covered porch. Her cheeks were flushing with concern. "Josephine! What are you doing here?"

"Hello, Matilda. I needed some time away, myself, and thought I would join you. Where's Leo?"

Cecil, Edwyn's brother, appeared behind Matilda. "Good heavens, Jo, what are you doing here? Didn't you get the wire?"

"What wire?"

"The wire we sent a few hours ago—no, obviously you didn't get it."

Icy dread began to coil through her veins. "Where's Leo?"

Matilda came down the steps and took Jo's bag. "Maybe you'd better come inside."

"No, I won't come inside until you tell me what's going on. *Where's Leo?*"

Cecil came down a step. "He went back to Dodge City."

"What!" Jo hollered. "You let him go?"

"He went on his own without telling us. He left a note and took the morning train."

"Let me see the note."

Cecil darted into the house and reappeared with the small piece of paper, handing it down to Jo.

"It says he knows who killed Edwyn," Jo read in a panic, "and he's going to take care of things. Take care of things! What does he mean by that?"

Matilda shook her head. "I don't know, Josephine, but he's probably arriving in Dodge right about now."

Jo stuffed the note into her bodice pocket. "When's the next train out of here?"

"The last one for the day will leave in about an hour."

Jo darted toward Cecil's barn, leaving her bag with Matilda for safekeeping. "I'll need a horse to get me to the station."

"I'll go with you," Cecil said, following. "Don't worry, Josephine. We'll find him."

"Just get me to the station."

With a hiss of steam and a coughing sputter of smoke from the smokestack, the train from Newton puffed wearily into Dodge City. Leo made his way down the aisle, holding on to the backs of the seats to keep his balance as the train shuddered to a slow stop. Local folk gathered on the platform, but none were there to greet him, he knew. For once, he was on his own, able to complete his business in town before going home to surprise his ma with the good news.

He patted his coat pocket one more time to check for his father's letter, then started off toward Zeb Stone's Dry Goods to see that it was delivered to the most powerful man in Dodge. If there was one person who could make use of such a letter, it was his good friend, Mr. Zeb Stone.

Chapter Twenty-Five

When the door to the jailhouse opened, Fletcher leaned forward at his desk, expecting a complaint about a drunken brawl or a stolen horse. He stood quickly when he recognized his sister. "Liz, what are you doing here?"

Elizabeth walked in wearing a dark blue afternoon dress and a matching velvet hat with ribbons and a face veil. She clutched her reticule in her tiny gloved hands, peering uneasily toward the jail cells. "Could I speak to you in private?"

"Of course. We'll go outside." Fletcher moved around the desk and escorted her out the door and around the side of the building. "What is it?"

She glanced over her shoulder. "Did you see Zeb today?"

"Yes, but I didn't talk to him. I waited for him to leave the store then checked out his office."

"Did anyone see you?" she asked anxiously.

"Don't worry. I have a knack for this kind of thing."

"I hope so."

Fletcher leaned against the wall. "What brings you here, Liz? You seem nervous."

"Well, I just don't want to get into trouble with Zeb. Ever since we went through his den this morning, I've been worrying. What if he notices something out of place?"

"He won't. I put everything back exactly where I found it." Fletcher stepped away from the wall. "You don't seem convinced."

"I'm just…well, the real reason I came here is because I have something more to tell you, and I fear I may be going too far."

Fletcher took her hand. "You can trust me, sis. I'll take care of everything."

Her chin began to quiver and she lowered her face and pressed her finger under her nose. "I'm not sure you can."

"Why not? What's wrong?"

She took a moment to regain her composure. "Zeb is my *husband*."

"I know that, Liz," he said gently. "But if he's guilty of something, I can't let it go because he's married to you. Do you understand that?"

Her gaze darted upward. "Of course I do. That's not what I mean to say." She paused, biting her lip. "If he is in some kind of trouble with the law, as his wife I will have to support him. But what if…what if I don't wish to?"

Fletcher relaxed against the wall, coming to understand her predicament. "Then you won't. I'll be here for you, sis, no matter what."

She wiped under her eye and sniffed. "Then I came here to tell you that Zeb came home this afternoon and went into his study for quite some time. After he left, I looked in and noticed the rug had been moved slightly." Leaning toward him, she quietly added, "It was not in the same place it was when we were in there this morning."

Fletcher's pulse quickened. "What are you telling me?"

"I'm telling you that he keeps papers under the desk. In the floor."

"Did you see them?"

"I pulled the rug aside and lifted the floorboard, saw what was there, but was afraid to touch anything. Matthews was hovering around in the front hall and, if he caught me, he would most certainly inform Zeb."

"You did the right thing. Where is Zeb now?"

"He said he was going back to the store, but I followed to come here and saw him go to the Long Branch."

"He likes his brandy, that's for certain." Fletcher took Elizabeth by the arm. "Let's go back to your house. I want to see what's under that desk."

"Are you sure, Fletcher? Perhaps this is too dangerous."

"Danger, my dear sister, doesn't exist in my vocabulary."

Zeb pulled his gold engraved timepiece from his coat pocket and squinted to read the time. "I suppose I should saunter down to the store," he said casually to the bartender. "I don't trust anyone but myself to count my cash."

The bartender snickered and gathered the empty glass and brandy bottle from Zeb's place at the bar.

"I'll settle up with you next week," Zeb said, turning unsteadily to leave the saloon. "And that brandy is putrid. Don't serve it to me again."

He staggered once, then gained his footing and

pushed through the swinging doors into the dusky evening light.

A few minutes later, Zeb reached the mercantile, walked in and shut the door behind him. He flipped the sign over to read Closed.

"Did we make a bundle today, Gerald? I certainly hope so. My tab at the Long Branch is getting out of hand."

Gerald laughed dutifully, then reached under the counter. "The O'Malley kid delivered this for you this afternoon."

"O'Malley, you say?"

"Yes, sir," Gerald replied, holding the sealed envelope out. "It's addressed to you, sir, as mayor of Dodge City."

Slowly Zeb moved forward and grasped the letter. "A bit premature, perhaps, but I do like the sound of it. Count the cash tonight, Gerald, and if you leave with one cent of my money, you're fired."

Zeb walked toward the back of the store and went into his office. He sat down at the huge oak desk, leaned back and crossed his legs. "This should be amusing," he said aloud to himself.

He ripped open the envelope and held up the first page to read:

Dear Mayor Stone,
I thought you should be the one to see this.

Sincerely,
Leo O'Malley

Zeb flipped to the next page to discover a letter written some time ago by the boy's father.

Dear Cecil,

I have a most disturbing matter to discuss with you regarding the cattle-rustling enterprise that I mentioned in my last correspondence. It seems the guilty party is a man named George Greer. I've finally come to suspect him after spotting one of his men branding cattle on my land. He drove them to town through a section of fence he removed and repaired afterward. I did not risk a confrontation, but I plan to inform the county sheriff and the town council anonymously. What will occur after that I can only hope will not involve me greatly. I have not told Josephine about this matter. You know how independent she can be. I trust you will keep it to yourself until I've had a chance to contact the right people.

Your brother,
Edwyn

Zeb stared silently at Leo's brief note for another minute, feeling his head begin to throb as he considered the boy's obvious meaning. Then, with an angry thrust, Zeb shoved back his chair and stood. The boy was ambitious to deliver this note the week before the election, Zeb thought with mounting fury. Too ambitious.

This would have to be taken care of immediately.

Quite some time after dark, Jo and Cecil leaped off the evening train and onto the wooden platform in Dodge City. Jo raised her skirts to hurry toward the jailhouse—her boots pounding over the damp ground as she went—all the while praying that Fletcher would be there.

She reached the calaboose and pulled open the door, but found the jailhouse and cells empty.

"Come on, he might be upstairs in the clerk's office," she said to Cecil, who was faithfully following behind her.

She dashed up the stairs on the outside of the building, but found the door locked. She clutched at the knob, shaking it in frustration.

"Where else would he be?" Cecil asked as they descended the steps.

"He might be patrolling the streets, but I can't spend all night looking for him. I have to find Leo."

Cecil glanced toward the saloons and theaters on the south side of the tracks. "That ain't no place for a lady. I'll look for Marshal Collins and explain things. You go home. That's the only place Leo would have gone."

"I hope so."

"Don't worry, I'll find the marshal and we'll search the city until we hear from you that Leo's safe."

Jo hesitated, trying to think if there was another, better alternative. "I wish I had my gun," she whispered, frustrated at the feeling of helplessness, then she wished Cecil luck and ran toward the boardinghouse where Fletcher had promised to leave her wagon.

Jo had no idea what time it was when she finally drove into her own yard, back aching and eyes burning from fatigue. She'd worked the horses hard to get there, fearing the worst, wanting nothing more than to find Leo safe in the house munching on sugar cookies, but when she saw the dark windows and dark bunkhouse, her hopes sank.

Still clinging to the possibility that he might be in his own bedroom upstairs at the back of the house, she hopped down from the wagon and went to the door. She ran up the stairs. "Leo? Are you here?"

The absence of a reply sent her bursting through every door, her prospects shrinking with the discovery of each silent, empty room. She gathered her skirts in her fists and ran down the stairs. "Leo!"

The kitchen, too, was empty. Where was her son?

Struggling to think clearly, Jo went into Edwyn's den and lit a lamp, took a rifle from the display on the wall and loaded it. She carried it through the dark hall to the front door and walked out of the house and into the cold night.

For a few seconds, she stood on the porch looking all around. She could make out the rolling pasture where crickets chirped and a cow called out somewhere in the distance. There was no wind, not even a whisper of a breeze.

She looked toward the barn and noticed light through a crack in the vertical plank wall. Her insides jolted with new hope. All she wanted now was to take Leo into her arms and know that he was safe, to hold him for a few minutes. After that, she would think of nothing but protecting him.

She ran down the porch steps and across the yard. She heard a horse nicker, a pig snort. Her feet tapped lightly over the damp dirt. She was getting closer and closer to the barn door.

Her heart began to pound against her rib cage.

Jo stopped just outside and leaned a hand against the wall. Last night, Fletcher had helped her go inside. Now, she was alone.

Struggling for breath, she tried to smother the white-hot terror that was smoldering inside her. She could not let it defeat her. She straightened and forced a deep breath into her lungs, reached a trembling hand through the darkness to the door latch and pulled it open. The barn was quiet.

She stood in the open doorway looking in, her blood pulsing through her body at an alarming speed. She wanted to call for Leo, but could push nothing from her fear-constricted throat. Again, she tried to get a breath.

Suddenly, a hand squeezed around her arm and yanked her into the barn. Her rifle was plucked from her grasp. Disoriented, she stumbled forward onto the hay-strewn floor, something struck her in the back of the head, and she lost all consciousness.

Feeling numb, not quite understanding where she was or what was happening to her, Jo tried to arrange her thoughts into something palpable. A dull ache throbbed at the back of her skull. She tried to open her eyes, but her injured body just wouldn't cooperate with her brain.

"What's happening?" she managed to mumble, but to whom she had no idea. She felt herself being lifted and placed on the back of a horse. She knew she was straddling it, leaning forward with eyes closed, her cheek resting on its coarse mane. Her wrists were bound behind her. Thoughts began to form.

Her eyes flew open just as a rope came down over her head and tightened around her neck.

Shock flooded through her and she bolted upright.

The horse took a startled step sideways. Nearly losing her balance and falling off, Jo realized with surprising clarity that the mare was the only thing keeping her from hanging.

"Whoa, girl," she said, trying to calm the horse, who had taken a few steps forward. The rope was stretched and pulling against Jo's jaw. "Move to the left, girl."

"I doubt she knows her left from her right."

The sound of Zeb's deep voice sent a wave a nausea through Jo. She looked down and saw him standing by the tack room door aiming a rifle at her.

"Where's Leo?" she demanded, but her voice was raspy under the tightening of the prickly rope.

"I was hoping you'd tell *me*."

Thank goodness, she thought, he hadn't found Leo. At least not yet.

If she was going to keep breathing, Jo needed slack in the rope. She pressed her knees together to get the horse to move.

"There's no point in trying," Zeb said, lowering the rifle to lean on it.

"You're going to slap her on the rump anyway, right?"

Zeb smiled sardonically. "I thought I'd just shoot her, but then it wouldn't look like a suicide, would it? Your idea is better."

Jo glared down at him, sickened by the self-satisfied glint in his eyes. "I should have killed you when I had the chance," she said.

"Yes, you should have. I guess Six-Shooter Hank wasn't as scary as the paper made him out to be. You're a coward, Mrs. O'Malley. You let your husband hang in front of your eyes and you couldn't even kill me for doing it."

"You won't get away with this, Zeb. Fletcher will know it was you. He already knows Will MacGregor worked for you and somehow he'll prove you killed him last night."

"So what if I did kill him? If Fletcher has a problem with it, I'll take care of him, too. But I'm tired of talking. I'm thirsty and I want to get back to Dodge to find that boy of yours before he blabbers all over town what he knows.''

The mere mention of Leo shook Jo to the core. Suddenly she felt powerless, at Zeb's mercy. ''Please, Zeb, leave Leo alone.''

''I told you I didn't want to talk anymore.'' He raised the rifle and pointed it at the peaked roof.

There was no way out of this! He was going to spook the horse and she could do nothing but watch! Just like the last time!

He pulled the trigger and the bullet ripped through the roof, booming in Jo's ears like a thunderclap.

The horse reared up. Jo held on with her legs as the noose tightened around her neck and chafed against her skin. She was barely on the mare's back anymore. Most of her weight was hanging in the rope. She couldn't breathe!

The mare's front hooves slammed onto the ground. Choking, feeling her heart rush, Jo shut her eyes and thought of Fletcher. She prayed he would save Leo. Surely he would.

Just then, the mare moved back, and Jo's weight lightened in the rope. She coughed and struggled for breath. Confused and trembling uncontrollably, she leaned forward onto the horse's mane again.

Somewhere in her numb consciousness, she heard Zeb laughing. ''Looks like I might just have to shoot her after all. To hell with a suicide.''

''Zeb, no…''

He raised the rifle and aimed it at the horse's head. Jo squeezed her eyes shut, feeling tears spill out as Zeb pulled the trigger again.

The gun clicked.

''Oh, for pity's sake,'' Zeb said, staring at the rifle.

Jo began to sit up, but fear flared through her anew when Zeb dropped the gun and walked toward her.

"What are you doing?" she asked, sobbing.

He didn't answer. He just slapped the horse on the rump.

The mare darted forward. Jo's body lurched with the horse, then whipped back and she fell off. All air was cut off. She was hanging from the neck, swinging and kicking, praying it would be over soon....

Fletcher didn't even have a chance to think. He walked into the barn and focused everything on shooting that rope in two. He aimed his rifle through the dim light, closed one eye and fired. The noise frightened the barn animals to shrieking and Jo dropped to the hard ground in a heap of skirts and petticoats.

Fletcher held his rifle in steady hands and fixed his aim on Zeb's black heart.

"Where the hell did you come from?" Zeb asked, his tone dripping with irritation. "I thought you were taking care of the saloon district tonight."

"It doesn't much matter. The only thing that matters is where you're going. And that's straight to hell."

Zeb raised his hands in the air. "You won't shoot me. You've never shot anyone in your life."

"I never felt much like it before now."

Zeb glanced down at Jo, who had wrestled her hands free and was tugging at the rope around her neck. "So...you *did* become infatuated with her."

"Shut up, Zeb. I'm taking you in."

Zeb spoke in a businesslike tone. "Why don't we talk about this."

"I said shut up and I meant it. Unless you want to leave here with your brains in a bucket."

Zeb considered it. "No, I don't suppose I do." He took a step forward and held out his wrists. "Go ahead, then. Take me in. You'll have a hell of a time convicting me, though. I have a lot of powerful friends."

Fletcher lowered the rifle to his side and pulled his cuffs out of the back of his belt. "It shouldn't be a problem."

"You sound full of confidence."

"I am, *Mr. Greer.*"

Zeb froze. "I beg your pardon?"

"I found your signature as Greer all over the papers under your desk. You're going to jail for a long time, Zeb."

But just as Fletcher flicked the handcuffs open, Zeb pulled a small revolver out of his pocket.

"Fletcher, look out!" Jo called, the rope still around her neck as she scrambled to her feet.

Zeb fired. Pain coursed through Fletcher's side and he stumbled back into a pile of hay.

"No!" Jo called out.

Zeb leaped onto Fletcher and went for his throat. Choking, Fletcher tried to push him off.

"No one's taking me in," Zeb said, growling between clenched teeth. He squeezed Fletcher's neck. "I've come too far."

Fletcher gasped for air, kicking and pulling against Zeb's hands. His gut was throbbing with pain; he could feel blood soaking his shirt.

Without warning, a garden shovel made an arc through the air and smashed against Zeb's head. He jolted under the blow and dropped like a sack of corn flour onto Fletcher's chest.

"Are you all right?" Jo asked, pulling Zeb off him. "You're shot!"

"No kidding." Fletcher tried to sit up and see the wound. His blood was staining the hay under him a deep, cherry-red. "Damn, this is the second time this week I've been shot. Maybe somebody's trying to tell me something."

Jo pushed him down onto his back. "Lie still. I'll get the wagon."

Fletcher's stomach churned. "I don't feel so good."

"Hang on!" she yelled over her shoulder, darting toward the barn door and pulling the double doors open.

He stared up at the gambrel-roofed trusses high above him and waited for Jo to come back. Damn, but his side hurt. And his heart was racing.

That fact worried him a bit, because he'd never truly been scared before.

He shut his eyes tight against the pain. Lord, he didn't want to die like this. He'd done none of the things he'd wanted to do with his life. He'd been wasting so much time....

Jo, where are you? I need you to hold my hand....

He heard her voice in his head. *You don't know who you are,* and he was beginning to understand.

Soon his body began to tingle, and though there was still so much he wanted and needed to think about and say, his awareness of things around him began to grow vague and unclear until he couldn't stop himself from drifting off to sleep.

Jo raced toward the wagon, leaped into the seat and slapped the reins hard against the horses' backs. "Yah! Yah!"

Startled into action, the team trotted into the barn. Jo jumped down. "Fletcher! Wake up! No, no!" She knelt beside him and tried to shake him, but he was completely out. Panic swept through her. She put her ear to his chest. "Where's your heartbeat?"

The soft thumping relieved her fears, but she still had to get him to the doctor. The horses were tired, but there was no time to unhitch and change them.

She pulled Fletcher up by the arm and felt every muscle in her body strain as she lifted him over her shoulder and tried to stand. "Hold on, Fletcher. Don't give up now," she said, wobbling under his impossible weight.

As gently as she could manage, she lowered him into the back of the wagon. Her heart ached at the sight of his unconscious form and the blood soaking his shirt.

She hurried to climb into the wagon seat, barely even aware of the noose still around her neck. She was about to flick the reins when she looked down and saw Zeb, sprawled in a heap beside a saddle horse.

Jo stared down at him. Was he still breathing, she wondered frantically, or had she killed him?

Without another thought, she jumped down and rolled him over onto his back, praying he was still alive. She placed her fingers under his nose and whispered a quiet thank-you when she felt the heat and moisture of his breath.

Quickly she dragged him by the arm across the barn floor toward the wagon, pulling with all her might, then let him drop for a moment while she searched around the dimly lit floor for Fletcher's handcuffs. After finding them a few feet away, she strained to roll Zeb over again onto his stomach, then fastened the cuffs onto his wrists behind his back. "That ought to hold you."

Struggling with his heavy, limp body, she groaned and staggered as she lifted him into the wagon to lie beside Fletcher, then she climbed back into the seat. "Let's go," she said to the horses.

They drove out the opposite door, and Jo slapped the reins to urge them into a gallop, praying with all her heart that she would make it to Dodge in time to save both the lives she took with her.

Chapter Twenty-Six

Jo sat by the front window in Dr. Green's office, tapping her foot on the floor, waiting impatiently while he operated on Fletcher in the back room. She thought of how she'd suffered earlier in the day when Fletcher had told her it was over between them, and how she'd not thought the heart-wrenching pain could be any worse. And yet, here it was, worse. The misery on the train had been compounded by fear when she learned about Leo's disappearance, and now it had swelled yet again to a kind of torture she'd not thought possible.

She dropped her forehead into her hands and shuddered with dread and trepidation, knowing she would be sick if the doctor came out and told her Fletcher was dead. *Please, let him live. Even if we can't be together, just let him live.*

Voices rose in the street and Jo sat up. The front door of the doctor's office swung open.

"Ma!" Leo called out, rushing to her and wrapping his arms around her waist.

She stood and cupped his head in her hand, bending forward to kiss his cheeks. "Oh, Leo! I'm so glad to see you!'' Tears welled up in her eyes and she sobbed with relief.

Cecil walked in behind Leo.

''You found him,'' she said, her heart overflowing with gratitude.

''Sure did. Just a short time after I sent Marshal Collins after you.''

''Where were you?'' she asked Leo, stroking his hair and lifting his chin so she could see his face.

''I was sitting on the steps at Jensen's Boardinghouse with John, waiting for Marshal Collins.''

''Whatever for?''

''To tell him about the letter I found, and that I gave it to Mr. Stone.''

''You did a very foolish thing, Leo. You should have come to me first.''

''I know, Ma. I'm real sorry. I only wanted to make you proud of me, but I won't ever go against what you say again. Uncle Cecil told me everything.''

She stroked the hair off his forehead. Ah, to see his face and hold him, her dear, sweet boy. She was so very, very grateful.

''And from now on, I won't keep things from you either, Leo. I'll try to give you more freedom. I'll agree to that because you're getting older. But you're still my son.''

''Yes, Ma,'' he groaned good-naturedly.

Jo held him close and he allowed it for a moment, then stepped back and straightened his shirt. ''So, is it true?'' Leo asked pointedly.

''Is what true?''

''What John told me about you and the marshal—that you two are in love.''

Caught off guard, Jo stepped back. "John told you that?"

"Yes, Ma, while we were talking at the boarding-house. He went there to have a word with the marshal about it. That's how we met up with each other."

"What exactly did John plan to say to the marshal?" Jo asked uncomfortably.

Leo looped a thumb through his belt. "He was going to tell Marshal Collins that if he didn't treat you right, he'd be sorry for it, because you deserve to be happy."

"I see," Jo replied, putting it in her mind to thank John one of these days, then worrying about how she was going to tell Leo that what he'd heard wasn't true, that it would never be true.

"Is there going to be a wedding like folks have been saying?"

Jo shuddered inwardly. "Well, no, Leo. Things are very complicated with the marshal and me." Not wanting to go into any of that, she stuck with the obvious. "Do you know what happened to him?" Her stomach rolled with nervous dread.

Leo looked up at her. "Yes, Ma, and I hope he's all right, 'cause I like him a lot. And I think Pa would've liked him, too."

An hour later, Jo sat next to the bed waiting, holding Fletcher's hand. "Please wake up," she whispered softly in his ear. "Don't die on me."

Touching him, so still and lifeless, made the pain in her heart resonate through her entire body.

She sat back and watched him. Teardrops fell from her eyes onto his bare forearm. "Please be all right. I don't know what would have become of me if you hadn't walked into my life when you did. You saved me, Fletcher."

Just then, his finger twitched under hers and her skin prickled everywhere. "Fletcher, it's me. I'm here," she said. "Try to open your eyes." He shook his head slowly back and forth, enough to give her a tiny fragment of hope. "You're going to be fine. The doctor got the bullet out. It was just lodged in the muscle."

He opened his eyes and looked at her for a long time and she wasn't even sure if he recognized her. Her heart was beating like a drum.

"You saved me, too," he said at last, groggily. "And I don't just mean from Zeb."

Jo stared at him in disbelief, her emotions flooding into her senses until she felt as if she might collapse from the weight of them. She leaned down to hug and kiss him. "Oh, Fletcher, thank goodness you're all right."

He pulled her in for a kiss and held her as their lips joined tenderly. "What happened to Zeb?" he asked, rubbing his temple.

"Deputy Anderson came and arrested him, took him to the county jail after the doctor made sure he was all right. He just has a bump on his head that'll be sore for a while."

Laughing quietly, then wincing from the pain it caused, Fletcher squeezed Jo's hand. "Now they can call *you* The Bruiser. It's time I retired the title anyway."

"Retired it," she repeated, not quite understanding his meaning.

A knock sounded at the door and Deputy Anderson walked in. "Marshal Collins, glad to see you're awake."

"Thanks," Fletcher replied. "What's up?"

Anderson removed his hat and turned it over in his hands a few times. "That's what I came here to find out. Mrs. O'Malley sent for me."

Fletcher gazed up at Jo, his eyes filling with concern. She squeezed his hand one more time, then stood up from the chair, feeling nervous butterflies invade her belly. "I called Deputy Anderson here so I could confess my crime."

Fletcher tried to lean up on his elbows. "Jo, you don't have to—"

"Yes, I do. I need to tell him this, or I won't be able to live with myself. It's the right thing to do."

Fully prepared to be handcuffed and taken to jail, Jo turned to face Deputy Anderson.

Fletcher tried to protest one more time. "Jo, please, don't—"

"I'm Six-Shooter Hank," she said quickly. "I was the one who broke into Zeb's store that night. Only I wasn't there to rob him. I was there to shoot him."

Anderson looked at Fletcher, as if he was searching for directions about what to say. Fletcher shook his head back and forth on the pillow. "Jo, you didn't have to do that."

"Yes, I did. I can't let you keep this a secret. You'll hate yourself for it and I care about you too much to do that to you."

Fletcher blinked a few times, a hint of a smile grazing his colorless lips. "I haven't told her yet," he said to Anderson.

Jo whirled around. "Told me what?"

His sleepy eyes glimmered in the lantern light. "While you were on the train to Newton, I got a wire from a lawman friend of mine in Chicago. Zeb's real

name is Jack Curtis. Stone and Greer were only two of
the names he's used. We're looking into the rest."
Fletcher wet his lips and paused for a break. His voice
was raspy with fatigue. He had to speak slowly.

"Zeb's been wanted in Illinois and in three other
states for murder and theft among other things, and with
the evidence I found in his house, he'll be convicted for
a lot more than that. There was a one thousand-dollar
reward out for his capture."

"A reward? Are you telling me that—"

"Yes, ma'am," Anderson interrupted. "He was
wanted dead or alive, so you won't be going to jail,
even if you had shot him that night. The way things
stand now, you'll be collecting a thousand dollars, seeing as it was you who cuffed him and dragged him all
the way to town. And that couldn't have been easy. He
ain't no lightweight."

Jo collapsed into the chair, too shocked to believe it.
"I had no idea."

Anderson replaced his hat on his head. "Is that all
you wanted me for, ma'am? To tell me about what you
did that night?"

"Yes, and to thank you, of course."

Anderson smiled and tipped his hat. "My pleasure,
ma'am. Take care, now." He turned and left the room.

Overwhelmed, Jo held Fletcher's hand. "What will
Elizabeth do?"

"My sister's a tough lady. She'll start over. We both
will."

Jo struggled with the painful yearning that was
squeezing around her heart, a yearning that would stay
with her and plague her forever, she was certain. She
loved this man so much, she would have given her life
for him tonight. How would she survive when he was

gone? "Will you take Elizabeth away from here?" she asked.

Fletcher tried to move but winced with pain. His face had no color; his eyes were underlined with dark circles. Jo felt suddenly guilty for being so selfish right now, for wanting to know what he planned to do with his future, when he planned on leaving Dodge City for good.

"Can I do anything for you?" she offered, rearranging his pillow under his head.

He touched her cheek. "You already have. You helped me. I...I feel like I understand things better now."

"What things?" she asked.

He wet his dry lips again. "What you said to me, on the train, that I didn't know who I was...you were right."

She sat patiently, waiting for him take an unsteady, painful breath before continuing.

"I'm not a lawman, Jo. It's just something I've been doing to make up for what my father did, to prove I'm not the same as him. But I am like him. I'm his son and he was a good man. It's time I remember that. I'm not saying what he did was right, and it couldn't have been easy for him—he was honest about everything. But he let those men go free because he loved us so much and he was afraid of something bad happening to us. Just like how I felt about *you*."

Jo nodded, still squeezing Fletcher's hand. "Can you forgive him?"

"I already have. I did a lot of thinking after you said what you said to me, and now, I just miss him."

Her eyes filled with tears. "It couldn't have been easy for you, carrying that burden."

"It wasn't. But it's lighter now, thanks to you. You showed me that feelings can be complicated when they're deep."

Hearing those kind words only made her love him more, and that didn't make this any easier, not when he still planned on leaving Dodge City. She at least had to make things right between them.

"Since you're handing out forgiveness today, do you think you could forgive *me,* too? I know I went against everything you believed in and I even asked you to break the law to let me go free, but I'm sorry for it now. I just want you to know that."

He pulled her down to hold her. "God, Jo, how can you ask that? You thought you wanted to kill Zeb, but you didn't, and I know you never would have been able to. You even dragged him back here to save his life. You were willing to confess everything just now, to go to prison because you felt it was the right thing to do. I don't know anyone with more integrity than that. There's nothing to forgive."

She dropped her cheek on his chest and closed her eyes with a surge of gratitude so strong it hurt. Everything she had feared so deeply—that she was a killer, that Fletcher would never be able to forgive her—it was all gone now. There was only the warmth of the man beside her and a feeling in her heart that was so sweet, so complete, it was almost unbearable. Perhaps now, she could live with letting him go.

"Still, I'm sorry that all this had to happen," she said, wiping a tear from her cheek. "I'm sorry that you were shot, that you had to arrest your brother-in-law, that things didn't work out for Elizabeth."

"I'm not sorry. Zeb was cruel to her. Now she has an excuse to be rid of him. And as for you and me..."

He raised her chin with a finger. "I never told you that I loved you."

She stared blankly at him, numb with shock, then a cry of joy broke from her lips. "You do?"

"Oh, yes."

"I love you, too," she whispered weakly. "More than I ever thought I could love any man."

He raised her hand to his lips and kissed it. "When I saw you in that noose, Jo, I thought I'd lost you. Then, I thought I was dying and all I could think about was how I'd been wasting my life doing something that just wasn't me, and how you're everything that I want and you make me everything I want to be. I can't miss this chance for happiness, Jo. I don't want to lose you."

Jo sat back, almost afraid to believe this could be happening, that he could be saying these things to her. "You won't."

"Is that a promise?"

"Yes." She kissed his hand, again and again. "Yes!"

"But there's only one thing that still bothers me about all this," Fletcher said, frowning. "Actually, about you."

At his words, Jo's heart flinched a little, but she forced herself to speak. "What would that be?"

He stared at her for a moment, looking reluctant to tell her. "Well...if you really want to know...it's your name."

"Josephine? You don't like it?"

"Oh, I like Josephine fine. It's Mrs. O'Malley I'm gonna have a problem with. You see, I was kind of hoping you'd change it—to Mrs. Collins."

Jo filled with warmth as Fletcher grasped her hand in his and brought it to his lips.

"Well, will you? Will you be Mrs. Collins?"

Laughing and crying at the same time, Jo flung herself at Fletcher and planted her mouth on his.

"Ow! Ow! My side!" he groaned, peeling her off him and laughing. "Have pity on an injured man! I take it that's a yes?"

"Yes," Jo sputtered, still wiping at the tears that flowed freely down her face as Fletcher reached up to kiss her.

"Hey," he said softly. "I guess that old saying is true after all."

"About what?"

He tilted his head for another kiss and smiled. "A rose by any other name does smell as sweet."

* * * * *

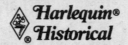

PRESENTS

SIRENS OF THE SEA

The brand-new historical series
from bestselling author

Ruth Langan

Join the spirited Lambert sisters in their
search for adventure—and love!

THE SEA WITCH
When dashing Captain Riordan Spencer arrives in
Land's End, Ambrosia Lambert may have
met her perfect match!

On sale January 2001
THE SEA NYMPH
Middle sister Bethany must choose between a
scandalous highwayman and the very proper
Earl of Alsmeeth.

In June 2001
THE SEA SPRITE
Youngest sister Darcy loses the love of her life
in a shipwreck, only to fall for a man who
strongly resembles her lost lover.

MONTANA MAVERICKS

Bestselling author

SUSAN MALLERY

WILD WEST WIFE

THE ORIGINAL MONTANA MAVERICKS HISTORICAL NOVEL

Jesse Kincaid had sworn off love forever.
But when the handsome rancher kidnaps
his enemy's mail-order bride to get revenge,
he ends up falling for his innocent captive!

RETURN TO WHITEHORN, MONTANA, WITH

WILD WEST WIFE

Available July 2001

And be sure to pick up
MONTANA MAVERICKS: BIG SKY GROOMS,
three brand-new historical stories about Montana's
most popular family, coming in August 2001.

*Harlequin truly does
make any time special. . . .
This year we are celebrating
weddings in style!*

To help us celebrate, we want you to tell us how wearing the Harlequin wedding gown will make your wedding day special. As the grand prize, Harlequin will offer one lucky bride the chance to **"Walk Down the Aisle" in the Harlequin wedding gown!**

There's more...

For her honeymoon, she and her groom will spend five nights at the **Hyatt Regency Maui.** As part of this five-night honeymoon at the hotel renowned for its romantic attractions, the couple will enjoy a candlelit dinner for two in Swan Court, a sunset sail on the hotel's catamaran, and duet spa treatments.

Maui • Molokai • Lanai

To enter, please write, in, 250 words or less, how wearing the Harlequin wedding gown will make your wedding day special. The entry will be judged based on its emotionally compelling nature, its originality and creativity, and its sincerity. This contest is open to Canadian and U.S. residents only and to those who are 18 years of age and older. There is no purchase necessary to enter. Void where prohibited. See further contest rules attached. Please send your entry to:

Walk Down the Aisle Contest

In Canada	In U.S.A.
P.O. Box 637	P.O. Box 9076
Fort Erie, Ontario	3010 Walden Ave.
L2A 5X3	Buffalo, NY 14269-9076

You can also enter by visiting www.eHarlequin.com
Win the Harlequin wedding gown and the vacation of a lifetime!
The deadline for entries is October 1, 2001.

HARLEQUIN WALK DOWN THE AISLE TO MAUI CONTEST 1197
OFFICIAL RULES
NO PURCHASE NECESSARY TO ENTER

1. To enter, follow directions published in the offer to which you are responding. Contest begins April 2, 2001, and ends on October 1, 2001. Method of entry may vary. Mailed entries must be postmarked by October 1, 2001, and received by October 8, 2001.

2. Contest entry may be, at times, presented via the Internet, but will be restricted solely to residents of certain geographic areas that are disclosed on the Web site. To enter via the Internet, if permissible, access the Harlequin Web site (www.eHarlequin.com) and follow the directions displayed online. Online entries must be received by 11:59 p.m. E.S.T. on October 1, 2001.

   In lieu of submitting an entry online, enter by mail by hand-printing (or typing) on an 8½" x 11" plain piece of paper, your name, address (including zip code), Contest number/name and in 250 words or fewer, why winning a Harlequin wedding dress would make your wedding day special. Mail via first-class mail to: Harlequin Walk Down the Aisle Contest 1197, (in the U.S.) P.O. Box 9076, 3010 Walden Avenue, Buffalo, NY 14269-9076, (in Canada) P.O. Box 637, Fort Erie, Ontario L2A 5X3, Canada.

   Limit one entry per person, household address and e-mail address. Online and/or mailed entries received from persons residing in geographic areas in which Internet entry is not permissible will be disqualified.

3. Contests will be judged by a panel of members of the Harlequin editorial, marketing and public relations staff based on the following criteria:
   - Originality and Creativity—50%
   - Emotionally Compelling—25%
   - Sincerity—25%

   In the event of a tie, duplicate prizes will be awarded. Decisions of the judges are final.

4. All entries become the property of Torstar Corp. and will not be returned. No responsibility is assumed for lost, late, illegible, incomplete, inaccurate, nondelivered or misdirected mail or misdirected e-mail, for technical, hardware or software failures of any kind, lost or unavailable network connections, or failed, incomplete, garbled or delayed computer transmission or any human error which may occur in the receipt or processing of the entries in this Contest.

5. Contest open only to residents of the U.S. (except Puerto Rico) and Canada, who are 18 years of age or older, and is void wherever prohibited by law; all applicable laws and regulations apply. Any litigation within the Province of Quebec respecting the conduct or organization of a publicity contest may be submitted to the Régie des alcools, des courses et des jeux for a ruling. Any litigation respecting the awarding of a prize may be submitted to the Régie des alcools, des courses et des jeux only for the purpose of helping the parties reach a settlement. Employees and immediate family members of Torstar Corp. and D. L. Blair, Inc., their affiliates, subsidiaries and all other agencies, entities and persons connected with the use, marketing or conduct of this Contest are not eligible to enter. Taxes on prizes are the sole responsibility of winners. Acceptance of any prize offered constitutes permission to use winner's name, photograph or other likeness for the purposes of advertising, trade and promotion on behalf of Torstar Corp., its affiliates and subsidiaries without further compensation to the winner, unless prohibited by law.

6. Winners will be determined no later than November 15, 2001, and will be notified by mail. Winners will be required to sign and return an Affidavit of Eligibility form within 15 days after notification. Noncompliance within that time period may result in disqualification and an alternative winner may be selected. Winners of trip must execute a Release of Liability prior to ticketing and must possess required travel documents (e.g. passport, photo ID) where applicable. Trip must be completed by November 2002. No substitution of prize permitted by winner. Torstar Corp. and D. L. Blair, Inc., their parents, affiliates, and subsidiaries are not responsible for errors in printing or electronic presentation of Contest, entries and/or game pieces. In the event of printing or other errors which may result in unintended prize values or duplication of prizes, all affected game pieces or entries shall be null and void. If for any reason the Internet portion of the Contest is not capable of running as planned, including infection by computer virus, bugs, tampering, unauthorized intervention, fraud, technical failures, or any other causes beyond the control of Torstar Corp. which corrupt or affect the administration, secrecy, fairness, integrity or proper conduct of the Contest, Torstar Corp. reserves the right, at its sole discretion, to disqualify any individual who tampers with the entry process and to cancel, terminate, modify or suspend the Contest or the Internet portion thereof. In the event of a dispute regarding an online entry, the entry will be deemed submitted by the authorized holder of the e-mail account submitted at the time of entry. Authorized account holder is defined as the natural person who is assigned to an e-mail address by an Internet access provider, online service provider or other organization that is responsible for arranging e-mail address for the domain associated with the submitted e-mail address. **Purchase or acceptance of a product offer does not improve your chances of winning.**

7. Prizes: (1) Grand Prize—A Harlequin wedding dress (approximate retail value: $3,500) and a 5-night/6-day honeymoon trip to Maui, HI, including round-trip air transportation provided by Maui Visitors Bureau from Los Angeles International Airport (winner is responsible for transportation to and from Los Angeles International Airport) and a Harlequin Romance Package, including hotel accomodations (double occupancy) at the Hyatt Regency Maui Resort and Spa, dinner for (2) two at Swan Court, a sunset sail on Kiele V and a spa treatment for the winner (approximate retail value: $4,000); (5) Five runner-up prizes of a $1000 gift certificate to selected retail outlets to be determined by Sponsor (retail value $1000 ea.). Prizes consist of only those items listed as part of the prize. Limit one prize per person. All prizes are valued in U.S. currency.

8. For a list of winners (available after December 17, 2001) send a self-addressed, stamped envelope to: Harlequin Walk Down the Aisle Contest 1197 Winners, P.O. Box 4200 Blair, NE 68009-4200 or you may access the www.eHarlequin.com Web site through January 15, 2002.

Contest sponsored by Torstar Corp., P.O. Box 9042, Buffalo, NY 14269-9042, U.S.A.

PHWDACONT2

If you enjoyed what you just read,
then we've got an offer you can't resist!

Take 2 bestselling
love stories FREE!
Plus get a FREE surprise gift!

Clip this page and mail it to Harlequin Reader Service®

IN U.S.A.	IN CANADA
3010 Walden Ave.	P.O. Box 609
P.O. Box 1867	Fort Erie, Ontario
Buffalo, N.Y. 14240-1867	L2A 5X3

YES! Please send me 2 free Harlequin Historical™ novels and my free surprise gift. Then send me 6 brand-new novels every month, which I will receive before they're available in stores. In the U.S.A., bill me at the bargain price of $3.94 plus 25¢ delivery per book and applicable sales tax, if any*. In Canada, bill me at the bargain price of $4.19 plus 25¢ delivery per book and applicable taxes**. That's the complete price and a savings of over 10% off the cover prices—what a great deal! I understand that accepting the 2 free books and gift places me under no obligation ever to buy any books. I can always return a shipment and cancel at any time. Even if I never buy another book from Harlequin, the 2 free books and gift are mine to keep forever. So why not take us up on our invitation. You'll be glad you did!

246 HEN C24S
349 HEN C24T

Name	(PLEASE PRINT)	
Address	Apt.#	
City	State/Prov.	Zip/Postal Code

* Terms and prices subject to change without notice. Sales tax applicable in N.Y.
** Canadian residents will be charged applicable provincial taxes and GST.
  All orders subject to approval. Offer limited to one per household.
  ® are registered trademarks of Harlequin Enterprises Limited.

HIST00_R   ©1998 Harlequin Enterprises Limited